Jessica ducked as a gunshot took out the passenger side mirror. "I'm sorry, Wes—"

"Save it."

This was the last time she was likely to speak with him, and he was going to hear her out. "There's no cover out here. I'll likely be dead before you get here, so shut up and listen. I truly am sorry for what I did to your career. But I genuinely believed you would be killed. And I cared—care—far too much for you to let you die. If that pisses you off, so be it. I forgive you for being mad at me. I don't want you to beat yourself up with guilt after I'm gone. I chose to come out here and warn you. This is on me. Whoever killed me did it because of mistakes I made in my past. There was nothing you could have done to protect me."

Wes's voice was ragged when he said, "If your shooter's zeroing in on you, he's in a stationary position, maybe in a sniper's nest. Get away from there."

* * *

D1005562

Dear Reader,

This book fulfills a long-held dream of mine to combine a military hero, because who can get enough of those, with a rugged, independent rancher, because who can get enough of those, either!

As if that weren't enough fun, I also got to throw in my love of mountains—Montana has some of the prettiest ones anywhere—and I got to write about cattle. Now, you might think cows aren't terribly sexy, but I grew up on a small cattle farm. My family bred and sold Herefords. I can verify that cows are truly like giant, sweet dogs. And in fact, the cow named Number 19 in this book was an actual cow on my family's farm.

At any rate, my heroine, Jessica, had to be a heck of a strong woman to stand up to an ex-Marine rancher who also happens to be one of the Morgan boys. I may or may not have channeled a tiny bit of my own life into her, too, but I'll never tell which parts!

I invite you to hunker down, pour yourself something to wet your whistle and saddle up for a wild ride in this cowboy's deadly reunion!

Happy reading!

Cindy

THE COWBOY'S
DEADLY REUNION

Cindy Dees

Recycling programs
for this product may
not exist in your area.

ISBN-13: 978-1-335-62887-9

The Cowboy's Deadly Reunion

Copyright © 2021 by Cynthia Dees

This edition published by arrangement with Harlequin Books S.A.

For questions and comments about the quality of this book, please contact us at CustomerService@Harlequin.com.

Harlequin Enterprises ULC
22 Adelaide St. West, 40th Floor
Toronto, Ontario M5H 4E3, Canada
www.Harlequin.com

Printed in U.S.A.

New York Times and USA TODAY bestselling author **Cindy Dees** is the author of more than fifty novels. She draws upon her experience as a US Air Force pilot to write romantic suspense. She's a two-time winner of the prestigious RITA® Award for romance fiction, a two-time winner of the RT Reviewers' Choice Best Book Award for Romantic Suspense and an RT Book Reviews Career Achievement Award nominee. She loves to hear from readers at www.cindydees.com.

Chapter 1

Wes Morgan looked out his office window at the Washington Monument across the Potomac River, rising like a spire of light into the night. He rubbed his eyes wearily. His boss, Marine General George Blankenship, was angling for a position on the Secretary of Defense's staff and had demanded a pile of briefings on current political issues ASAP. It had been a long day, and it was going to be a longer night. The general was hard-core bordering on a little maniacal. Only an aide as motivated and hardworking as Wes could keep up with the guy.

His private phone line rang. Great. The boss had thought of more work to pile on his long-suffering aide. He picked it up and said briskly, "Captain Morgan."

A frantic female voice whispered barely intelligibly, "Wes, it's Jessica. I'm in trouble."

He snorted. What was new? General Blankenship's only daughter was always in trouble.

"Puh-lease, Wesh. I need helllllp."

He frowned. She sounded drunk. Or high. Which was strange. She partied harder than most, but she was not a substance abuser. Sure, she drank through a long night of clubbing. Her thing was dancing. She could do it all night long. And she was good at it, sexy, flirty and fun on the dance floor. But word-slurring drunk? Not her thing. She was far too much of a control freak for it. In that regard, she was a lot like her old man.

He heard a crashing noise, as if something had been knocked over.

"Oopsies," Jessica mumbled.

Okay. Jessica was never clumsy. She was arguably the most graceful woman he'd ever dated. And he'd dated a ballerina from the National Ballet before.

"Where are you, Jess?"

"'M in a club." She was starting to sound groggy.

She'd gone from coherent and worried to stumbling drunk to near passing out awfully damned fast. He swore under his breath. Had she been drugged?

"I got that. Which club?" he asked urgently.

"Pop-up. Shh. I's seeeecret."

He swore in earnest now. A pop-up club could have been set up in any abandoned building, warehouse or vacant office space anywhere in the suburban sprawl of Washington, DC, and its surrounding areas. It might have been in place for weeks or just for a single night.

"Where are you, Jessica? Did you see any buildings or street signs on your way in?"

"Don't know."

"*Think*. This is important. What's the last place you saw that you recognized?"

"Cons…constitu-shuh…"

"Constitution Avenue?" he tried.

"No. Buil…ding…" Her voice faded.

"Stay with me, Jess. *Don't* pass out. That's an order!" He lurched to his feet, adrenaline screaming, on full battle alert. Sure, she'd pulled stunts on him before, but nothing like this. She sounded genuinely trashed and in real danger.

"Talk to me," he bit out as he grabbed his keys and raced out of the office.

"Whadya wanna…know?" she mumbled.

"Did you have to go up or down stairs to get into the club? Or are you on the ground floor?"

Silence stretched out for so long he thought she'd passed out. He bolted out into the long corridor of the Pentagon's E-Ring and sprinted down the nearest stairwell, taking a half-dozen steps at a time.

Jessica surprised him by mumbling, "Up. Wen' up."

"Great. Can you see any windows from where you are?"

"Uh-huh."

"Move over to the nearest one and look out. I need you to tell me what you see."

"Tired," she mumbled.

"Move!" He used his best Marine command voice to bully her into motion. Anything to keep her conscious. There was no way Jessica had gotten this smashed by herself. Someone had fed her much stronger booze than she'd realized she was drinking. Or, worse, she'd been drugged. Either way, Jess was in big trouble.

Panic hummed in his gut as he raced past the startled security guards, burst out of the Pentagon into the damp chill of early winter and tore across the parking lot to his pickup truck.

He'd rescued Jessica from her ridiculous and impulsive follies more times than he cared to count during the past four years of working for her father on battalion staff and then here in Washington. But her stunts ran more to speeding tickets or getting caught gluing mustaches to statues on base. This time, however, his gut told him she was in serious danger.

"Are you at the window yet?" he demanded as he jammed his truck into gear and peeled out of the parking lot.

"Uh-huh."

"Tell me what you see."

"S'dark."

"It is nighttime," he replied drily. "Do you see any buildings?"

"Wash…wash…ton. Mon…ment."

She was up high, then. "The Washington Monument? How far away is it?"

"Phal…lic…symb…"

"Yes, I know, sweetheart. Is it close or a long ways away?"

She giggled a little. "Tiny."

"Can you see the Potomac River from where you are?" he tried. If she was on the Virginia side of the river on the high hills overlooking Washington, DC, the wide river should be in sight, also.

"No."

Okay. The Maryland side of the river then. She'd mentioned the Constitution Hotel earlier. That was on the north side of DC in a posh part of town. He frantically calculated the fastest route to the swanky hotel. It was nearly ten o'clock. Traffic wouldn't be a serious factor. The Beltway it was. The multilane highway ringed the city and would bypass the congested and convoluted city streets of Washington, DC, proper. At rush hour, the Beltway was a parking lot. But at this time of night, it would more closely resemble a NASCAR track. Perfect.

"What else can you see?" he asked.

"Ho…dell."

"The Constitution Hotel?" he confirmed sharply. She was fading on him.

"Uh-huh."

"Okay. I'm on my way. I need you to fight. Stay awake."

"Luf…yooo…"

The mumbled syllables stunned him. She loved him? For real? Shock pounded through him. He and Jess had been hot and heavy last summer, and he'd been pretty infatuated with her, too. She was an exotic creature—beautiful and brilliant and wild—and he'd been amazed that she saw anything in him to attract her. He'd worried that he was some sort of revenge against her father with whom she was pretty much constantly at war. But, against all odds, she had seemed to genuinely care for him.

And now this declaration of love? His pulse leaped exultantly—

Stop right there, soldier.

She was stoned out of her mind on something. She didn't know what she was saying. He had no business getting all worked up at anything she said in her current state. But a little voice in the back of his head whispered, *What if the drugs coursing through her system had actually revealed a hidden truth?*

Even if she did secretly have feelings for him, getting back together with her was a nonstarter. General Blankenship had been blunt with Wes. Quit dating his daughter or face career ruin. A dutiful soldier, Wes had backed off dating Jess before they could fall any harder for each other. She'd been furious and accused him of being a wimp and not deserving to have her if he wouldn't stand up to her father.

Yeah. That had hurt to hear. Because she was not wrong.

But he had an overbearing father of his own to deal with. Wes was the Morgan clan's great hope to follow in his father's footsteps and have an illustrious career in the Marines. His older brother had come home under a cloud from the Navy and, as the second son, *the good son*, all the pressure had landed on Wes to uphold the family name.

Hang on, baby. I'm coming for you.

"Wes?" Jessica's voice was barely a whisper.

"I'm here. Keep talking to me."

"'Fraid."

He'd never known Jess to be scared of anything, and she sounded *terrified* right now. If he'd had any doubt about the seriousness of her predicament, that one word had just erased it. "I won't let anything bad happen to you. I promise."

She had a thing about promises. She hated them because she said people always broke them. He prayed he wouldn't end up breaking this one to her.

"Sleepy…"

"I know you are. Fight it, baby. You're the strongest woman I know. You can do this."

"Dec…deca…dec…"

He frowned, listening intently, trying and failing to decipher what she was trying to say. She was clearly fading. Clearly losing all ability to form words. But she was fighting like crazy to say something.

"Deca…dence," she finally got out. A note of triumph sounded in her voice.

The line went dead.

Sonofabitch.

He alternated between panic and…well, more panic… as he drove like a maniac around the Beltway toward the north side of town.

What the hell did she mean by that? Decadence?

Jessica hadn't been talking about herself, had she? She was a known drama queen, spoiled rotten and a bona fide pain in the ass at times. She was decadently beautiful and, God knew, she'd blown his mind in bed with her decadence there. But why would she say something like that with such urgency just before she passed out?

He made it to the Continental in record time and miraculously managed not to encounter any police as he destroyed every speed limit between the Pentagon and the hotel. He pulled into the circle drive in front of the hotel and looked around frantically. A pop-up nightclub would need a large, open space. Easy access. Plenty of parking. There. Across the street. A tall, ugly office building with a huge banner hanging across its front declaring the space for lease.

He sprinted across the street, eyeing the building.

There. A flash of blue and then red out of a top-floor window. That looked like disco lighting. That had to be it.

A chain hung unlocked on one of the front doors. He stepped into a deserted lobby lit only by the dim glow of exit signs. God. If he didn't know Jessica was upstairs somewhere, he would never guess anyone at all was here. He jammed the elevator button and waited impatiently for it. The only reason he wasn't running up the stairs was this would be faster. Plus, if Jessica was passed out and being carried from the building, the douchebag who'd drugged her would inevitably drag her into the elevator and not try to carry her down a dozen flights of stairs.

Girding himself for he knew not what, he watched the elevator door slide open.

Empty.

He jumped inside and mashed the button for the top floor. It was the longest elevator ride of his life. Every second was agony. Was someone dragging Jess into a bathroom or coatroom right now? Taking advantage of her? Doing unthinkable things to her?

He forced the grisly images from his mind, along with the red haze of rage accompanying them. It had been less than ten minutes since she'd mumbled that last word to him. That wasn't long enough for anything bad to happen to her, right?

Cripes. It was a lifetime.

C'mon, c'mon. He exhorted the elevator to go faster.

Finally, at long last, the doors began to slide open ponderously. He slipped sideways through the opening as soon as it was wide enough to accommodate his muscular chest. He gathered himself to take off running, but spied a man standing at the end of a short hallway. Wes checked himself and strode toward the guy.

On full combat alert, Wes took note of details instantly—Asian. Late twenties. Same height as Wes—six feet on the nose. Ripped like a bodybuilder.

As Wes approached, the dude said woodenly, "Password?"

Password? What the hell? Clearly this was some sort of private pop-up party. Which meant drugs, booze and girls were likely involved. What on earth had Jessica gotten herself mixed up in?

Thinking fast, he slurred his words a little. "Crap. I forgot it. My friend said the best action in DC was here. I've got cash…" He dug for his wallet, praying that he had enough bills in it to look like more than a few bucks.

"No password. No entry."

Dammit. Then inspiration struck. "Wait. I've got it. Decadence." And if that didn't work, Wes was clocking this guy and taking him out.

As Wes's fist balled tight, the bodybuilder nodded. Stepped back. Opened the solid wood door.

Praise the Lord and pass the potatoes. Wes stepped into a large open space with exposed vents and conduit overhead. Concrete floor. Exposed concrete columns broke up the expanse. Four big guys lounged just inside the door, obviously to keep the riffraff out—or throw the riffraff out as the case might be.

The music was deafening, and a dozen young women lolled at a bar built of cases of beer. Beyond the bar a crowd gyrated to the music in a near orgy on the dance floor. As far as he could see, people were standing, sitting and—holy crap—lying down in various stages of undress and orgy.

How in the hell was he ever going to find Jessica in this morass of bodies, booze and sex? Stone-cold terror washed through his gut. He wasn't going to get to her in time. Someone was going to assault her, and she was utterly defenseless. He'd been in killer firefights in hot combat zones that scared him less than this.

Jessica, what in the hell have you done?

"Yo, brah," one of the thug/bouncers said, coming forward to greet him. "You look uptight as hell, man. Can I get you something to drink? Snort? Shoot? You know, get you in the mood?"

He was in the mood to hurt someone. "No. I'm good," he bit out.

He moved into the crowd, bypassing the dance floor on the assumption that she was currently unconscious. He had to step over and around people shooting drugs, engaged in near sex acts or simply passed out. Class in a glass, man.

He gazed around in search of Jessica's wavy golden hair but didn't spy her. Last he'd talked with her, she'd been looking out a window. He didn't see any windows on this side of the building. Damn. He was going to have to cross the dance floor. Taking a deep breath, he plunged into the writhing mass of sweaty, gyrating bodies and flailing limbs.

Instantly, hands were on him, pulling at him and blatantly groping him. He batted away the grabs at his crotch as best he could. But breasts and bellies and asses rubbed up against him suggestively in spite of his best efforts to slip through the crowd. Women shouted in his ear, but he ignored them, focusing his efforts on finding a path through the human maze.

All at once, he popped out the back side of the mosh

pit. It was dark on this side of the floor, and the debauchery was even more pronounced as he picked his way through the partyers.

A new and improved layer of fear exploded inside his skull. He had to find Jessica, and *soon*. She was wild, but her brand of wild didn't extend to *this*. He skirted around a guy snorting lines of cocaine off a girl's bare stomach, and spied a flash of pale, golden blond against the far wall over the shoulder of a guy in a suit.

Wes charged forward, grabbing the guy by the shoulder a spinning him around.

"Get your own piece of ass," the guy growled as Wes saw the girl's face.

Not Jessica.

Wes spun away, moving quickly along the long wall containing a half-dozen floor-to-ceiling glass windows. He was almost on top of another couple—a huge, muscular man totally hiding the girl he had smashed up against the wall—before Wes caught a glimpse of a tear-streaked cheek.

He would know the classic elegance of that cheek anywhere.

A strand of wavy blond hair fell forward as she turned her head weakly from side to side. She was tall, but her head barely reached the shoulder of the guy pinning her to the wall.

"Hey!" Wes said sharply, grabbing the guy's shoulder and yanking him back from her.

"What the—" the big man growled.

Jessica's dress was pushed down around her waist, exposing her black lace bra and a whole lot of creamy, satin flesh that even now looked touchable as hell. Wes spied the hemline of her dress, and it was bunched up nearly to her waist, exposing Jessica's long, slender legs and a scrap of black lace that passed for a thong. The bastard had been well on his way to molesting her, obviously. Wes appeared to have gotten to her in the nick of time.

"I'm going to have to ask you to step away from the lady," Wes ground out, barely hanging on to his cool.

"And I'm going to have to ask you to take off, asshole."

"She has been drugged," Wes retorted. "You need to leave her alone and let me take her home."

"Of course, she's drugged. Bitch blew me off when I asked her nice. So I slipped her a little something to change her mind."

Wes could've reasoned with the guy. Could've threatened the guy with legal action for taking advantage of a defenseless woman. Could've accused him of drugging Jessica and assaulting her and called the police.

But it was a hundred times more satisfying to punch the guy in the nose with all of his considerable strength.

"Sonofa—" the guy roared, holding his bloody face. The guy came up swinging, and Wes danced back from the larger man, who was faster than he looked and not nearly as drunk as Wes had hoped he might be. "I'll kill you," the big man growled. "She's mine, and you can't have her."

For some reason, the assertion that Jessica belonged to this jackass infuriated Wes beyond all reason.

The guy charged Wes, coming shoulder first like a football player. Crap. This guy was going to be fully as strong as his bulk suggested.

But Wes had both righteous fury and a burning need to protect Jessica on his side. His rage transformed in a blink of the eye, becoming an icy calm that focused his senses and distilled his purpose into a single pin-point to make this man pay for what he'd intended to do—hell, had nearly done—to Jessica.

The fight was brutal and one-sided. Despite the other man having easily fifty pounds on him, Wes was a combat-trained and battle-hardened Marine. And he was pissed.

By the time the bouncers heard the commotion, made their way past the mosh pit and finally pulled Wes off the guy, Jessica's assailant looked more like hamburger than human.

Wes, still in the grips of adrenaline-enhanced strength, pulled away from the bouncers who had him by the arms and rushed over to kneel in front of Jessica where she'd slid down the wall and was now huddled on the concrete floor, hugging her knees.

"Jess?" he murmured. "Are you okay?"

She looked up, mascara streaking her porcelain skin. She launched herself at him, throwing her arms around his neck with a sob of relief. He stood, taking her with him, and her slender body plastered against his, trembling. Her head lolled against his shoulder and renewed fury coursed through him.

He held her close, doing his damnedest to make her feel safe and protected. Her legs gave out, but he supported her weight easily with an arm around her waist. Lord, he'd forgotten how good she felt in his arms. She tended more toward lean and angular than round and lush, but her body was soft in comparison to his, and she had all the curves he needed.

"You…came," she mumbled against his neck. He felt wetness through his shirt. She was crying.

Holy Mother of God. Jessica Blankenship, force of nature and formidable femme fatale, was *crying*?

"I've got you, babe," he murmured, comforting her as best as he could.

Hands grabbed at him, tugging him away from her. He fought as hard as he could, but there were a lot of hands, and they were collectively stronger than him. People were shouting about police coming, patrons ran in every direction and the chaos was incredible. In the middle of it, a pair of bouncers pulled him away from Jessica.

Wes locked stares with her, and she looked at him in fearful entreaty as the bouncers dragged him, still struggling violently, away from her.

He reached out for her, and her hands came up to reach for him. Then something cracked him painfully across the skull, and everything went black.

Chapter 2

Wes tugged his black dress uniform down, adjusting the white belt at his waist carefully. This hearing was just a formality, but the Marines followed the rules obsessively. He'd assaulted a civilian and was subject to the Uniform Code of Military Justice for doing so. Of course, he'd been rescuing an innocent woman from assault or worse, and everyone knew he would walk away today with a slap on the wrist and an unofficial attaboy for saving Jessica.

He walked into the pale wood military courtroom and nodded at his boss, General Blankenship, who was seated beside his daughter and her lawyer. Oddly, the Old Man didn't nod back. In fact, he was scowling rather thunderously at Wes.

He passed Jessica, who was staring down at her twined fingers in her lap, and took his place at the defendant's table beside his own lawyer, murmuring a quick greeting, then asking, "Any reason why the general's looking so annoyed?"

His lawyer opened his mouth, but the judge entered the courtroom just then, and the bailiff intoned in a rolling baritone, "All rise."

Legalese passed back and forth between the government's lawyer and Wes's lawyer for a minute or so, and then the other lawyer stood up. "In the matter of conduct unbecoming an officer, we call Jessica Blankenship to the stand."

Wes didn't relish hearing the story again of her drugging nor her urgent call to him for a rescue. Still, he pasted the most supportive look he could on his face for her. He was just abjectly grateful he'd reached her before anything worse than some groping and embarrassment had happened to her.

He hadn't been allowed to see her since he'd been hauled away in handcuffs that night a month ago. Which annoyed the hell out of him. He'd desperately wanted to hear from her directly that she was okay. That she wasn't scarred by her near miss with disaster. That he'd kept his promise to her and that no harm had befallen her.

She looked slightly ill as she raised her hand and swore to tell the truth. Worried, he studied her closely. She was too thin. She was wan and had chosen not to wear any makeup to relieve the purple smudges beneath her eyes. Her hair looked odd, tamed into a conservative twist on the back of her head like that. Its lush, long waves were her pride and joy. And for good reason. He'd spent hours trailing his fingers through the lustrous, silken strands.

The hairdo showed off her lovely, slender neck, though. A string of lustrous pearls competed with her skin to be paler and more luminescent. Her skin won.

The prosecution lawyer asked her to relay what had happened to her on the night of his arrest.

This was the part where she would tell about being roofied and calling him, and how he'd charged to her rescue. If Wes was lucky, she would remember how the guy had admitted to drugging her and had refused to leave her alone.

Her sultry voice sounded strained as she said, "Captain Morgan approached my…date…and demanded that he leave. Then Captain Morgan insisted that he wanted to take me home, himself. When my date refused, Captain Morgan, uh, assaulted him."

Wes stared in utter disbelief. She was lying! Not to mention, he would *never* force any woman to go home with him, and she damned well knew it.

"Did you witness this assault by Captain Morgan on your friend?" the lawyer asked.

"Yes."

"How would you describe it?"

"It was violent. One-sided."

"Did your friend fight back?"

"He tried. But Captain Morgan is a lot stronger than him."

"Of course he is. He's a Marine. He's trained in the use of lethal force, isn't that right?"

"I guess so," she answered.

"Would you say that Captain Morgan intended to harm your date?"

"I would say Captain Morgan intended to kill him, sir."

Wes's jaw dropped. She wasn't wrong that an urge

to kill the guy had certainly passed through his mind. But the guy had admitted to drugging her with the intent of forcing himself upon her sexually!

More to the point, he hadn't killed the bastard, no matter how richly he'd deserved to die. He'd restrained himself, dammit. Wes was fully willing to face the music for beating the crap out of that jerk. But attempted murder? Not so much.

The prosecution lawyer pressed on. "I'm entering into evidence these photographs of the victim of Captain Morgan's beating obtained from the emergency room where he was admitted. They are graphic and of a disturbing nature, and in deference to my client, I would like to ask the judge to view the images in chambers and not subject my client to viewing them."

The judge nodded his assent to the request and rose to go into his office to look through a stack of photos the lawyer handed over.

Wes leaned over to his lawyer, whispering, "The guy was huge and said he was going to kill me."

"I'll cross-examine her about it and hope she can corroborate that."

The judge came back, the look on his face grim to say the least. And he was refusing to make eye contact with Wes anymore. A sick feeling lodged in the pit of Wes's stomach. He had pounded the crap out of the bastard, and the list of injuries he'd inflicted had included broken ribs, a ruptured spleen, broken wrist, separated retina and, of course, the broken nose. He expected the guy had copious contusions and bruises to go along with the major injuries, too.

Wes leaned over and whispered urgently to his lawyer, "Ask her about the phone call. She called me.

Begged me to rescue her. Check the damned phone records!"

His lawyer whispered back, "She didn't have a cell phone on her at the time of the raid. I can't prove that she called you. If she won't testify to it, the existence of a phone and of a call to you becomes a he-said-she-said."

"She. Called. Me," he ground out. "Surely the Pentagon has records of it."

But she had likely called on an unsecured public line. No log was made of calls to or from those lines.

His own lawyer was gestured forward to cross-examine Jessica, and he asked, "Did you call anyone for help on the night in question, Miss Blankenship?"

"No."

Wes stared at her. What in the hell was she *doing*? She refused to look at him and was staring fixedly at his lawyer instead.

"Did you contact anyone at all while you were in the nightclub?"

"No."

"Did you ask Captain Morgan to help you? To rescue you from your date? To interfere in any way between you and the man you were with on the night in question?"

"No."

"Did you have any communication at all with Captain Morgan prior to his assault upon the victim?"

Jessica did glance up at Wes then, for just an instant. Her gaze seemed agonized, and then it hardened. Became determined. Shifted back to the questioning lawyer. "No, I had no communication with him."

Wes burst out, "You called me! Begged me to save

you? How would I have even known where you were if you hadn't called me and told me where to find you?"

The judge pounded his gavel and glared at him. Wes got the message loud and clear. This hearing wasn't about justice. It was about railroading him in the name of protecting the reputation of Blankenship's precious daughter.

Hell, didn't it count for anything that the guy he'd beat up hadn't pressed any charges against him at all? Didn't that speak to the man's guilt in drugging Jessica and trying to sexually assault her?

Wes sat back, flabbergasted. Jessica had just single-handedly destroyed his career. He was going to be thrown out of the Corps at a minimum, or even sent to Fort Leavenworth for assaulting that bastard. Was she really that pissed off that he'd broken up with her last summer? Or was Blankenship himself behind this travesty? What had he threatened Jessica with to get her to perjure herself like this?

Wes would refute her testimony, of course. But the fact remained that he'd beaten a civilian man half to death, and her word would be taken over his as to why he'd done it. Not to mention Daddy Dearest was one of the most politically connected officers in the entire Marine Corps. The Blankenships had thrown him under the bus but good. The general might be behind this, but Jessica was bloody well going along with him in this travesty.

What. A. Liar.

Cold rage built in his gut until it consumed his entire being. He literally shook with it. The hearing proceeded around him, and he heard none of it. Only the stark truth that Jessica Blankenship had destroyed him remained in his mind. And there wasn't a damned thing he could do about it.

The judge called a recess for lunch and they reconvened afterward in chambers. It was just Wes, the two lawyers and the judge in the meeting. There was no sign of Jessica or her father in the halls leading to the courtroom.

The judge informed him that, in light of his exemplary service record and heroic service to his country in time of war, he would generously be offered an opportunity to resign his commission before court-martial proceedings were initiated against him.

His lawyer looked at him in open pity. "Take the deal, Wes. Otherwise you'll have a criminal record and a dishonorable discharge that will follow you the rest of your life."

Numb, stunned and utterly devastated, he nodded. A couple of official documents were shoved at him. He signed where indicated and, just like that, his distinguished career was over. He was no longer a Marine. He was…nothing.

Chapter 3

Jessica drove her 1960 red Corvette into Sunny Creek, Montana, wearily. Main Street looked like a picture postcard of an Old West town, with square storefronts of various heights, some brick, some clapboard. Hanging signs were labeled with old-fashioned lettering, hitching posts stood in front of some stores and wagon wheels stood upright in planting beds along the street.

She guided her little sports car down the broad avenue, and it banged along over what felt like cobblestones. How…quaint.

Sunny Creek actually looked like a friendly sort of place. She only prayed it was a friendly sort of place with a hotel. She was exhausted after driving for three days nonstop with only brief pauses for naps and to get more coffee. Her car was a classic, but it was not designed for long road trips.

The happening place on Main Street seemed to be a diner called Pittypat's. She parked in one of the diagonal parking spaces lining each side of the broad street and headed inside. And entered a time warp from the 1950s. It was all turquoise and peach with vinyl booths and the front end of a vintage car coming out of the back wall. There was even a jukebox across from the soda fountain.

"You look ready to drop, sweetie," a gray-haired woman said kindly. "Would you like a booth and a cup of coffee?"

"I'm all coffeed out. What I need is food."

"We have plenty of that around here. Take a look at the menu and let me know what looks good to you. Everything's tasty."

"I could really use some comfort food. What do you recommend?"

The woman laughed. "My sister makes a mean beef stew. We could add some of her homemade yeast biscuits to that, and finish it off with a piece of pie, and you'd have a nice meal."

"Sold."

"What's your favorite kind of pie? Petunia's the best baker in these parts. Her pies are famous."

She must have been more exhausted than she realized, for all of a sudden Jessica was back in the lake house, about age five, sitting at the kitchen table with her mother—who was only a vague, beautiful ghost of a memory—digging into a piece of made-totally-from-scratch lemon meringue pie, so tall and fluffy she could barely see over it.

"Do you have lemon meringue?" she asked wistfully.

"Sure do. I'll save you back a piece for when you're done with your supper."

The stew was hot and thick, savory and bracing. She had a second bowl of it, and a second satiny-soft yeast roll the size of her fist to go with it.

When the waitress, whose name tag declared her to be Patricia, put the pie in front of Jessica and she bit into the tart lemon filling and airy, sweet meringue, she surprised herself by tearing up.

"What's wrong, sweetie?" Patricia asked quickly.

"It tastes just like my mother's. She died when I was a little girl."

The waitress slid into the booth across from her and reached out to hold her hand. "Well, I'm glad we could help you conjure up a memory. Tell me about her."

Jessica blinked, startled at the woman's kindness. "I don't remember much. Only a few images of her laughing. She was tall and elegant and beautiful."

"Do you take after her?"

"My father says I do."

"Well, I'm not surprised. You look like an old-time movie star."

Jessica smiled. "I get that a lot. I suppose it's the way my hair waves."

"It's more than that. You've got good bones. Breeding. If you'll forgive my saying it, you look like old money."

Which wasn't wrong. Her mother's family had been East Coast money from way back, complete with summers in the Hamptons and a mansion on the Hudson River. Her father had been a handsome young Marine officer who'd swept her off her feet and hauled her off to be a military wife. But apparently, she'd always insisted on living off base in beautiful old homes she restored to their former glory. Jessica took after her in that, too.

Jessica said, "I remember her picking me up and spinning me around. Oh, and she used to go swimming with me in the lake. She wore a red one-piece bathing suit. She drowned when I was six."

Patricia patted her hand sympathetically, which almost made Jessica cry again. She dug into the pie to distract herself.

"What brings you to Sunny Creek, dear?"

"I'm looking for an old friend. We have some unfinished business to attend to. His name is Wes Morgan. Perhaps you know him?"

"Everyone in this town knows the Morgans. They own Runaway Ranch, up in the high country north of town."

"Do you know where I can find Wes? Is he at his family's ranch?"

Patricia leaned forward and lowered her voice. "Wes came home from the Marines a few months ago. He and his papa had a huge falling-out and aren't speaking to each other. Way I hear it, Wes has bought himself some land adjoining his daddy's ranch and is setting himself up in the cattle business. Gonna go up against his daddy, supposedly. That boy always did have a lot to prove."

"Why's that?"

"His father's a hard man. Demanding of his boys. Wes is the only one who followed his daddy into the Marine Corps. John Morgan was a war hero in Vietnam, and he expected Wes to live up to the family name."

Jessica winced. She knew what came next in this tale because she'd caused it.

Patricia continued, "John was mighty miffed when

Wes left the military under a cloud. Nobody around here knows what happened, but it was some kind of scandal."

"Is that why Wes and his father argued?"

Patricia shrugged. "Who knows with those Morgan men? They're a stubborn bunch, they are."

God. Yet another sin to atone for. She'd destroyed Wes's career, and now she'd ruined his relationship with his family, too.

"Where can I find Wes's house?"

"It's north of town on the Westlake Trace Road. But you don't want to head up there, now. It's getting dark, and there's a storm coming."

Jessica glanced out the window into the twilight and was startled to see that while she'd been eating, it had started to snow. Small crystalline flakes fell in deep silence, floating down gently to kiss the earth like diamond dust.

"I'll be all right. And I'm in a hurry to see Wes. My business with him is urgent."

Patricia looked dubious but gave her directions across town and up into the mountains. Jessica settled her bill, left a big tip for the kind woman and headed out of town.

On her way out of Sunny Creek, she drove down a street lined with a dozen grand old Victorian mansions—and every last one of them in sad disrepair. Her restoration designer's soul perked up.

The Westlake Trace turned out to be a decent road, but it twisted and turned up into the mountains and forced her to go slow and pay close attention to her driving. Which was hard because vast vistas of towering mountains and deep valleys kept opening up beside her, drawing her eye to them.

The mountain peaks disappeared into a blanket of clouds as the last light faded and black, deep night fell around her. She had to slow down even more as the snow intensified and her headlights struggled to cut through the darkness. The road disappeared under a layer of snow, and she slowed to a crawl in order to stay on the road at all.

Man, it was snowing hard. Snow was accumulating fast. There had to be three inches on the road already, and more piling up.

She almost missed the turnoff to Wes's ranch. A dilapidated arch crossed over the driveway, built of old gray wood rails. A name was burned into the wood in rough, black lettering that looked recently done. *Outlaw Ranch*.

Her heart contracted in pain. Wes was the soul of law and order. He'd been a fast-burner up through the Marine ranks, and her father had said from day one that Wes was destined to be a general. Everyone who met Captain Wes Morgan admired and respected him. They all thought he was bound for greatness.

And now he called himself an outlaw.

God. She'd *wrecked* him.

She'd had no choice. The voice on her phone had told her in no uncertain terms that Wes would die if she didn't do what the voice said and testify against him.

Tears choked her throat. She'd resisted at first. But then her pocket puppy, a sweet little Chihuahua named Paco, had died abruptly.

He'd been sixteen years old, but he'd been in seemingly perfect health. One day he was fine, and the next, he was acting strange and died that night at the vet's office. The veterinarian thought he might have ingested rat poison. But where? How? The little dog had never left the Blankenship house.

And then the voice had called back. Told Jessica that the same thing would happen to Wes if she said anything about that night, about the assault and about her being drugged.

A sob ravaged her chest, and she drew a shaky breath as she put the car back into gear.

She *had* to find a way to make it right. To help him put his life back together.

She rattled over a metal grate under the arch and then followed the gravel drive across what looked like a cattle pasture. It rose steadily toward a pair of mountains looming close like craggy giants. A light cut through the snow, and she pulled up in front of one of the saddest houses she'd ever seen. Once upon a time, it would have been a warm and inviting home. Now, it was falling into ruin.

It was a sprawling one-story ranch house with a steeply pitched roof and a long, deep porch across the entire front facade. Gray vertical wood siding was split and badly weathered, and the metal roof was rusty, the remaining shutters sagging badly. Two stone chimneys rose up above the structure, both of them putting out a thin thread of smoke.

Good Lord. Mr. Neat-and-Tidy lived here? How low had Wes sunk?

An equally sorry-looking barn sagged behind the decrepit house. She thought she spied some outbuildings, though it was hard to tell in the darkness and snow. The light she'd seen came from a window at the far right end of the porch.

She climbed out of her car, slipping and sliding

through ankle-deep snow to the porch. A board for one of the steps was missing, and she stepped over the gap. The porch floor looked ready to collapse at any minute and she picked her way across it carefully.

The front door stopped her in her tracks, and she paused to examine it in the faint glow from the window beside it. The panel looked made of solid oak, a rich golden color. The entire thing was magnificently carved with eagles and wolves and horses and buffalo. Mountains rose in relief behind the animals, and the vertical door handle was bronze, cast to look like an aspen tree whose branches spread up one side of the panel.

She had never been a great fan of Western decor, but this carving rose to the level of art. The animals were so detailed and realistic she almost expected them to jump off the panel and head out into the wilderness.

She felt the carving with her fingertips, marveling at how fine the texturing was. She couldn't imagine how many hours the artist must have put into this. The carving was sharp. Fresh. Not weathered with time or age. Huh. A local artist must have made it. Maybe she could find him or her and commission some pieces for her design business back home—

Oh, wait. That life was over. Gone. Turned out she'd wrecked herself nearly as badly as she'd wrecked Wes.

It dawned on her that a frigid wind was cutting through her thin jacket, swirling snow around her feet and sending ice picks of cold into her body. She realized with a start that tears were freezing on her cheeks, or maybe that was just snow stinging them. Either way, she needed to get inside before she got frostbite.

She lifted the burled knot of wood mounted in a

brass fitting and knocked it firmly against the metal plate behind it.

She waited a minute.

No answer.

She knocked again.

This time she heard movement inside the house and waited, shivering, praying to get out of this biting wind.

At long last, the door opened. A man wearing a bulky Aran knit sweater, jeans and heavy work boots stood there. His hair was thick and dark and shaggy, his face covered with a dark, thick beard.

She stepped back, startled. She'd been expecting Wes. "I'm sorry," she stammered. "I must have the wrong house. I was told this was where I could find…"

She trailed off, staring at the man's eyes. They were dark, almost black in the dim light spilling out from behind him. But she still spied their sapphire hue, as deep as the ocean and more blue.

"Wes?" she asked in disbelief.

The door slammed shut in her face. Hard.

She would take that as confirmation that she did, indeed, have the right house. And, furthermore, that Wes was no happier to see her than she'd expected. Guilt ripped through her, tinged with disbelief. That wild mountain man was the trim and sharp Marine she'd known for years?

Temptation to turn and walk away coursed through her. He would never forgive her. She had ruined his life. It was insanity to even try to make up for what she'd done to him.

Still, she'd vowed to try. At a minimum she owed him a face-to-face apology.

She shouted through the door. "Please let me in! Just for a minute."

A muffled voice came back through the door at her. "Go away."

"Wes, we need to talk. I—" she added lamely "—need to apologize to you." Which was the understatement of the century.

The door cracked open again. "I don't need your apology. I don't *want* your apology. Go back to wherever you came from and don't ever come near me again."

"I can't. I'm sorry."

"I told you not to apologize!"

She explained reluctantly, "It's snowing really hard, and my car isn't cut out for winter driving. I barely got this far. I don't think I can make it back to town to-night."

"You drove the Corvette up here? Oh, for the love of Mike. You never did have a lick of sense."

She smiled sadly. "No, I never did. And I'm afraid I'm stuck up here."

The door remained almost closed for a moment more and then opened wide. "Get inside, then. But I'm not interested in hearing your tearful confession. You can spend the night, but you're out of here first thing in the morning, even if I have to tow you down the damn mountain with my tractor."

The bitter tone in his voice was unlike him. But she surely didn't begrudge him some bitterness. "Fair enough," she said as evenly as she could manage past the lump in her throat.

She stepped inside and was surprised by the vaulted ceiling and log rafters over a spacious great room. This place had tons of potential. Of course, the inside of the ranch house was nearly as battered and worn as the outside. But the bones were there.

To her left, a fireplace was made of gray rocks that started basketball-sized and gradually got smaller as they rose up from a broad hearth to the ceiling. A fire burned brightly in it, and heat radiated from it and from the stones to warm the entire room.

At the right end of the large room, an island covered in peeling linoleum separated a big kitchen toward the back of the house from the living space. In front of the kitchen was a dining space. Nice open floor plan. Good flow. That hideous wagon-wheel chandelier over the table had to go, though. To her left, in front of the fireplace, a hallway stretched out, no doubt leading to bedrooms.

"Give me your keys. I'll pull your car into one of the barns."

She handed over her keys and Wes disappeared outside. She wandered around the living room and kitchen, redecorating it in her mind. A Rocky Mountain theme. Gray slate and blue granite. Oversize furniture in muted colors, maybe a pop of red here and there. Hardwood floors—wide hand-scraped planks would look best.

The log rafters were magnificent, actually. They just needed sanding and staining to regain their original glory—

Wes blew in on a howling gust of wind. "Got the place redecorated yet?" he asked sourly.

He knew her too well. "It'll clean up nicely."

"Not happening on your watch. I'm not kidding. You're out of here in the morning."

She nodded her understanding. Wes never had been the most flexible soul. Her artistic, free-spirited ways had often bumped into this rigid side of him. She suspected she actually needed the stability of someone like him in her life, but she'd spent so long rebelling against the choke hold her father kept on her that she'd never tested the theory.

"Have you eaten?" He asked the question reluctantly, as if he didn't want to be polite to her but his manners were too ingrained to stop himself.

"Yes. I stopped at Pittypat's."

"Guest bedroom is the first door on the right. Bathroom's the door beyond that."

And with that pronouncement, he headed down the hallway, leaving her standing in the middle of the living room. It was barely nine o'clock. Surely he wasn't going to sleep this early. No, he was just retreating to his own room to avoid having to make nice with her. She sighed and followed him down the hallway.

"Wes, I really need to talk with you—"

He whirled so fast she barely saw him move. He had her backed up against the wall, hands on her shoulders pinning her in place, before she could draw a single shocked breath. Her body responded violently, recognizing and remembering him, heck, lusting after him. Her insides went liquid and molten in an instant, and her mind exploded with a single thought. She *wanted* him. She'd never stopped wanting him.

The crazy magnetism that had always flared between them when they were in proximity to each other exploded again tonight. Awareness tore through her with his strong fingers digging into her shoulders, with the rapid rise and fall of his muscular chest, with the way her own breathing accelerated to match his.

She lifted her shocked gaze to his…and froze.

The rage burning in his eyes was so white-hot he almost looked as if he'd lost his sanity.

They'd always had sparks between them. Always felt the pull of attraction. Sure, they'd fought it for a while, given in to it for a while, seen that it was a huge mistake and backed off. That didn't mean the sizzling attraction had ever gone away. Why was he looking at her like this? Was he that angry that she was still attracted to him? Or, worse, was he still attracted to her and reacting this angrily to the idea?

He snarled, "Get this through your pretty, spoiled little head. I do *not* want to talk with you. *Ever.* I don't give a damn what you have to say to me, and I don't care if your guilty conscience is driving you crazy with the need to apologize to me. I don't want to hear it. In the morning, you'll leave. And don't ever come back here. You get out of my life and stay out of it. Understood?"

"Well, I understand, but I really need to—"

"Don't push me. I'm perilously close to hurting you right now." And with that growled warning, he shoved away from her and strode to his bedroom, slamming the door shut behind him.

She would be indignant at being shut down like that if she didn't understand the source of his rage. She'd destroyed his career. Actually, she'd nuked it in spectacular fashion. He had every right to be angry with her. But she really did need to speak with him. Beyond the apology she so desperately owed him, she had a problem. And it impacted him, too.

Still, it hurt to have him look at her like that. Like he genuinely despised her. If only he would listen to her. Give her time to explain that she'd never meant him any harm. Quite the opposite, in fact. She'd never stopped caring about him. A lot.

What was it going to take to get through to him? She considered going down the hall and knocking on his door. But that slightly mad expression in his eyes was enough to give her pause. In the morning would be soon enough to talk with him. After he'd had some sleep and gotten over the initial shock of her showing up at his front door.

She wandered back to the living room. The furniture arrangement was all wrong. The couch needed to be parallel to the hearth, and the recliner should face the back wall where the television was mounted—

She stopped herself. It was his house. She really shouldn't rearrange the furniture, but he would thank her for it when he realized how much more functional the layout was…and it wasn't that big a change…

She gave the long couch an experimental tug. It was heavy. But it did move. That did it. She pushed the sofa to where it properly belonged and dragged the chair to its left. Better. The coffee table's edge was scarred like one too many pair of boots had been propped on it. The thing really needed a rug under it to anchor it, but the great room was entirely rugless. Drat.

She flopped down on the couch and watched the fire burn. The dance of white-yellow flames hypnotized her, lulling her into a relaxation she hadn't felt since that fateful night at the underground club in Washington.

As best she could tell, the guy Wes had dragged off her had spiked the drink he'd bought her. Thank God she'd only sipped at it and hadn't consumed the whole thing. She'd stayed conscious for Wes on the phone much longer than she'd expected to. As far as she could tell, she'd only been fully unconscious for a little while. And then Wes had arrived and saved her. It had been a close call with disaster. Far, far too close.

Now when she looked at men—all men—she saw a threat. Intellectually, she knew that most men were respectful and kind to women. But her gut didn't want to play along with trusting any of them.

As if that wasn't bad enough, the emails had started coming, threatening the life of the one man she did trust. She couldn't lose Wes. Even if he hated her for the rest of their lives, she needed to know that one good man existed out there somewhere.

Every time she waivered and considered contacting Wes to explain herself, another email arrived. It was uncanny how the sender seemed to sense when she was on the verge of cracking and telling Wes everything. She began to suspect that whoever was writing the emails either knew her or was watching her. Which turned out to be a surefire recipe for soul-sucking paranoia, terrible sleep and a destroyed appetite. Sometimes, she seriously thought she was losing her mind.

Unable to take the stress any longer, she'd finally snuck out of Washington without telling even her father where she was going or that she was leaving town. She'd just thrown a few clothes and toiletries in a bag and started driving. And here she was.

She had to find a way to get Wes to listen to her. She *had* to warn him. *In the morning.* Before he kicked her to the curb—or to the cow pie, as it were—she would force him to hear her out.

There had to be some way she could make all of this up to him. If only she wasn't tired all the way to the depths of her soul. If only she could think. Tomorrow. She would find it tomorrow.

Her head nodded forward on her chest, then jerked upright. She kicked off her sheepskin boots, tucking her feet under the ragged throw blanket across the back of the couch. She pulled the scratchy wool across her shoulders and drifted off, staring into the flames of her life.

Wes woke with a start. What was that noise? Someone was in his house. He went on full battle alert before he remembered that Jessica had shown up at his door unannounced and unwelcome. A bitter taste filled his mouth. Talk about nasty shocks. Opening his door to see her standing there, tall and elegant and more beautiful than ought to be legal, her eyes bright with worry and her cheeks rosy with cold—sheesh. His heart couldn't take too many shocks like that.

He heard the sound again. A moan of fear and pain. Swearing, he threw back the covers and yanked on jeans. He grabbed a T-shirt and pulled it on as he headed into the hall. He poked his head in the guest room, but the bed was still made. Frowning, he headed for the living room.

Jessica was stretched out on the couch, tangled in the old saddle blanket he'd thrown over the back of the thing to hide the threadbare cushions. She twitched and then thrashed as some nightmare stalked her.

He tossed several pieces of split oak onto the almost dead fire and used the bellows to blow on the embers until they glowed brightly. The seasoned wood caught fast, and bright new flames licked at the logs.

He sat on the hearth and contemplated the woman

on his sofa. The firelight kissed her skin, which was as silky and dewy soft as he remembered. If anything, the past few months had made her even more beautiful than he remembered. He had never tired of looking at her. It was just when she was awake that he had a huge problem with her. She was selfish, scheming and childishly vengeful if history was any indication.

Jessica quieted and he caught himself staring hungrily at her perfect features, remembering her slender body wrapped around his, all that fiery passion for life spilling over onto him. Nope. Not opening that can of worms again. He'd been burned too badly the first time.

He nursed his rage, cloaking himself in its protection from the niggle of hurt gnawing at his gut. He didn't care why she'd done it. He knew why. She was a self-serving bitch who'd chosen to protect her own dubious reputation rather than telling the truth and exonerating him.

He stood up to go back to bed. But his movement must have woken her, for Jessica's luminous, sky blue eyes opened, and she looked around wildly, lurching upright. He stared at her, shocked.

That was stone-cold terror on her face. Since when did she experience that kind of fear? She was ballsy and bold, charging headfirst into life with courage he'd seen matched in only a few of the most confident of warriors. But here she was in the deep silence of a Montana snowstorm acting like the boogeyman was about to snatch her up and eat her alive.

Frowning, he murmured, "You had a bad dream."

She reached up…and dashed away wetness from her cheek. She was *crying*? There was a snowball fight happening in hell at this very second.

"Sorry I woke you up," she mumbled.

Apologetic Jessica was another first. Since when did she regret anything she did? Maybe that scare with getting drugged had taught her a much-needed lesson in caution and humility.

Still, this was the woman who'd told bald-faced lies in a court of law and had forced him to pay the price. He muttered, "If you're done thrashing around, I'll go back to bed now."

"No more thrashing. I promise."

"Thrash all you'd like. It's no skin off my nose. You might want to go back into the bedroom, though. That couch puts a mean kink in a person's back." He should know. He fell asleep out here in front of the fire more nights than not. He had demons of his own waiting for him in dreamland. And most of them were elegant blondes who tied him up in emotional knots he was helpless to resist.

Shaking his head, he padded back to his room to do some thrashing around of his own as sleep eluded him and rage and betrayal wrestled in his gut. *One night.* He just had to survive this night. And then he'd get rid of her forever.

Chapter 4

Jessica woke with a start for the second time and lurched upright. Shabby room. Giant fireplace with a dead fire. A deep, bone-chilling cold pervaded the room.

Montana. Wes. And a snowstorm.

He hated her guts as he rightfully should and was refusing to let her explain anything to him. She *had* to make him listen. Poking her feet into her boots, she laid some wood on the ashes and used the bellows to blow on them. Nothing. The fire had gone out completely. Depressed by the cold gray ashes, she spotted some kindling and a newspaper folded in the wood holder. She wadded up a few pieces of it, laid the kindling and went hunting for matches. She found some in a drawer in the kitchen and carried them back to the hearth.

It took a few minutes of babying it along, but eventually the wood lit and the fire became self-sustaining. That task taken care of, she headed for the kitchen to see how stocked it was with food. She found a half-dozen eggs and some bacon. And then she spotted a pint of cream and some cheese. Now she was talking! She hunted around in the cupboards and found a bag of flour and some old-fashioned lard. Now for a pie pan. She found only an old cake pan stuffed in the back of a cupboard. That would work. She rolled up her sleeves and went to work, mixing a pastry crust, shredding cheese, frying bacon and putting together a quiche lorraine. Carefully, she placed it the oven and went looking for something to go with it. A bag of potatoes in the pantry and an onion became a fried hash while the quiche cooked. As the meal came together, she frowned at the ancient drip coffeepot on the kitchen counter. If she could work a French press, surely she could figure this out.

The cantankerous machine was finally dripping coffee through a paper filter when Wes said from behind her, "What's all this?"

"A peace offering. That, and I was hungry."

"It would take a hell of a lot more than a nice breakfast to make peace with me, darlin'."

At least he thought it was a nice breakfast. She didn't, however, take him calling her darling as anything other than the sarcasm it was meant to be. She poured him a cup of coffee and used the bit of cream she'd saved to gunk it up the way he liked it. "Try this. I wasn't sure how to work your coffee maker. How is it?" she asked anxiously.

He sipped it and grimaced. "Strong."

"I'm sorry. I'll remake it."

"Stop fussing, Jess. I can add a little more milk and some sugar, and it'll be fine."

Anxiously she served him a slice of the quiche and some hash.

"Will you stop hovering long enough to get yourself a plate of food and sit down?" he finally grumbled.

Too tense to eat now that the moment was upon her to talk with Wes, she settled for pouring herself a cup of coffee. She took a sip and grimaced. No amount of cream or sugar was going to save that. It tasted terrible. Well. Wasn't this conversation off to a spectacular start?

She dived in, blurting, "Aren't you going to ask me why I lied?"

He froze in the act of taking a bite of the quiche. Laid his fork down slowly without taking the bite. Wiped his mouth and folded his napkin with exacting precision. Leaned back in his chair. And finally looked up at her. He pinned her with a stare that would freeze a polar bear. He hadn't been a Marine officer for nothing.

It took every ounce of self-discipline she had not to fidget under that accusing glare.

He spoke from between clenched teeth. "I know why you lied."

She stared. "You do?"

He shrugged, but the movement was so tense she wasn't sure what that jerk of his shoulders was at first. "You threw me under the bus to save your reputation and your father's. I hope you both find them to be cold comfort when you end up alone."

He stood up abruptly, startling her, and carried his plate over to the sink.

"That's not why!" she exclaimed.

Another exaggeratedly slow movement, this time to

turn around and stare at her from over by the sink. She noticed with dismay that his hands were balled into fists at his sides.

"Fine. Why?" he bit out. His voice didn't quite shake with rage but wasn't far from it. With that beard and wild look in his eyes, he looked lke some sort of crazed mountain man. Where was the spit-and-polish Marine she'd fallen so hard for before? She searched for any sign of him, and the only remnant she spied was the rigid set of his shoulders and ramrod-straight spine.

She explained urgently, "I was threatened. I got a bunch of anonymous emails saying that if I didn't destroy you professionally, they would kill you."

"They who?"

She stared down at her fingers, twined together, tugging at each other until they turned red. "I don't know. But they knew things about me. Like what I was wearing and where I was. They were following me."

"Why didn't you go to the police?"

"Because I believed them," she answered desperately.

He huffed. "You know better than to give in to anonymous threats. You should have called their bluff."

"I did. They killed my dog."

"Paco? How do you know someone killed that little rat? Wasn't he about a hundred years old?"

Paco had been more than a little neurotic and he'd had lots of quirks. But he surely hadn't deserved to be murdered. "The veterinarian did a tox screen, and he died from ingesting large quantities of rat poison."

"Dogs get into stuff like that if it's left where they can reach it."

"We didn't have anything like that in the house. And

he was never let out of the house. Someone came into my father's house and deliberately fed it to him."

"So because someone poisoned your dog, you decided you had to destroy my life?"

"Of course not. Because someone poisoned my dog and threatened to harm you, I took the threats against you seriously. That's why I—" she choked on the word but forced it out anyway "—lied."

Wes demanded, "Do you have any idea how insane that sounds?"

"Yes. I do. But you have to believe me. They promised me—*promised me*—they'd kill you if I didn't get you thrown out of the military."

"That's a pretty specific threat. What did your father think about it?"

She winced. "I couldn't tell him. They threatened to kill him, too."

"You seriously expect me to believe this ridiculous story?"

She opened her mouth to ask him why she would lie about something like that and then realized in the nick of time how stupid that would sound to him. "Someone has been following me."

"So you've seen whoever's threatening you? Who is it?"

"I haven't seen anyone's face. Cars tail me, and I see strangers lurking behind me in doorways and down the street."

"That sounds more like paranoia than a problem."

"I got more emails after the hearing. They continued to threaten you and my father."

"You definitely should have called the police."

"Wes, I was afraid! I still am!"

"Why? You already ruined my life. Who cares if someone knocks me off?"

"I care! And you should, too."

"Drama queen, much?" he muttered.

"I drove all the way out here to warn you that someone is threatening to kill you. Look, I was pretty sure you wouldn't accept my apology if I tried to say I was sorry for tanking your career. I get it. But you have to believe me when I tell you someone is threatening you and my father. I lied to save the only two men in the world I lo—" she broke off and corrected herself "—that I care about."

The look on his face made it clear she had wasted both her time and her breath by coming out here to see him. Her heart ached far more than it should have at the way he was shutting her out. They'd been broken off for a while when the whole catastrophe happened. She wasn't still harboring *love* for him, was she?

Why else would the anger and disgust in his eyes be so hard to look at?

She stood up, her spine rigid. She wasn't going to get out of this exchange with her honor intact. But she could at least leave with her dignity intact. She said quietly, "I thought I at least owed you the courtesy of letting you know you may be in danger."

He snorted. "This is Montana. Strangers stick out like a sore thumb around here, and everyone owns a rifle. Not much crime happens in these parts that the locals don't take care of immediately. Hell, the sheriff is my cousin."

"Great. Then I'll just take my warning and leave you to your vigilante justice. Good luck with that."

The least he could do was show a tiny bit of gratitude for the dire warning she'd delivered to him. Even if he did decide to completely blow it off, she'd gone to a lot of trouble to get here to share it with him. Not that she expected him to care. She should have expected him not to believe her.

She grabbed her coat, opened the front door and stopped cold. A wall of snow that came nearly to her waist confronted her. She turned around to ask for another way out and spied Wes leaning against the edge of the kitchen island, arms crossed, studying her like she was some kind of unwelcome bug.

She asked reluctantly, "Is there another way out to my car, or am I going to have to bust through that?"

"The barn your car is parked in has a bigger drift than that in front of it. You're not going anywhere today."

She swore colorfully. She *really* didn't want to spend the entire day with Wes glowering at her like she was sharing some contagious disease with him.

He shrugged. "If you're gonna be stuck here, you might as well make yourself useful."

Her gaze narrowed. That sounded ominous. She wouldn't put it past him to exact some sort of petty revenge on her now that he had her at his mercy. "What did you have in mind?"

"This is a ranch. There's always work to be done."

Yup. Petty revenge. Well, two could play that game. She smiled brightly. "Great! I've been cooped up in a car for three days. Getting out and doing something physical sounds wonderful."

She glanced down at her leggings and silk blouse. "But I'm not exactly dressed for it."

"Change into something else."

"I grabbed my purse, left my father's house and

started driving. I didn't pack a suitcase to signal to anyone that I was leaving town. I have the clothes on my back until I can get back to an actual town with stores and do a little shopping."

Wes rolled his eyes. "City slicker. I don't suppose you have a heavier coat than that skimpy jacket you wore last night, either, do you?"

"March is springtime in Washington!"

"Newsflash—it's still winter here."

She made a face. "I figured that out as I drove up here in a blizzard last night."

He grinned sardonically. "*That* was not a blizzard. That was a minor late-season snowstorm."

She rolled her eyes.

"I suppose I can lend you some work clothes."

He strode down the hall to his room and emerged in a minute with a pair of jeans, a belt, a black T-shirt and a hoodie sweatshirt. "Leave your leggings on under the jeans. You'll need the layers. While you put this stuff on, I'll go see if I can find a pair of my old work boots that might fit you."

Work boots? Good grief. He really was planning to torture her!

She emerged from the guest bedroom feeling like a snowman. Wes was in the living room with a pair of what looked a lot like combat boots but clunkier, if that was actually possible.

"If you wear a couple pairs of socks, these should work."

He held out the boots and she grimaced at their weight. "Are there lead blocks in these?"

"Steel toes. You need them when working around large animals and heavy equipment."

Animals? Equipment?

Deeply skeptical of whatever he had planned for her, she donned the three pairs of socks that he lent her and the boots. Silently he handed her a pair of wool-lined leather work gloves. She followed him out the side door between the kitchen and dining room. A mudroom extended the full width of the end of the house. Cold bit through her clothes instantly, and she shivered as Wes passed her a thick parka and an ugly knit cap. Fashion be damned. It was freezing out here. She yanked on the cap and pulled the parka's hood up over it for good measure.

Wes donned a big sheepskin coat and led her outside. Bright sunshine glittered off the snow, blinding her. She squinted against the glare and followed the dark blob of Wes down the porch steps. He broke a path through the drifts and she followed close on his heels. An icy wind picked up the powdery snow, coating her clothing and stinging her skin everywhere it was exposed to the air.

He slid open a big barn door on a squeaky track, and she slipped inside the decrepit barn behind him. It was warmer in here. Quiet. It smelled of sweetgrass on a summer day. And it was crammed with fuzzy red cows with curly white faces.

She cringed beside Wes as one of them turned to sniff her with its wet pink nose.

He spoke soothingly, no doubt so he wouldn't upset the animals—because God knew he didn't give a damn about her feelings. "They won't hurt you. They're Herefords. One of the gentlest breeds of cattle. Think of them as giant, docile puppies, and you'll have their temperament about right."

"Really? They seem so…big."

He laughed. "Bulls—they're big. And muscular. These are all cows. They'll start calving in the next month or so. See their big bellies? And how their sides stick out?"

"They're pregnant ladies? That's so cool. Can I pet them?"

"You don't pet a cow. But you can scratch them. They like to have their shoulders scratched right here or, if they like you, around their ears or under their chin. Like this." The cow he demonstrated on all but lay down on his hand, so happy she was to be scratched.

"That's adorable!" Jessica exclaimed under her breath.

Wes gave her a withering look. "Cows are not adorable. They're good-looking or well built or have nice conformation."

"Well, yours are adorable. Look at those curly faces! I'm dying."

Wes rolled his eyes. "Good thing you won't be here to see the calves. They have knobby knees and whiter, curlier faces than their mamas. Now *they* are adorable."

"Isn't it too cold for calves to be born?" she asked in concern.

"Spring will be here in another month. There will be green grass in the pastures and it'll be warm in the daytime. I'll bring the cows inside at night for a few extra weeks so the calves aren't killed by predators."

"Killed?" she exclaimed. The nearest cows threw their heads up in alarm, and she muttered, "Sorry."

"You don't have to say you're sorry to cows. Since when did you become such an apologizer, anyway?"

She looked over at him in surprise. "What do you mean?"

"You never used to be sorry for anything. You were fearless and took life head-on. No regrets. No looking back. What happened?"

She shrugged. "The nightclub happened."

"How'd you get drugged?" He sounded reluctant, like he hated to ask but had been dying to ask the question for a long time.

"The guy you pulled off me tried to pick me up and I turned him down. He came back a few minutes later carrying a drink and apologized really nicely. It didn't even occur to me that he would try to get even by dropping a roofie on me. God, it was so easy for him to incapacitate me."

"Scary," he muttered.

"*You* think it's scary! It terrifies me how close I came to being raped. I never did get a chance to thank you for charging in to the rescue like you did. You saved my life."

"If you're trying to tell me it was worth destroying my life for, don't. There were other ways to save yourself that didn't involve me. You could have called the police directly."

She rubbed the shoulders of the nearest cow absently and was surprised when the animal leaned into her hand a little. She confessed, "I was afraid the police wouldn't believe me. Or that they would think it was my fault for ingesting the roofie in the first place. I knew you would believe me and come right away."

He scowled. "Gee. Thanks for the vote of confidence. I'm so glad my reliability and gullibility made me behave as forecast."

"I didn't mean it like that—"

"Don't." To punctuate his order, he moved away from her, winding into the closely packed herd of cattle.

"Where are you going?"

"To feed," he answered unhelpfully.

She debated staying here by the door, on her own with the unknown feeding behaviors of cows, or following him. She opted for Wes. He might hate her guts, but he was a known quantity.

She stepped in something squishy, and a pungent odor immediately rose up. *Oh. My. God.* Horrified, she didn't look down and kept on going, praying Wes wouldn't be furious that she'd stepped in a fresh cow pie in his boots.

He stood behind a long feeding trough on the other side of a gate made of steel pipe. She quickly unlatched the gate, slipped through and relatched it behind her. Wes handed her a big metal scoop. "Start throwing corn in the trough. Don't stop until I tell you to."

She dug with gusto into a huge burlap bag of dried cracked corn and dumped a scoop of corn into the long, V-shaped feeder. The cows moved into a line, side by side, every one poking its nose into the trough eagerly.

She moved a little bit down the line to scoop and dump again. And again.

By the twentieth time she'd scooped and dumped, she'd added pain to the rhythm. *Scoop. Pain. Dump. Pain. Scoop. Pain. Dump. Pain.* Her shoulders and back ached, her arms burned and even her hands ached from the weight of the corn.

"More?" she called. She'd lost sight of Wes and had no idea where he'd gone off to.

"Keep scooping." His voice was muffled and came from above her. She realized a partial second floor jutted out to right about where she stood. A hayloft, maybe?

She looked up at the loft just in time to catch a face full of fine green hay leaves. They got in her eyes and mouth and tasted sweet and green, but the hay dust made her sneeze violently. She stepped back under the overhang hastily and realized with dismay that her hair was *full* of hay. He had done that on purpose!

Scowling, she combed her fingers through her hair in a futile effort to get the bits of clinging hay out. No luck. She was covered in the stuff.

"Are you scooping?" he called down. "Those poor, pregnant cows are hungry."

Jerk. She resumed scooping, keeping a wary eye on where big flakes of hay were flying down into the feeder from above. Any time he neared her, she prudently stepped back out of the way. Eventually, when she'd laid down a line of corn along the entire fifty-foot-or-so length of the trough, and had gone back to the beginning and replenished it again, Wes called down, "That's enough corn."

She sagged, exhausted. She must have scooped three hundred pounds' worth of the kernels. Wes came down from the loft and joined her. She asked him, "Do you scoop all that corn every day?"

He shrugged. "I just pick up the bags and walk down the feeder with them. Takes me about thirty seconds."

"And you made me do it one scoop at a time?" she exclaimed.

"I didn't think you could pick up a hundred-pound sack of corn."

Oh. Well, there was that. She looked up at him side-long, and for a fleeting moment his dark, dark blue eyes glinted with humor. It was just a glimpse of the old Wes, the man she'd fallen for, but he was still in there. Hiding, maybe, inside the angry, bitter man he'd become.

She looked down the line of contentedly munching cows. "Will you keep them inside until the snow melts?"

"Good Lord, no. They'll go outside as soon as they're done eating. Because they're in the late stages of pregnancy, I'm supplementing their forage to make sure they're getting plenty of high-quality nutrition. They'll go outside and graze on the exposed grass and will dig through the snow to expose more roughage for themselves."

"Won't they get cold?"

"Have you taken a look at their coats? Their fur's nearly three inches long. If anything, I have to guard against them getting too warm inside this barn and shedding out their winter hair too soon."

"I had no idea you knew so much about cows."

He rolled his eyes. "What part of 'I grew up on a ranch in Montana' didn't you get?"

"It's one thing to hear it. It's another to see exactly what that means."

"Well, now you've seen it. You can go back to DC and resume your regularly scheduled jet-set life."

But that was the thing. She couldn't go back. Her previous life had been irrevocably taken from her when she'd realized how terribly vulnerable her party-girl lifestyle had made her to predators like the man who'd drugged her.

Aloud, she mused, "I'm not sure what my regularly scheduled life should look like anymore."

Wes snorted. "That makes two of us."

She frowned. "It looks to me like you've settled right

back into your old life. You own a ranch. Some cows. A house."

He turned on her abruptly, and the fury in his stare made her step back from him. He ground out, "I never wanted this life for myself. I joined the Marine Corps to escape this. But you took my escape away from me and forced me right back here to the one place I swore I would never end up."

He might as well have punched her in the stomach. Only now was the true enormity of what she'd done to him starting to sink in. She hadn't really given any thought to what he would do after he left the military. Her father was always talking about how he couldn't wait to be a civilian again. It had never dawned on her that all soldiers might not feel the same way.

"Wes, I'm really sorr—"

"Save it. I already told you, I don't want your apology."

"Is there some way I can make it up to you?"

"Yeah. Get me my commission back."

If only. Her father had supposedly pulled all kinds of strings to keep him out of jail. No way could anyone, not even her father, get Wes his rank and position back. Not after he'd half killed a man with his bare hands.

The temporary truce between them while feeding the cattle was apparently over.

"Go inside the house," he bit out.

"What are you going to do?"

"Plow my damned driveway so you can get the hell out of here."

Stung, she retreated along the path they'd created before. She stopped in the mudroom to doff her boots and outer layers of clothing. Dispirited, she cleaned up the breakfast dishes and tidied the kitchen. Except for the quiche in the fridge and the new furniture arrangement, no one would know she'd ever been here. Wes could get on with his life, and she...

She didn't know what she was going to do.

Chapter 5

Where did one go when one's life was in danger? Was a run-down ranch in Montana far enough out of the way that she would be safe here or not? Or would she lead the killer straight to Wes if she stayed here?

Maybe she should decamp to some exotic island far away, take up a new identity and sit on a beach watching sunsets. With the trust fund from her mother, she could afford to do it. But she would be bored out of her mind in about a week. And then what? She would go totally stir-crazy. She was a project kind of girl. She needed to stay busy and have something to do.

In the past, she had put her energy into knowing the best restaurants, finding the most on-trend clubs, spotting the latest fashion craze just before it hit. Her it-girl blog and YouTube channel had amassed a substantial following over the past few years. She'd parlayed that popularity into an interior design business that had been growing quickly before she'd fled Washington.

But Sunny Creek, Montana, couldn't have more than a handful of houses in need of redecorating. And it wasn't like the locals would hire her after Wes got done trashing her reputation. Which she probably deserved. Still, it would leave her at loose ends with nothing to do.

The sound of a tractor engine fractured the deep silence, and she listened glumly as Wes attacked Mother Nature with a vengeance, all in the name of getting rid of her.

She moved over by the living room window to watch him on the tractor. For a man who professed to hate this life, he seemed pretty good at it. He handled the tractor like a pro, dragging aside snow with an angled blade on the back of the tractor and shoveling away the big drifts with a bucket on the front of it. Gradually a path emerged, heading across the pasture toward the main road.

Panic began to set in. He hadn't listened to her. Maybe he wasn't in danger, as isolated as he was and with all his neighbors looking out for him. But she—she had no such protections. All of a sudden, the isolation of this decrepit little homestead began to look a lot less terrible. In a place like this, no one would ever find her. She could hunker down and be safe from the world. Too bad Wes despised her with a burning passion.

She heard the tractor drive back up toward the house and, a moment later, the sound of her car starting. Taking one last, wistful look around Wes's sanctuary, she stepped outside onto the porch.

Wes was just unfolding his tall, athletic frame from her little car, and she was riveted by the sight of his broad shoulders and long, muscular legs encased in denim. From the first moment she'd ever laid eyes on her father's new aide, she'd wanted him. There was something so magnetic about him—she just couldn't look away. Even now, with that awful beard and shaggy hair, he was still one of the best-looking men she'd ever seen.

If everyone in the world had their own personal kryptonite, he was hers.

Too bad she'd completely alienated him and would never get to be with him again. She didn't relish the long years ahead, knowing he was out in the world somewhere, hating her.

She strode across the porch, head held high, determined not to cry in front of him again. That was probably why she didn't see the missing porch step and stepped down into thin air. She pitched forward as her foot went down between the slats of wood. Her ankle wrenched violently, and she fell hard to the frozen ground. Only the thick layer of snow prevented her from racking up further injuries.

Wes rushed forward and was by her side in an instant. "Don't move," he ordered sharply.

Dammit, she felt tears squeezing out of the corners of her eyes. "I wasn't looking where I was going," she mumbled.

"Did you hit your head?" Wes demanded.

"No. I'm fine. No need to make a big deal out of me being a klutz." She sat up and Wes put an arm behind her shoulders, raising her the rest of the way upright. Lord, she'd forgotten how strong he was. Apparently, life on a farm did nothing to diminish the toned power of a Marine.

She tried to stand up and her right ankle gave a mighty shout of protest. She went right back down to the ground, and Wes immediately reached for her ankle.

"Cripes. I can feel the swelling through your boot," he muttered. "You've sprained your ankle, at a minimum. You might even have broken it. A doctor's going to have to look at it."

She closed her eyes in mortification. Of course, she would choose this exact moment to lose her natural grace entirely. Wes helped her to her feet again, and this time she held her right foot off the ground, making no effort to put any weight on it. "If you'll tell me where I can find a doctor, I'll be on my way—"

Wes interrupted briskly, "You can't drive with that foot injured. You won't be able to operate the gas pedal and brakes safely."

"I'll drive with my left foot."

"On these roads? Just after a snowstorm? I think not," he snapped. "I'll drive you to Hillsdale. There's an urgent care clinic there. Doc Cooper will take care of you."

And now she was an even greater pain in the butt than she'd already been to him. Great. She was undoubtedly upgrading from hated to pariah in the man's mind. "Just call me a cab or something."

"This is Montana, not Manhattan."

She rolled her eyes at him. Without further words, he grabbed her right hand, pulled it across his shoulders and hoisted her over to the front porch. "Sit," he ordered. "I'll pull the truck up to the porch. Back in a minute."

She followed orders and sat glumly. If it was possible to make a bigger hash of seeing Wes again, she didn't think she could have done much better than this. A big pickup truck plowed through the snow from the barn onto the cleared path he'd made for her car. Wes parked and jumped out to fetch her. She hopped on one foot to the truck with his help and then awkwardly climbed into the vehicle.

Wes climbed onto the driver's seat, jaw clenched, and headed off his property.

As they clattered over the metal grate under the entry arch, she asked, "What's the grate for?"

"It's called a cattle grate. Cows won't walk over it, so it acts like a fence to keep them on the property. But vehicles can still get through without having to open and close gates behind them."

"That's so clever!"

He threw her a vaguely scornful look as if she was a hopeless city slicker. Which would not be wrong. He drove for a solid half hour, which made her feel worse than she already did about inconveniencing him.

Hillsdale looked a lot like Sunny Creek without the charming old-fashioned Main Street. She waited in the truck while he went inside the urgent care clinic. A tall, handsome man with coffee-colored skin pushing a wheelchair came back out with Wes.

"Hi. I'm Dr. Cooper. I hear you tried to fly and it didn't go so well."

She grinned ruefully at him. "I'll get it right next time."

"I like your optimism, ma'am," the doctor replied.

"Oh, Lord. Don't ma'am me. I grew up in a military family and I despise the whole sir and ma'am thing."

Dr. Cooper shrugged. "Gonna be mighty hard to break folks of that habit in these parts… Miss."

She smiled warmly. "You can call me Jessica."

"Only if you'll call me Ben. Or Doc."

She happened to glance over at Wes and was startled to see his jaw as hard as a rock. He didn't like her flirting with the hot doctor, huh? Too bad. Ben was good-looking, and had a great smile and a winning personality. She continued to banter with the doctor as he wheeled her inside and took a quick X-ray of her ankle.

He pushed her into a hospital-style room to wait while he read the X-ray.

Wes poked his head in the door. "You okay?" he asked reluctantly.

"Look, Wes, I know you hate my guts, and that being polite to me is the last thing you want to do. You don't have to keep up appearances for my sake. If you want to go on home, I'll figure out some way to get back to my car and pick it up. And then I'll be on my way."

The look of indecision that entered his eyes would have been funny if it weren't for the cause—his hatred of her warring with his innate good manners.

"Go home, Wes," she said firmly. "I'll take care of myself. You've made it crystal clear you want nothing to do with me. I'm sorry I bothered you by warning you that you're in danger. I won't make that mistake again."

He frowned and backed out of the room. She immediately felt bad. She shouldn't have snapped at him. After all, it wasn't his fault she'd taken a header off his porch.

"Well, Jessica, I have good news and bad news for you," Dr. Cooper announced, coming around the corner into her room.

"Do tell."

"The good news is your ankle isn't broken. The bad news is you've sprained it pretty badly. I'm going to tape it up, and I'll need you to elevate and ice it, and stay off it for a couple weeks."

"Weeks?" she squawked.

"Like I said, it's a bad sprain. If you don't let it heal properly before you start gallivanting around on it, you'll have lingering problems with the joint forever and will risk repeat sprains down the road."

"Great," she huffed.

"Where are you staying?" he asked.

"Nowhere at the moment."

A momentary frown puckered Cooper's brow. "You're not with Wes, then?"

"Emphatically not."

He studied her thoughtfully. "There's a story behind that answer, but I won't pry. There's a nice bed-and-breakfast in Sunny Creek I can recommend. My mother runs the place, actually."

"Well, then, clearly that's where I have to stay to recuperate."

"Will Wes give you a ride over there, or can you hang on for an hour till I'm off shift here? I can drive ov—"

"I'll take her," Wes interrupted from the doorway.

Cooper looked up, startled, along with Jessica. "Um, okay, then." The doctor turned back to her. "I'm going to prescribe you a painkiller and some anti-inflammatories for the next week. Take the pain pills only as needed and stop taking them as soon as you can tolerate the pain."

She nodded, half listening to the remaining instructions about propping up the foot and icing it for twenty minutes every hour while she was awake. She stood and got fitted for a pair of crutches—which were total overkill, by the way—bemused over why Wes had insisted on taking her back to Sunny Creek. Surely he wasn't jealous of Ben, was he? Jealousy would connote him giving a damn about her and wanting her not to have feelings for other men.

The ride back to Sunny Creek was silent. Wes seemed distracted and irritated, and her ankle throbbed enough that she didn't have the stomach for a fight with him.

The truck turned onto the street of dilapidated Victorian mansions, and she roused herself enough to ask, "Where did all these big homes come from?"

"Copper barons built them at the turn of the century. But the mines are all played out, and the copper boom busted decades ago."

"They're beautiful. Too bad someone's not restoring them."

Wes looked at her askance. He pulled up at the end of the street in front of one of the few restored Victorians. A small, wrought iron sign in the front yard announced it to be the Brock House and a historic bed-and-breakfast.

Wes hovered as she tried out the crutches and hop-stepped up the sidewalk. She was careful not to slip on the steps and made it to the front door all by herself. "I'll take it from here," she murmured to Wes. "Thanks for your help. Again."

He scowled darkly and all but ran back to his truck, obviously eager to get away from her.

The front door opened, and a tall, attractive woman from whom Ben Cooper obviously got his good looks stood there. "You must be Jessica. I'm Annabelle Cooper. Ben called and told me to expect you. I've made up a room for you, and we've got an elevator, so you won't have to use the stairs."

Jessica smiled gratefully. The elevator turned out not

to be much larger than a phone booth, and it was a cozy fit for her and Ben's mother together. Her room was a lovely space with great light from a big bay window with a cushioned window seat in it. But Jessica made her way directly to the bed, exhausted by, frankly, the whole past several months.

"I brought in some extra pillows for you to use to prop up your ankle. And there's an ice bucket beside the bed with an ice bag in it. Here's a pitcher of water and a glass for your pills, and that's a buzzer for you to call downstairs if you need anything."

"Good grief. You've thought of everything! I can't thank you enough," Jessica said warmly.

"We'll have you up and around in no time. You look tired, honey. Why don't you just go on and take a little nap. I'll wake you in time for supper."

Without further ado, Jessica collapsed, staying awake only long enough to stick her foot on some pillows and swath her ankle in ice packs. And then she passed out. For the first time since her drugging, she fell asleep and really slept, deeply and dreamlessly.

The next few days passed in a painkiller-induced blur. She slept constantly and followed the doctor's orders in caring for her ankle. By day five, her ankle felt much better, and she was so housebound she could scream in spite of the steady stream of books and movies her hostess supplied to her.

Annabelle, who took being a perfect hostess to a whole new level of greatness, suggested that Jessica ride along with her on a trip to a new antiques store in Hillsdale, and offered to swing by the clinic first to let Ben have a look at her ankle.

Ben declared her to be mending nicely, took off the

tape around her ankle and replaced it with a thick sports bandage. He said that she could drive a little and put some weight on it if she was careful. But she was to continue using the crutches for another week.

The antiques store had apparently just been purchased by a newcomer to the area, a pretty young woman named Charlotte Adams. Jessica hop-stepped inside and smiled in delight. Whoever had bought the inventory for this place had taste extremely similar to hers. The furnishings and decorations were authentic, elegant and occasionally just quirky enough to be fun and young.

The proprietor, a pretty brunette, welcomed them to the store and apologized for being thin in selection. She had apparently bought an existing antiques store and culled the old inventory but was still in the process of finding new suppliers.

Annabelle was shopping for a new sofa for the downstairs sitting room, and Jessica gently steered the woman away from a piece that would have overpowered the room, instead suggesting a smaller sofa that was slightly less opulent in its carved decorations. Jessica and Charlotte agreed the piece needed reupholstering, and all three women put their heads together over fabric books in search of the perfect fabric. The other two deferred to Jessica's trained design taste and went with the rich burgundy fabric she suggested.

The bell rang at the front of the store just as Charlotte was starting to write up the sale with Annabelle, and Jessica murmured, "I'll go say hello. You two finish up here."

She made her way on her crutches to the front of the store and spied a tall, striking woman with snow-white hair and patrician features. "Hi. I'm Jessica. Charlotte will be with you in a minute."

"Nice to meet you. I'm Miranda Morgan."

Whoa. The formidable Morgan matriarch in the flesh. Wes had told her stories about this woman. She trained horses when she was younger and apparently could shoot the eye out of a squirrel at fifty paces. The way Wes told it, even his tough-as-shoe-leather father was intimidated by her, and she ran the Morgan clan with an iron fist.

Jessica blurted, "Wes's mother?"

"You know my son?"

"Um, yes. We've met." In an effort to avoid the inevitable question of how she knew Wes and from where, Jessica added quickly, "Can I help you find something while Charlotte finishes up with another customer?"

Of course, Jessica didn't work here and had no idea what the inventory was, but she was frantic to avoid awkward questions about herself and Wes.

"I need to redecorate a cabin on my ranch. It's tiny, but big men use it, so I don't know what to do for furniture in the space."

Jessica spied a drawing pad on the counter with graph paper ideal for sketching out a room. She opened the pad and picked up the pencil conveniently beside it. "Tell me about the layout of the cabin."

Miranda described the space, estimating its size, and Jessica quickly drew it out. "Like that?" she asked when she was done.

Miranda nodded. "I'm not sure on the dimensions, honestly. It has been a while since I spent any time there."

"It will be necessary to measure the space because a

foot or two either way will make a big difference in what will fit in the space. For example…" She trailed off as she sketched out two possible layouts for the cabin's main room, one for a larger space and one for a smaller space.

"I gather you're an interior designer?" Miranda asked.

Jessica nodded modestly. "I specialize in restoring old properties to the historically correct plans and decorations."

"Really? That's fascinating. Did I mention that this cabin is the original homestead of the first Morgans to settle on Runaway Ranch?"

"No! That's so cool! I confess, Old West isn't my forte, but I could certainly research the period and give you some suggestions if you'd like. The trick, of course, is to blend modern comfort with authentic period feel."

"Exactly!" Miranda smiled broadly at her. "I'm not fond of dealing with this design stuff. I like my house to look nice and be comfortable, but I leave making that happen to professionals."

"Is there another designer in the area who's already up to speed on Western decor?"

Miranda shook her head. "I paid a fortune to bring in a designer from Denver when we built the new main house. He did a fine job, but it seems silly to fly in some fancy designer for a tiny hunting cabin. Would you be willing to do it?"

Jessica blinked. She loved a challenge and getting this small space right would be one. Every detail would matter because of the limited space to set a mood and make an impression. Light-colored woods would brighten up the space. She could lay a hardwood floor diagonally to trick the eye…

She looked up, blinking. "Since I'm already redoing the space in my mind, I guess you've got yourself a designer. When can I come up and see the space and measure it?"

"Anytime. No one's staying there since my son, Chase, moved to Sunny Creek to be with his fiancée. They're renovating a house she bought a few months back."

"I'll have to pick up my car before I can drive out to see you. I got snowed in at the Outlaw Ranch last week. I'm hoping the snow has melted enough with this warm snap the past few days for me to go get it soon."

"Outlaw, you said?" Miranda asked sharply.

Jessica winced. Crud. The whole point had been to avoid nosy questions about her and Wes. She said quickly, "I didn't realize how fast snow could accumulate in the mountains, and I got stuck up that way. Wes was kind enough to take me in for a night. But then I sprained my ankle and haven't been back to pick up my car."

"Wes took you in? As in he was actually sociable with you?" Miranda asked in surprise.

"Well, more or less. He wasn't thrilled to have me show up at his door unannounced. But he was certainly courteous about letting me spend the night until the storm blew out."

"Huh. Interesting."

Now why on earth would his mother find that interesting?

Miranda continued, "Runaway's property adjoins the Outlaw Ranch. It's right by where I live. How about I give you a ride to my son's place? You can pick up your car and then follow me to Runaway Ranch. I'll show you where the cabin is."

Charlotte came out of the back room just then, and Jessica asked to borrow a measuring tape and the design pad. Charlotte grinned. "Only if you'll throw a little of the furnishing business from your project my way."

Jessica gave her a quick hug. "I promise."

In short order, Jessica's crutches were put in the back seat of a sleek German sedan, and Jessica was installed in the passenger seat. Miranda took off driving for home, speeding like a Formula 1 driver and taking the winding mountain roads like she was in a race. Jessica liked to drive fast, but she had nothing on Wes's mother in the vehicular-daredevil department.

Jessica's knuckles were white as she gripped the door handle, and she held her breath for most of the ride to Outlaw Ranch. When the grimy arch over the driveway came into view, she actually sighed in relief to have made it there alive.

Miranda sped across the pasture on the gravel drive and pulled up in front of the house, which looked even more decrepit in bright sunlight. "Now there's a house I'd love to see you redo. I can't believe Wes insisted on buying it. But he was determined to make it on his own. My husband offered him the position of ranch manager at Runaway, but that stubborn boy was having no part of it."

"How long has Wes owned this place?"

"Just a few months. He bought it when he left the military and came home to live."

"I imagine he'll fix the place up as he has time, then. He struck me as a rather organized and neat person."

Miranda's eyes darkened with pain. "He used to be

that way. I don't know anymore. His military career changed him, and not for the better. I'm sure something bad happened to him, but he won't talk about it."

"I'm sorry," Jessica said softly.

Miranda shook herself out of her worried reverie. "Don't mind me. Wes will be fine. We Morgans always bounce back from adversity."

Jessica wasn't so sure about that. She'd done a heck of a number on Wes. She sighed. "Let me go see if Wes is home. If not, maybe he left the keys in my car."

Just then, the front door opened and Wes jogged down the front steps. Jessica noticed that the missing one had been replaced by a new step that was bright, fresh wood, yellow in contrast to the weathered gray of the other steps.

He wore jeans, cowboy boots and a flannel shirt with the sleeves rolled up to reveal his muscular forearms. He looked like a model out of a television commercial.

"Lord, I hate that beard," Miranda muttered.

Jessica hid a smile. She preferred Wes clean-shaven, too, but she could still see the strong jaw and lean cheeks in her mind's eye and tended to look past the dark, shaggy beard.

He came across the yard to stand beside Miranda's car window, one hand on the roof of the car, leaning down to peer inside. "Well. This is a surprise."

He didn't sound as if he found it a particularly pleasant one.

"What brings you here, Mother?"

"Can't a parent stop by to check on her son and say hello?"

"They can. But you didn't come here for that and we both know it."

Jessica was startled by the anger in his voice. Not happy to see Mommy Dearest, was he? Had Miranda been included in the big falling-out with his father that Patricia at the diner had mentioned?

"I just came by to drop off Jessica so she can pick up her car."

That was her cue. Jessica stepped out of the German sedan and fished her crutches from the back seat. Wes stared at her over the roof of the car, an entire unspoken tirade turbulent in his dark blue eyes. Nope. Still not the least bit happy to see her.

As for her, however, her stomach was jumping nervously and she felt the pulse pounding hard in her neck. How was it he still had that effect on her after all this time? She *knew* it was over with him. But her body totally hadn't gotten the memo. She still reacted like a girl in the presence of her first crush when he was around.

"How the hell did you two meet?" he demanded suspiciously.

Jessica answered quickly lest Miranda reveal more than was prudent to Wes, especially in light of their shared past of which Miranda knew nothing. "We met at the new antiques store in Hillsdale. We struck up a conversation and your mother ended up offering to bring me here to get my car since it was on her way home."

Wes looked dubious of that explanation and included her in the general scowl he was shooting at his mother. "Should you be driving on that ankle yet?"

She took off on crutches toward the small barn where her car was parked, and Wes kept pace beside her. She answered, "I just had a follow-up visit with Ben Cooper, and he told me I could drive a little if I was careful and took it easy."

He snorted. "Since when do you know how to take it easy in a car?"

She snorted back. "Have you ridden in a car with your mother? She's a menace!"

"That's why my father insists on her driving that German tank. He figures if she crashes she has a better chance of survival in a well-made car. She has actually slowed down some in her latter years."

That was a scary thought. They walked in silence for a minute, and then Jessica asked, "How are the cows doing? Any calves yet?"

"Nah. It'll be three more weeks or so before calves start dropping."

"At least it's warming up before they get here."

"Don't be fooled. We'll have at least one more big snowstorm, if not two, before spring really arrives."

"Crazy weather you people have out here."

"It's the mountains. They make the weather unpredictable." He pushed back a big sliding door and revealed her little car parked in the barn. It was clean and waxed and polished.

She looked over at Wes in surprise. "You washed my car for me?"

He shrugged. "I was bored, and it had salt on it from the road. If you don't get that stuff off, it'll corrode the paint right off. It's a nice old car, and I didn't want Montana to ruin it."

"That was so thoughtful of you!" She smiled at her vintage 1960 Corvette fondly. "She is a sweet ride. Thanks for taking care of her."

His scowl was back, even deeper and darker than before. "Trust me, I didn't do it for you. I did it for the car."

Hurt speared into her. When would she stop feeling

his jabs like this? With previous boyfriends, when she'd been done with them, she was done with them. Their opinions ceased to matter to her. But for some reason, she still cared—deeply—what Wes thought of her.

Weird. Did it have something to do with him being a Marine like her father, or something else? Except, she didn't care what her father thought of her for the most part, either. He'd smothered her as a kid and controlled her far too aggressively as she'd gotten older. She had long ago given up on ever pleasing the man and had committed to living her own life.

Of course, look where that had gotten her. Rebelling against the Old Man hadn't turned out so well.

She sighed and climbed into her car, awkwardly positioning her bandaged ankle. Wes put the crutches in the passenger seat, leaning from the floor up to the passenger headrest.

Without a single word of farewell, he moved over to the barn door to wait for her to leave. She blinked back tears that took her by surprise. He really did hate her.

Chapter 6

Wes watched Jessica drive away, his gut roiling wildly. Why in the hell did he still react so strongly every time he saw her? If only he was sure it was just hatred tying his stomach in knots like this. But he feared it wasn't. And that ticked him off. He had to get her out of his head!

He'd dreamed of her again last night. A hot, sexy dream of lust and love, naked bodies and naughty deeds. The kind of dream that he woke up from restless and horny and with a huge chip on his shoulder.

And what the hell was his mother doing palling around with his ex, anyway? God knew what Jessica was saying about him to his mother. Not that he cared, of course. But Miranda always had been a meddler of the first water.

Well, she and his father could just get the hell out

of his life and stay out. Irritated, he turned to face his house. Its decrepit state grated on his nerves, but he didn't have the money to do anything about it yet. The first order of business was to establish a high-quality herd of cattle, care for them and then put decent facilities around them—solid fences, a good barn and improved pasture.

He'd vowed to himself not to touch his trust fund that came from his share of the proceeds of Runaway Ranch. This was about doing something on his own for himself, by himself. No politics, no favors traded, no ties or debts to anyone. He was done with all of that. It was bad enough to be forced to come home with his tail between his legs. He'd be damned if he came crawling back to his family for a handout, too.

And Jessica Blankenship was to blame for it all.

Irritated at the world in general, he loaded up the bucket of the tractor with tools for repairing fences and headed out to work on the fence line between the Outlaw Ranch and Runaway Ranch. It was a warm afternoon, and he knew that particular fence had been in bad shape when he bought this place. Hard winter had come before he could repair all of it, however.

Sure enough, as he headed up into the high pasture above the barns, he found a whole stretch of fence that was completely down. Worse, there were plenty of fresh tracks in the mud around it. Crud. Had some of his cows wandered through the broken fence to join the herd at Runaway? He would have to take a head count when he got back to the barn.

This was, of course, why ranchers still branded cattle. It was the only way to know which animals belonged to which ranch when something like this happened.

Sure enough, when he drove back to the barn and banged on the metal feeder to call in the cows for food, only about half his herd showed up. Great. He counted heads and was down forty-six cows. Like it or not, he was going to have to make a trip over to Runaway.

It galled him to have to get in contact with his father to ask if he could come over and retrieve cows that had managed to slip off his ranch. It made him look like an amateur who couldn't control his own herd. He might hate the idea of being reduced to being a cattle rancher, but, by God, if he was going to be one, he wanted to be a good one.

He should have known when Jessica showed up earlier that this day was going to suck from top to bottom. He finished feeding the remaining cows, stomped up to the house and jumped in his truck. He hooked it to his cattle trailer and reluctantly drove next door to Runaway Ranch.

He couldn't help being envious of the miles of steel fences, the manicured pastures and the massive log-and-stone mansion that proclaimed the ranch's wealth and success. Not to mention the sprawling, handsome barns and neat row of farm equipment parked under an open-sided shed. His father had close to two million dollars' worth of tractors, plows, hay balers and other equipment, alone. The real wealth of the ranch was in the land and animals, however. John Morgan kept one of the best cattle herds in this part of the country.

Someday, Outlaw Ranch would be every bit as successful. He would work day and night until it was. And he would do it on his own, dammit. He would show his father. He would show everyone.

As he passed the main house, he got a nasty shock.

What the hell was Jessica's car doing parked here? What plot was she hatching against him now? Hadn't it been enough to destroy his career? Was she going after his family, too? Or maybe she was just trying to poison his relationship with his family. News flash: he'd already done that for himself.

Scowling ferociously, he parked his truck beside her sports car and stormed into the main house to give her a piece of his mind.

Willa Mathers, daughter of the long-time ranch foreman, Hank Mathers, looked up from a desk tucked into a corner of the massive kitchen. She'd grown up alongside the Morgan children and was, for all intents and purposes, one of them.

"Hey, Wes. What brings you here? I thought you and John were on the outs."

He scowled at his surrogate little sister. "We are. But I had a fence line go down and some of my cattle appear to have wandered onto Runaway land."

"Oh, man. That sucks. How many cows are you missing?"

"Forty-six." Which was more than half of his herd and a bigger loss than he would be financially able to absorb. Not that he was about to admit that to anyone over here. Runaway's herd numbered in the many hundreds, and forty-six cows would be an annoying inconvenience to them. "Do you know where my father is?"

"Last I heard, he was down in the cattle barn checking out a couple of new bulls."

He didn't want to ask the question, but he couldn't resist. "What's Jessica Blankenship doing here?"

"Is she the girl on crutches that your mother was talking to earlier?"

"That would be her."

"Miranda's taken her up to the old hunting cabin."

"What the hell for?" he blurted.

"Miranda's redoing the place. I got the impression that Jessica is some sort of interior decorator or something."

"She is."

"Well, there you have it. Miranda must have hired her to redo the cabin."

If possible, his scowl deepened. Leave it to Jessica to worm her way into his family and continue making his life a living hell.

"Want me to give her or your mother a message when they get back?" Willa asked.

"No!" He glared at her fiercely. She was far too damned observant for her own good.

She grinned at him unrepentantly as if she'd known she was poking at a sore spot by asking.

"Twerp," he grumbled.

"Jerk," she retorted fondly.

"How's school coming?" he asked her, relenting.

"Almost done with my dissertation. Anna has given me the last piece I needed for it. I used the way she helped Chase recover from his combat experiences as a case study."

"What are you going to do with this PhD of yours when you finish it?"

"I'm going to help ex-military buttheads like you learn to reintegrate with civilian society to lead productive— and socially pleasant—lives."

"I'm socially pleasant!" he exclaimed in response to her obvious dig.

"Ha. And I thought Chase was a curmudgeon when

he came home! You're grouchier than Attila the Hun, Wes."

Offended at the comparison, Wes retorted, "Chase had PTSD from a mission gone wrong. I don't."

"And yet, you're possibly more messed up in the head than he was. Why is that?"

"Don't try to play amateur shrink with me, Willa."

"In a few months, I won't be an amateur. Will you answer me then?"

"No. Keep your nose out of it."

"So you *do* admit you have issues."

He threw up his hands in disgust and marched out of the house. He wasn't interested in arguing in tricky circles with his almost-shrink, almost-sister. He jumped back into his truck and headed for the big cattle barn that would shelter upwards of a thousand heads of cattle if the weather got bad.

Today, the barn was empty. His father's main herd must be out in one of the back pastures taking advantage of the warm sunshine and first grass of spring. The next barn over was the calving barn, and he headed there on the off chance that some of his very pregnant cows had ended up being sorted out in the past day and sent there for supplemental feed and monitoring as they approached calving.

As he stepped into the relative dark of the calving barn's dim interior, his father boomed, "Well, well, well. The prodigal son has come home already?"

Cursing mentally, Wes gritted his teeth and said evenly, "I'm short some cattle, and I found a stretch of busted fence this afternoon. Any chance forty-six of my cows have found their way into your herd?"

"Let's take a look."

A quick check of the cows munching hay and resting in the barn's main loafing shed showed that about a dozen of his most pregnant cows were in here.

John asked, "You want to leave these cows with me? I can have my guys oversee their deliveries. Make sure nothing goes wrong. I'll have a vet here full-time starting next week until calving season is over."

"I can take care of my own cattle, thanks," Wes bit out, his jaw hardening even more in his effort to be polite.

"Too bad we turned the herd out up in the high pasture this morning. We're gonna have to bring them back in and run them through the chutes to sort out your cows from ours."

Wes winced. That would be an all-day job.

John suggested, "Why don't you spend the night here, and we'll get to it first thing in the morning?"

He hated the suggestion, but it made sense. His own herd was already fed for the day, and he really did want his cows back as quickly as possible and to get back to living his own life on his own land.

"Besides, your mother will be thrilled to have you for supper."

His gaze narrowed. Staying the night would give him a chance to tell his mother to steer clear of Jessica and the trouble that seemed to follow her around. He nodded briskly. "Fine. I'll stay."

But when suppertime arrived and Jessica accompanied Miranda into the house at the last minute before the meal, Wes had a change of heart. Just looking at Jessica made his gut tighten into impossible knots.

"Wes!" his mother exclaimed. "What a lovely surprise!"

She stepped forward to kiss his cheek, and he took advantage of the moment to mutter, "What's *she* doing here?"

"Oh, you mean Jessica? She's redecorating the hunting cabin for me. I told her to stay here at the ranch until she's done with the job. It'll save her a ton of driving back and forth to town while she's working on the place."

Perfect. Now he knew where *not* to be for the next few weeks.

For her part, Jessica was silent, standing behind Miranda and looking uncomfortable. What did she have to be uncomfortable about? He was the one whose life had been destroyed.

Scowling, he took his place at the big plank table as Willa and the housekeeper, a young woman named Ella who was new at the ranch since he'd left to join the Marines, served supper. He dug into the sour cream enchiladas, arrested by how good they tasted.

Miranda commented, "Ella's a chef by training. I keep offering to set her up in business with a restaurant of her own, but she keeps insisting she likes it out here on the ranch."

Wes nodded at the pretty young woman. "You really should take my mother up on the offer if everything you make is this tasty."

A shadow passed across the young woman's face—the kind of shadow he'd seen from victims of war and violence when he'd been deployed in the field as a combat officer. What the hell had put that expression in her eyes?

He was distracted, though, by dessert—cinnamon ice cream and crispy sopaipillas so tender they practically fell apart on his fork. Jessica had been notably silent during the meal, which was unusual for her. Usually, she was in the thick of conversation, outgoing and vivacious. She had a gift for making everyone around her feel at ease.

He'd seen it any number of times when she'd acted as her father's hostess at official dinners and the cocktail parties so vital to advancing a senior officer's career. After all, it wasn't what you knew, rather who you knew, when it came time for political appointments to be made. And George Blankenship had been nothing if not ambitious. The man aimed to be chairman of the Joint Chiefs of Staff one day.

Personally, Wes had found the man overbearing and arrogant, too willing to throw others under the bus in the name of advancing his own career. And that trait had transferred to the bastard's daughter.

As coffee was poured all around, John asked his wife, "So how much is this renovation of the cabin going to cost me?"

Miranda deferred to Jessica, and all eyes turned on her. She answered smoothly, "It's a small space, and I want to keep the design simple and functional. It won't be ridiculously expensive."

She quoted a figure that actually sounded cheap, given the quality of work Wes knew she was capable of. In Washington, Jessica had commanded shocking fees for redoing the homes of the wealthy who wanted authentic historic renovations.

"I'll hold you to that, young lady," John said, smiling.

Wes interjected, "He means it, Jessica. If you want to revise your estimate upward, do it now."

She glanced over at him, her expression impossible to read. "You forget that I am my father's daughter. I know exactly what to expect out of your father, a military man himself."

John pounced on that. "Your father was military? What branch?"

"He's a Marine, sir. Stationed at the Pentagon at the moment."

John grinned. "Ugh. He's hating every minute of it, isn't he?"

Jessica shrugged. "He seems to have adapted pretty well. He considers politics to be just a different form of warfare. It's combat in a conference room instead of in an armored personnel carrier."

Wes snorted mentally. Truer words had never been spoken.

Jessica neatly turned the conversation back to a discussion of what color John and Miranda would like the inside of the new cabin to be.

For his part, Wes leaned back, studying Jessica. Why hadn't she admitted who her father was? Surely she wasn't trying to protect him. What was she up to, then?

He waited until after the meal, when his parents had settled down to read newspapers in front of the giant stone hearth that dominated the great room, and he followed Jessica down the hall to a bathroom. When she emerged, he grabbed her elbow, steered her into his father's office and closed the door.

He backed her up against the wood-paneled walls and planted a hand over her shoulder to trap her in place.

He looked down and her chest was heaving in the most disconcerting way.

All of a sudden, he was thinking about other times she'd breathed that hard. Times when she'd arched up into him, kissing him senseless, wrapping her leg around his hips and teasing him until he'd stripped her clothes off and sunk into her hot, welcoming body and lost himself—

"What are you playing at?" he growled at her.

"What do you mean?"

Their gazes locked, clashing. Sparks flew between them, sparks of friction and anger and betrayal—and of something else. Something he didn't want to acknowledge. Something he refused to name.

"What are you doing here, insinuating yourself into my family's life?"

"Contrary to popular belief, Wes, not everything revolves around you. I bumped into your mother in an antique shop, and she and I got to discussing the cabin she's looking to redo. One thing led to another, and she hired me for the job. There's no deep, dark plot afoot. It's just a job."

"Is that really what this is?" he snarled. "Tell me the truth."

Her eyes widened as she stared up at him. He saw the moment her gaze dropped to his mouth. How her throat worked as she swallowed convulsively.

"Quit looking at me like that," he muttered.

"Like what?" she asked breathlessly.

"Like you want to eat me up."

"But I do."

The words zinged through him with the jolting shock of electricity. She wanted to eat him up? An image of her red, juicy lips on his flesh, doing just that made blood race to his groin. All of a sudden, he was hard as a rock and his pulse pounded through his erection demandingly.

"Stop it," he bit out from behind clenched teeth. Whether he meant it for her or for himself, he wasn't sure. Maybe both.

"Stop what?" she breathed.

"Dammit," he snapped. He closed the distance between them, all of twelve inches, and kissed her roughly. He didn't want to be doing this. Didn't want to remember how damned soft and welcoming she always was to him. How she tasted like cinnamon and cream, and how he wanted more of that taste. More of her...

Her body surged forward against his, her slender arms going around his neck. Her head tilted to fit their mouths together better, and her tongue sipped tentatively at his.

The wet slide of tongue on tongue was so sexy, so blatantly sexual, that he lost his mind a little. His arms swept around her, dragging her up against him. Oh, man. Those curves. The way they fit against his hard body was perfect. She was perfect. So hot. So eager.

He wanted her. Like he wanted to breathe.

Wrong. This was wrong.

But so damned good. His hands plunged into her silky, lush hair, drawing her closer so he could deepen the kiss, explore her mouth more fully, taste that seductive sweetness—

There was a reason he shouldn't be doing this—

Didn't care. He couldn't get enough of her. His kiss gentled and slowed. It had been so long. So. Damned. Long. All those nights of dreaming about her. All those

nights of wanting her. And here she was, real and warm
and eager in his arms, every bit as lithe and sensual and
irresistible as ever. More so.

"I've missed you so much," she murmured against
his mouth between kisses.

He peppered her jaw with kisses, tracing the artistic
line of her neck with his lips, tasting the pulse leaping in
her throat. A need to take her right here, right now, came
over him. He plunged his hand down the waistband of
her peasant skirt, found the skimpy thong—she always
did have naughty taste in lingerie—and eased his fingers between the soft, plump folds of her womanhood.

She groaned and shifted her stance to give him access to her core, and then she rode his fingers, shame-
lessly groaning into his mouth as he rubbed the bud of
her desire, rolling it between his fingertips. He plunged
a finger into her wet heat and she gasped, arching up
against him sharply.

"Like that?" he mumbled.

She let out a half sigh, half groan, and rocked her
hips forward, impaling herself more deeply upon his
finger. He added a second finger and her hips moved
more rapidly. Using his thumb to rub across the hard,
wet little bud, he drove her out of her mind.

As her cries increased in volume, he captured them
with his mouth, tasting her pleasure with dark satisfaction. It didn't take her long to shatter around his
hand—it never did. And then she was trembling in his
arms, her forehead falling to rest on his shoulder, her
chest heaving with pleasure, her internal muscles still
spasming around his fingers hungrily.

An urge to unzip his jeans, free his erection and
plunge into all that wet heat and make her his once more

nearly overcame him. And then, all of a sudden, reason came crashing back in upon him, breaking over him in a cold rush of terror.

Lord, the hold this woman still had over him—

He stumbled back from her in horror. What had he just done? No way did he want to get back into a relationship with her. She was lethal. Deadly. She'd sucked him back in so easily. And he'd gone along with her, a lamb for the slaughter. What fall was she setting him up for this time?

"What the hell do you do to me?" he mumbled hoarsely. "How do you do that?"

She stared at him in what looked like shock. "What are you talking about? You did that to me."

"I didn't want to. How did you manipulate me *again*?"

"I didn't manipulate anything, Wes. We just have chemistry between us. We always have—"

He cut her off, half in fury, half in panic. "It has to stop. I want nothing to do with you. Do you understand? *Nothing*."

"Are you sure about that?" she asked. She reached forward boldly to cup the erection that still strained at his zipper. "You don't feel like a man who wants nothing. Seems to me you'd like quite a bit more than we just did. And that's fine by me."

She reached for the zipper and he swatted her hand away, staggering back from her. "You're poison. An addiction. I can't. Won't—"

He turned and bolted from the room before he could give in to temptation—to disaster—again.

Chapter 7

Jessica tossed and turned in the guest bedroom of the Morgan mansion for hours, unable to forget the screaming orgasm that had ripped through her earlier. She had known she still wanted Wes. She'd just had no idea how much she still wanted him until she'd gotten a little piece of him. A very little piece. The man had held his body completely apart from her, never sharing more than a few kisses. And then he'd reached for her. Played her body like a finely tuned musical instrument. He always had known how to draw pleasure out of her like no one else.

And now she was sleepless and so turned on she could hardly stand it. Sure, she could scratch the itch herself, but she wanted Wes to scratch it. Why had he turned her down when she'd directly offered him more? She knew he wanted it. The bulge behind his zipper had been rock hard and filled her entire hand. He seriously wanted her.

Was he so stubborn that he would deny both of them the pleasure they both craved just to prove his point? What was his point, anyway?

That he had more self-discipline than she did? That he was a better person than she was? Lord knew, that was true. She was wild and undisciplined and had gotten both of them into trouble, dragging him down against his will. But she'd changed since the kidnapping. Grown up. She had no more desire to be the bad girl or break all the rules. Although she would never get along with her father, she no longer needed to enrage him like she once had.

If only Wes would give her a chance to show him the new Jessica. He might never forgive her for wrecking his career, but maybe he could at least see that a little good had come of it.

And he had his own ranch now. That was good, right?

His life didn't totally suck.

If she had truly been out to ruin his life, she would have done a better job of it than this. Surely he could see that. Right? Was that what he was hung up on? Didn't he know she would never have hurt him just for the sake of hurting him? She *really* liked him. Heck, she still cared for him after everything that had happened between them. Or maybe he didn't know that.

A need to tell him, to make sure he was aware of how she felt about him, came over her. The clock on the nightstand said it was nearly two in the morning. He must be asleep by now.

Although, maybe that wasn't a bad thing. The more

alert he was, the more hostile he tended to be. When she'd caught him off guard, surprised him in the office by kissing him, that was when he'd let his real feelings for her show.

She climbed out of bed, the sleep shirt she'd bought in Hillsdale skimming her thighs. She opened the hallway door, glad for the small lamp on a table at the end of the long passage. The girl named Willa had helpfully told her that Wes's room was the last one on the right. Jessica crept down the hallway now, heading for the closed door. She was startled to see that the door was beautifully carved, much like the front door on his current house. Except this panel depicted mountains with a stream running through a broad meadow. A deer grazed by the stream, and an eagle flew overhead. She made a mental note to ask Miranda tomorrow who the artist was.

And then she was reaching for the doorknob, and all thought fled her brain except letting Wes know how she really felt about him and, moreover, getting him to admit to himself how he still felt about her.

It did register that this was potentially insane and that he might very well tell her to go to hell and toss her out on her keister. But, hey, she'd always been a risk taker. Why stop now?

Memory of that throbbing erection behind Wes's zipper spurred her forward. He did want her. She had to believe in that.

She tried his doorknob and it turned silently under her hand. She slipped inside the room, and faint moonlight crept around the curtains. A sleeping form stretched under the covers on the bed. She eased forward until she could see the planes of his face, the bushy beard that seemed to be such a source of contention with his parents. If he'd wanted to find a rebellion that would drive his folks nuts, he'd succeeded with that beard. They'd pestered him over it at length at supper, exhorting him to shave and cut his hair like a civilized human being.

Amused, she studied his beard. With a little trimming, it wouldn't look half-bad. But she still preferred him clean-shaven. In her mind he would always be that spit-polished Marine she'd first met in her father's office.

Carefully she lifted the covers so as not to wake Wes and slipped into bed beside him. She rolled to face him and gently reached across his body with her arm. Yay. He still slept commando.

He shifted a little but didn't wake. She slid her hand ever so lightly down the flat, hard plane of his stomach. Her fingertips slipped through the curls at his groin and stroked lightly down the length of him. Immediately she felt a swelling response. She stroked him again. In seconds, his body was raging in response to her. Ha. And he'd claimed to be unaffected by her earlier tonight. Liar.

Of course, she was not immune to him, either. Her own body went limpid and wet in response to his obvious, if unconscious, desire for her.

She leaned in close to kiss his shoulder, and he woke—or half woke to be more accurate—groaning and turning toward her to wrap his arms around her. He rolled her beneath him, his muscular thigh pushing her legs open for him. His beard tickled her neck as he nuzzled her ear, and she lifted her chin to give him better access to her neck. He took the invitation and nibbled her neck, working his way across her jaw to her mouth. Their tongues tangled sexily, his plunging into her mouth and hers swirling around his, teasing him and inviting him in. His hips pushed against hers, his erection pressing into her core with only her flimsy sleep shirt separating their bodies.

"Take me, Wes," she whispered.

His eyes opened then, and he stared down at her as if he was disoriented, as if he couldn't tell if she was a dream or not. She lifted her head to capture his mouth with hers, to kiss him before logic could get the better of him and make him overthink this. That was his problem. He needed to go with the flow more.

She undulated invitingly beneath him, rubbing herself against the length of his erection. Her breasts pressed against his chest, her nipples pebbling through her sleep shirt. She drew a deep breath and the cotton fabric dragged across her skin, making her shudder with pleasure. She was so highly sensitized at the moment that his mere breath against her cheek was doing things to her—sending bolts of pleasure zinging through her body where they were gathering at her core into a tight ball of desire.

"I want you so much," she murmured. "I dream about you. About doing things with you. Asking you to do things to me…"

"What things?" he mumbled.

"Anything you want. Take me any way you want. Ravish me."

He groaned and one of his arms snaked out to the side. He opened a drawer in his nightstand and groped around while he kissed her again, deeply. Druggingly.

She arched against his thigh, unable to stop her body from seeking the release she so craved.

She heard foil tear and a snap of rubber. And then Wes was back, pressing her deeply into the mattress, his thighs pushing hers apart. The blunt, hot tip of him touched her throbbing flesh and she cried out. His mouth closed on hers instantly, absorbing the sound into him.

"You sure about this?" he muttered against her mouth.

"Take me. Please. Do whatever you want to me. I want it all."

"Don't say that," he groaned. "I've been having some pretty dark fantasies about you."

"Show me," she panted as he remained tantalizingly poised at her entrance, so close but so very far away.

"How bad do you want it, Jessica?"

"Worse than I've ever wanted anything."

"Do you want it bad enough to cry?"

She wasn't sure what he was asking. If he needed to cause her pain to work out his anger at her betrayal, she was honestly okay with that if it meant he would forgive her. "Uh-huh."

"Bad enough to beg?"

"I'm begging you now. Please." She squirmed beneath him, so hungry to have him inside her she was struggling to find words.

"Tell me what you want."

"I want you inside me. Filling me. Pounding into me. Driving me out of my mind. Driving you out of your mind—"

He plunged into her swiftly, without warning, filling her all the way.

She cried out against his shoulder, muffling her outburst so the whole family wouldn't hear what they were doing. But it was hard not to scream with pleasure.

He withdrew all the way and she whimpered.

He slammed home again and she shuddered around him, teetering on the brink of something spectacular.

"Again," she panted.

"Beg for it."

"Please, Wes. *Please*. I want it so bad. I want you. Give it all to me."

"On one condition."

"Anything. Name it."

"You can't make any noise."

He rose up above her, taking her hips in his big hands and lifting her up. He slammed into her again, and that did it. She shattered into a million pieces. She dragged a pillow across her mouth and shouted into it, shivering and shaking as he set up a rhythm, pounding into her like a piston, using her body hard yet never hurting her. Wes always had known exactly where that line lay and didn't cross it.

His callused thumbs rubbed across her nipples and she surged up into his hands, silently urging him to use her breasts for his pleasure, as well. His mouth closed on her right nipple and he sucked hard enough to make her shudder with ecstasy. All the while, he surged into her over and over, filling her to bursting, withdrawing until she wanted to sob and then ramming home again.

It wasn't elegant sex. It wasn't slow and sexy and seductive. But it was exactly what she needed—a mutual plundering that left no doubt whatsoever about how much he'd wanted and missed her or how much she'd wanted and missed him.

Again and again she orgasmed, shattering around him more sharply each time, until she was nigh unconscious with pleasure.

A lifetime later, when she was little more than a quivering mass of jelly, more pleasure than person, he finally picked up the pace, driving her over the edge one last time. And this time, he joined her, plastering his face in the pillow beside her head and shouting with his own shuddering release.

His body was covered with perspiration and she held him tight, her own perspiration-slicked body shaking like a leaf. Their legs twined together intimately, and she relished the crushing weight of him pressing her deep, deep into the mattress. They panted in unison, and their hearts pounded in unison, which was gratifying. She would hate to be the only one whose world had just been rocked.

Eventually Wes gathered himself and rolled away from her onto his back. He stared up at the ceiling for a long time before finally growling, "What are you doing in my bed, Jess?"

"Isn't it obvious?"

"Not to me."

"I never stopped wanting you, Wes. And I know you've never stopped wanting me. You wouldn't listen to me when I tried to tell you how I feel, so I thought I would show you instead."

"Message received."

He threw back the covers and paced across the room, opened a door and disappeared into what must be an attached bathroom. She heard the sink run. Then nothing. She lay in his bed for a long time waiting for him to return, but he never did. Eventually she got up, found her nightshirt wadded on the floor and pulled it over her head. She knocked on the bathroom door. No answer.

Tentatively she opened it. It was empty! She spotted a door to the hallway and realized he had slipped out and abandoned her. Again.

She sat down on the closed toilet seat, buried her head in her hands and cried.

Wes's silver-blue truck was gone when she got up in the morning. Which was just as well. She was bleary-eyed from crying much of the rest of the night. She truly had lost him. Even the explosive attraction that always erupted between them hadn't been enough to convince him of how much she cared for him—or more importantly, to lure him into staying.

That was it. She had no more ammunition to fire at him. Her gun was empty.

They'd shared the best sex she'd ever had, they'd connected intensely the way they always had, they'd fallen into the perfect simpatico they shared, and he'd still walked away.

He really was never coming back to her.

And her heart was officially broken.

In Washington, DC, a laptop computer beeped an alert on the highly illegal search that had been set up the day Jessica left town without warning. Apparently, she didn't tell anyone she was going or where—even her closest friends and family knew nothing. Damn her. Who did she think she was, running from him? She was bought and paid for. He owned her.

He opened the computer file, which hacked the FBI search system and piggybacked upon its powerful capabilities. Her debit card had been used earlier today in some town called Sunny Creek. In Montana. Montana? Really? Did she think she could hide from him, even in some hick town across the country from him? He would use whatever means, go to any lengths to find her, no matter where she ran. And, by God, he would grab her and bring her back to where she belonged. To finish what he'd started with her. No one walked away from him like that. No *woman* turned her back on him!

Wes Morgan would rue the day he'd stormed into her life to save her from him. Oh, yes. That bastard would pay, too. With his life.

Chapter 8

Wes worked like a fiend for the next several days, mending fences and welding the cattle chutes he would need to inoculate his herd come spring. He cleaned out and repaired the decrepit barn he'd decided to turn into a calving shed, and ran electricity to it so he could hang heat lamps for the new calves. He hauled in fresh, clean straw and filled the barn with a knee-deep layer of the stuff for the cows to be comfortable lying in and the calves to nest in for warmth.

He never stopped moving, frantic to exhaust himself each day.

It didn't help. Every night when he fell into bed sore and worn-out, he still couldn't get Jessica out of his mind. He still felt her hands roaming seductively down his body, still felt her tight internal muscles gripping him, still heard her muffled cries of ecstasy against his shoulder, felt her shivering in release around him.

Her pleasure sliced right through him, eviscerating him. It destroyed his resolve. Made him question his sanity in turning his back on her.

He probably owed her a thank-you for barging into his life and claiming that someone was out to kill them both. It was a stark reminder of how much she loved a good drama. So much so that she would make one up if there wasn't already one to wallow in. He was so done with all of that. He wanted to be left alone. To live a quiet life. To raise some cattle. Pay the bills. Carve out a place for himself in the world that didn't depend on anyone else. He was sick and tired of trying to live up to everyone else's expectations of him. They could all go to hell.

On the morning of the fourth day after that disastrous night with Jessica, he trudged down to the calving barn a little before dawn to check on the half-dozen cows closest to delivering.

Cow number 19, according to her ear tag, was down on her side, straining to deliver her calf. One white hoof stuck out, encased in the semitransparent, rubbery amniotic sac. But there was no sign of the other hoof or of a pink nose.

Crap. The calf must be cast. That was when the head turned to the side instead of entering the birth canal, or one of the legs got stuck facing backward instead of pointing down the birth canal.

Number 19 gave another push, but it was weak. She was clearly nearing exhaustion. She must have been trying to deliver this calf for a while before Wes found her. Swearing, he yanked off his shirt and quickly sterilized his right arm by splashing it liberally with iodine. He lay down in the straw behind the cow and gently slid his hand inside the birth canal, following the calf's leg carefully. Nope. No sign of the nose. When he was inside the cow up to nearly his shoulder, he tried to feel around for the nose and missing front foot to guide them into the birth canal.

No luck.

Number 19 had another weak contraction. It should have cut off the circulation in his arm, but he barely felt the squeeze. The cow was exhausted and would never deliver this calf without assistance. He backed out of her and pulled out his cell phone. He had no choice. As much as he hated to put himself in debt to his old man, he hated more the idea of losing this cow and her calf. Reluctantly, he hit the speed dial for his father.

Predictably, John was terse. The man knew Wes would never have called him if it weren't an emergency, nor at this ungodly early hour. "What's wrong?"

"Sorry to wake you so early, Dad. Is that calving vet you were going to hire at your place yet?"

John answered with the quick alertness of a rancher—or a longtime soldier—sensing a crisis. "She got here yesterday."

"Any chance I could borrow her? I've got a cow with a cast calf and I can't straighten out the baby. I need her help."

"We'll be there as fast as we can, son."

Crap. He hadn't particularly wanted his father to come with the vet. The man drove him crazy with his stubbornness, hardheadedness and sheer cussedness. The last time they'd talked it had turned into a shouting match over how Wes had let down John by leaving the Marines so abruptly and under a cloud of scandal. John had made no secret of how disappointed he was in his son, who was supposed to uphold the honor of the family name and serve with distinction.

It had been frustrating as hell not to be able to share the details of why he'd resigned his commission. But to do so, he would have had to drag Jessica through the mud. And as much as he hated her, it still wasn't in his DNA to throw anyone—not even a lying, deceitful, selfish woman—to the wolves.

Not to mention, he really didn't want his father around to witness his very first cow's calving go badly. It would *not* be an auspicious start for his attempt to ranch on his own.

He made Number 19 as comfortable as he could while he waited for the vet to arrive. Every minute that ticked by was agony for him. He couldn't stand to see any animal suffer, nor could he afford to lose a single cow or calf. Especially not this first and most vulnerable year financially, before the ranch started producing income.

He heard a truck rumble up the driveway and prayed the vet had gotten here in time. Number 19 was showing signs of going into shock.

John and a tall, striking woman who might be part Asian strode into the barn. The woman was carrying a big leather satchel.

All business, John said, "This is Sherry Hamilton. My new vet. What can we do for you?"

Thank God. His old man was offering an unspoken truce between them to aid an animal in crisis. No strings attached. Rancher to rancher, here to help.

Wes started to nod and then froze. A third person walked into the barn. *Jessica*. What the hell was she doing here?

He didn't have time for her right now. He turned to the vet and tersely brought her up to speed. Young cow. First calf. One hoof presenting. No nose or second front foot. Briskly Dr. Hamilton gave Number 19 an injection of a powerful muscle relaxant and donned a plastic surgical sleeve that went to her shoulder.

"I already tried to palpate her and reposition the calf," Wes said. "It didn't work."

The vet shrugged. "I want to give it a try before I cut her open. With that muscle relaxant in her, I may have better luck."

Wes waited impatiently as the vet slowly and carefully felt around inside the cow. Eventually she announced, "I've found the nose. Now I just have to locate that other foot."

The cow grunted and began to push weakly as another contraction claimed her.

"Easy, girl," Wes crooned. "Let the doctor help you."

The cow's big brown eyes fixed on him, and he continued to speak soothingly to her.

From the other end, the vet announced quietly, "I've got the second foot. The calf's positioned properly now, but I've knocked out your cow. She won't be able to push out the calf. We'll have to pull it."

John said, "Want me to get a tractor?"

Wes replied sharply, "No. We'll try it by hand. I don't want to rip up the mama any more than I have to, and I don't want to risk killing the calf if I can avoid it."

John shrugged.

On a ranch the size of Runaway, they might have the luxury of sacrificing a calf to save a cow. But here on Outlaw, every single cow and calf mattered to him. Wes was barely going to make ends meet this year if he was lucky, and if the price of feeder steers stayed halfway decent.

"Jess, come here and talk to the cow. Rub her forehead and try to keep her attention on you."

Looking alarmed, Jessica nonetheless moved to the cow's head and knelt gamely beside her.

Wes murmured, "Keep eye contact with her and just talk to her calmly and quietly. She's pretty drugged up at the moment, but I don't want her to be too afraid if I can help it. Think of her as a giant, gentle dog."

"Got it." Jessica started talking in a voice so sweet and mellow it would knock him out if he weren't so damned worried about his cow and calf.

He moved back beside the veterinarian, who had, indeed, managed to get both front hooves and a pink nose presenting properly. Using a clean towel, he took hold of one of the calf's front legs above the ankle joint while the vet took hold of the other. Sitting in the straw and bracing their feet against Number 19's haunches, they began to pull slowly and steadily.

As if the cow sensed help was at hand, she roused herself to attempt to push. But the humans ended up doing most of the work.

Wes strained with all his strength, and finally the calf's shoulders popped free of their constraints. From there, it was one more easy pull to deliver the rest of the red-and-white calf. The vet pulled the amniotic sac free of the baby and went to work examining the placenta to make sure the entire thing had also been delivered properly.

Meanwhile, Wes rubbed the calf's sides vigorously and heaved a mighty sigh of relief as the little heifer shook her head and drew her first breaths. Normally, the cow would stand up quickly to bathe and dry the baby, but Wes did the honors for Number 19, who was still resting.

It took nearly an hour for Number 19 to finally get back on her feet and for Doc Hamilton to declare her none the worse for the rough delivery. All four of the humans backed off and let the little Hereford heifer figure out how to manage four legs and gravity and finally stand up, her legs splayed like a sawhorse. An adorable, fuzzy sawhorse. She took her first tottering steps, collapsed and stood again.

In a few minutes, the calf was bumping mama's udder and getting her first meal. Quiet slurping sounds were all that disturbed the early morning silence. Jessica smiled in wide-eyed wonder.

Wes always felt much the same way at witnessing the birth of a new life. Calving season was hard, but it was his favorite time of year on the ranch. Even his father had a softer than usual look in his eyes.

"I think we can safely leave mother and daughter to their own devices," Dr. Hamilton murmured.

Exhaustion slammed into Wes. The emotional roller coaster of the past two hours had drained him, and pulling that calf had been hard work.

The humans left the barn and Wes invited everyone up to the house for a cup of coffee. He glanced at Jessica in time to see her look back over her shoulder toward the calving barn, one last look of awe on her face.

"First time you've ever seen an animal born?" he asked her as they strode across the yard.

She nodded.

"Pretty miraculous stuff, isn't it?"

"Yeah," she breathed.

"Normally, they're not that rough. Most times, the cow does it all herself and we humans are only spectators."

"I'm so glad you were there to help her," Jessica said fervently.

He shrugged. "Doc Hamilton saved the day."

The vet replied from his other side, "I couldn't have pulled that calf by myself. She was really wedged in there. You might want to consider breeding to a smaller bull next time. You'd get smaller babies."

Wes pulled a face. "I bought these cows already pregnant. And you can be sure I'll be careful when it comes time to choose my own bull."

They went inside, and Jessica shooed him out of the kitchen. "Go take a shower. You're covered in gunk and straw. I know how to use the coffee maker."

The vet excused herself to wash up in the guest bathroom, and Wes retreated to the master bath to take a fast shower. He was disgusted to realize how eager he was to get out of the shower and back to the kitchen, however. He was done with Jessica, dammit.

Then why was he still smiling over that look on her face as she'd watched the new calf take its first steps? Everyone reacted that way the first time they saw a baby animal born. Jessica's reaction was nothing special. Except he'd loved seeing that look on her face. Loved sharing this most magical part of life on a ranch with her.

What in the hell was wrong with him?

He was just feeling all sappy and sentimental after the scare of nearly losing his first cow and calf. That was all. He steeled his resolve not to respond to Jessica. *Not* to let her worm her way back into his life. He knew better.

As they sat around the kitchen table, John commented, "You ought to see what Jessica's doing with the hunting cabin. It looks like a million bucks. You should let her redo this place."

Wes rolled his eyes. "Right now, I'm putting all my money into the cattle."

John snorted. "You have a trust fund. Use the damn thing. You can afford to fix up this house and the barns and have ten times as many head of cattle and still have money left over."

Wes winced. Sure enough, Jessica's eyebrows sailed up toward her hairline. He had never let on to her that he came from any kind of money, although that cat was probably out of the bag the minute she'd set foot on Runaway Ranch. The place screamed of wealth. But it was not his home anymore.

This place—as crappy as it was—belonged to him and him alone, bought and paid for with money he'd saved over the course of his entire military career.

He got up from the kitchen table and carried a handful of coffee mugs over to the sink. Jessica set the coffeepot down beside him and murmured under her voice, "A trust fund, huh? Why'd you always give me so much crap about mine, then?"

"You use yours."

"Why don't you use yours?"

He glanced over at her, his eyes narrowed. "Because I give a damn about being my own person."

She retreated from the sink looking stung. Good. The sooner she was out of his house and out of his life, the better. He hadn't been kidding when he'd called her poison and an addiction.

Thankfully, John, the vet and Jessica loaded up in

John's truck soon after that, saving him from any more awkward revelations by his father or any more unpleasant exchanges with Jessica.

Except as the truck disappeared from view, a sense of loneliness washed over him. What was the point of building all of this if he was never going to share it with anyone? He looked around the yard at his ramshackle barns and even more ramshackle house and seriously wondered if he'd done the right thing. Maybe he should have kept right on going when he'd hit the city limits of Sunny Creek a few months ago. Maybe he would be better off far, far away from here. Away from his family. Away from Jessica and her damned, irresistible sex appeal.

After her eventful morning and upsetting exchange with Wes, Jessica decided to head for Hillsdale and do a little shopping for the cabin. Miranda and John had agreed on a color palette of mossy greens and light woods, and she needed to pick a fabric for the vintage sofa Charlotte had found for her yesterday and agreed to reupholster.

Why hadn't Wes ever mentioned that he had all the money he could ever want? He'd always insisted on paying for their dates and had refused to let her take him on any expensive vacations or buy him extravagant gifts because he couldn't reciprocate in kind. But he could have all along! How hypocritical was that?

Sure, he had issues with his father. And having met John, she could see how the man could be overbearing. Lord knew, her own father was at least as domineering and controlling as John Morgan, if not more so. If her trust fund had come from him instead of her mother, would she have been less inclined to use it?

Nah. She would have wanted to burn through his money to punish him. But then, she was vindictive that way. Wes wasn't. She supposed she could see how he would refuse to take handouts from his father.

She'd been driving for perhaps twenty minutes when she heard a loud bang. Startled, she swerved a little. Another bang, and her car swerved on its own this time. Hard. The distinctive flapping-rubber-on-concrete noise of a blown tire made her groan. She eased onto the brakes and fought the steering wheel grimly as the little car fishtailed wildly. It took several long, heart-stopping seconds to wrestle it to a stop.

Well, hell. Good thing her daddy was a Marine who believed in preparedness. He'd taught her how to change a tire well before she'd even gotten a driver's license. She climbed out of the car and headed for the trunk. Just as she bent over to lift out the tire, something metallic pinged above her head. She looked up, startled, and spied a tiny hole in her lifted trunk hood.

She dropped to the ground instinctively. Nope, she hadn't been raised by a Marine for nothing. That was a freaking bullet hole!

Replaying the noises of the last minute in her head, she decided that the gunshots had been coming from behind her. She crawled frantically around the side of the car, using it for cover from the shooter.

Why in the hell was someone shooting at her?

Surely whoever had been threatening her hadn't found her out here in the middle of nowhere!

Another shot zinged off a rock behind her. She huddled against the side of the car and searched the hillside rising above her for a hiding place with decent cover. Nothing. It was bare dirt and rock. She was going to *die* out here.

She fished in her pocket and pulled out her cell phone. She started to dial 911, and thought better of it. The police were in Sunny Creek, a good half hour away. Wincing, she hit the speed dial number for Wes. He was going to blow his stack at getting called again to rescue her.

The line connected and Wes growled without greeting or preamble, "What the hell do you want now?"

"Someone's shooting at me. I'm on the Westlake Road. I left Runaway Ranch and was heading toward Hillsdale—" She broke off and ducked as another shot pinged off rock just above her head. The shooter was zeroing in on her position. She *had* to get out of there.

"That was a gunshot!" Wes said urgently.

"I *know*. Like I said. Someone's shooting at me. Took out one of my tires. It's shredded. Undrivable." Weird. She'd dropped into some strange state of calm, detached from her emotions and focused on dealing with the crisis. She ought to be scared out of her mind. Instead, she was thinking at hyperspeed and feeling nothing.

"Do you have a gun?" Wes asked tersely.

"No. You know I hate the things."

"Damn." She thought she heard gravel crunching from his end of the call.

"Look. I don't expect you to come rushing to my rescue again. But could you call your father and have him send some of his men out this way? I figure they'll get here faster than the sheriff could, coming from Sunny Creek. I don't have John's cell phone number or I'd have called him myself."

"I'm on my way." She heard an engine roar in the background.

She ducked as a gunshot took out the passenger side rearview mirror. "I'm sorry, Wes—"

"Save it."

This was the last time she was likely to speak with him, and by God he was going to hear her out. She talked right over his objection. "There's no cover at all out here. I'll likely be dead before you get here, so shut up and listen. I truly am sorry for what I did to your career. But I genuinely believed you would be killed if I didn't lie. And I cared—care—far too much for you to sit around and let you die. If that pisses you off, so be it. I forgive you for being mad at me. I know you, Wes, and I don't want you to beat yourself up with guilt after I'm gone. I chose to come out here and warn you. This is on me. Whoever kills me will undoubtedly have done it because of mistakes I made in my past. There was nothing you could have done to protect me."

Wes's voice was ragged when he said, "Get in the car. Drive it away from there. If your shooter's zeroing in on you, he's in a stationary position, maybe in a sniper's nest. Get away from there."

"The car's not drivable—"

"Sure it is. You'll wreck a rim, but that's replaceable. Move!"

He made an excellent point. She reached up over her head and opened the passenger door. Immediately, a gunshot ripped into the white leather door lining. She dived across the seats, and awkwardly jackknifed her body. It was nearly impossible to stay low, turn around and get into a position to drive. Who knew it would turn out to be a lifesaver to have fooled around in this

Wes. And she knew without a shadow of a doubt that he hadn't tried to kill her. Not that she hadn't given him plenty of reason to do so. But he was too honorable, too *good*, to ever harm her, no matter how enraged he might be at her.

A truck rounded the curve behind her and she tensed. Had the shooter caught up with her, or was it Wes charging to the rescue? The vehicle drew closer, and she spied its silver-blue color—Wes.

She slowed and guided her broken car over to the side of the road. Wes had barely pulled to a stop behind her before she spilled out her door and ran to him.

He got out of his truck and his arms opened. She ran straight into them, plowing into him, tears already flowing down her cheeks. He wrapped her in an embrace that unquestionably bruised a few of her ribs. He buried his face in her hair, and they stood like that for an endless moment of pure relief.

Then Wes broke the spell, saying tersely, "Get in the truck. I want you out of here in case that bastard's following you. He undoubtedly had a vehicle hidden nearby and could be here any second."

"Oh, God. I hadn't thought of that." She ran around to the passenger side of Wes's truck and jumped in as he gunned the engine. She was silent as he drove grimly, breaking all the speed limits. Thankfully, he seemed familiar with the road, and he was a combat-trained driver. Which was good because he was driving like their lives depended on it. And, for all she knew, they did.

They drove for about a half hour and came down out of the high mountains to a relatively flat plateau before she finally asked, "Where are we?"

"We're taking a circular route back to the west side of the McMinn Mountain Range."

Okay. That meant nothing to her. But she wasn't about to bicker with Wes over it. He'd saved her life, and she was more grateful than she had words to express.

The road finally started to look familiar, and she realized they were only a few minutes from Runaway Ranch.

She was surprised, however, when Wes turned into Outlaw Ranch and didn't take her on up the road to his parents' place. But she held her silence. Did she dare hope he was actually concerned about her?

She'd done it again. She'd called him and dragged him into the middle of her insane life. And he'd come running. *Again.* Did it mean he secretly—way down deep—had actual feelings for her? Or was he just acting out of human decency? Either way, he seemed to have declared a temporary truce with her and wasn't being a gigantic jerk at the moment. Thank God.

He parked in front of his house and she climbed out silently, following him up the front steps. As he fiddled with his key ring looking for the house key, she ventured to ask, "Who carved this door? It's magnificent."

"Thanks. I did it."

Her jaw dropped. "You? Are you kidding?"

He looked at her, frowning slightly. "No. If you want to see my workshop, I'll show it to you later."

"I never knew you were such a talented artist!"

"You never asked." He pushed open the front door and she followed him inside.

Her eyes adjusted to the dim interior and she commented reflectively, "When you and I were together, talking wasn't exactly at the top of our activity agenda.

Which is a shame. I would have liked to know more about you."

His gaze lifted to hers, and a combination of wry humor and heated memory swirled in his dark blue gaze. Oh, Lord, he looked edible when he had that particular expression on his face. She walked toward him slowly, never breaking eye contact, giving him plenty of time to run for cover if he chose.

He didn't choose, apparently. He stood there as if rooted in place, staring at her as she came toward him, his gaze burning down her soul. She stopped in front of him, less than an arm's length away.

"Thank you for saving my life, Wes. Again. I seem to keep going deeper and deeper in debt to you."

A frown twitched on his brow. "Helping other people isn't a thing you keep track of in a ledger."

She took the last step toward him and wrapped her arms around his waist. Her head fit perfectly in the hollow of his neck, and she laid it there just like she used to. He stood there, unmoving and stiff as a board for a long time, but she persisted, holding her ground. Eventually his arms came up around her but felt reluctant. Her heart hurt at that, but it was no more and no less than she deserved.

"I know you're not the kind of man who keeps a tally of debts owed," she murmured. "But you keep doing the right thing, and I keep putting you in danger. I have never meant to cause you any harm." A shudder that was half sob and half self-hatred passed through her.

"Look at me, Jess."

She lifted her head and stared into the depths of his beautiful eyes. Something moved deep in her belly that had less to do with lust and more to do with genuine feelings for this man. She confessed, "You have no idea how much I would love to go all the way back to a year ago and have a complete do-over with you." His arms tightened a little more as she added, "I owe you so much. And not just for the rescues."

One dark, sardonic eyebrow rose.

Her gaze did fall away from his then. But she forced herself to look back at this man upon whom she'd inflicted so much damage. "You changed me, Wes."

The eyebrow inched a bit higher.

"When you broke up with me, you forced me to see myself through your eyes. As I really was. And I didn't like the person I saw. I was angry that you made me examine myself. Honestly, it put me in a really bad headspace for a while. That was why I went to the pop-up club that night. I knew I was taking a big chance going there alone and accepting a drink from a stranger. But I was determined to act as shallow and stupid as you saw me to be."

"I never thought you were stupid. Shallow, maybe, but not stupid."

One corner of her mouth quirked up wryly. "Fair enough. I think we can both agree, though, that I was stupid to let myself get drugged."

"It's not your job to assume that every guy is a criminal creep—"

"And yet I knew better. It was my fault. Let me own that."

He shrugged. "All right. You did something stupid. We all do from time to time."

Yeah, like him barging in to rescue her and losing his temper and assaulting her assailant.

"Getting drugged scared me. Really scared me."

"Good."

"I beg your pardon?"

"You needed a hard scare. Maybe it'll help you make better decisions in the future."

"The best decision I've made since then was coming out here to see you." She smiled sadly. "But I doubt you see it that way."

For an instant, humor glinted in his gaze. "I was pretty furious when you showed up at my door unannounced."

She got the impression he wasn't just talking about the night she'd arrived. She sighed. "You have a right to feel that way. I'm impulsive and selfish and don't stop to think about the consequences of my actions for other people."

"You don't have to put yourself down all the time, you know," he murmured. "You're not a completely bad person."

"Gee. Thanks," she responded drily.

His chest shook with a silent chuckle.

"Where does all of this leave us?" she asked.

"Hell if I know."

"Do you still hate me?"

"Sometimes."

That was progress. At least he hadn't answered with an unqualified yes. And he was still holding her in his arms.

"I am a horrible person sometimes," she declared.

"Agreed."

"But sometimes I'm not." It felt strange admitting that after all this time of self-castigation and self-recrimination.

Wes didn't respond to that other than to stare down

at her intently, as if he was waiting for something. Although she had no idea what, exactly.

She always had leaped before she looked, and that would never change. Following her gut, she lifted her chin and murmured, "Sometimes, I go after what I want."

"What do you want, Jessica?"

She leaned in the last few inches and kissed him.

Chapter 9

A thousand emotions exploded in Wes's gut as Jessica kissed him. Disbelief. Caution. Anger. *Relief.*

And foremost among them was desire, burning hot and bright and strong. He had never, not for a second, stopped wanting this woman. No matter how much he hated her. How much he wanted to *hurt* her. Not even when she destroyed everything he did and ripped away who he was.

It was fair to say he'd passionately hated her after the debacle in Washington. But, as it turned out, hate was a passion not entirely in opposition to lust…or to other, deeper emotions.

He shouldn't kiss her back. He should walk away from this woman. She was Trouble. Capital *T.*

And yet he slanted his mouth across hers hungrily, and she opened for him, her tongue tangling eagerly with his. Her entire body undulated hungrily against his, and he absorbed her desire into himself, reflecting it back tenfold.

This was a mistake. She was nothing but bad for him.

But cripes. Hearing that gunshot in the background as she'd called him—again—frantic and sure she was going to die, had scared ten years off his life. He couldn't very well just listen to her die.

If only he could find a way not to give a damn about her. To let her go completely. To walk away from her. Of course, that assumed she wouldn't follow him and suck him back into her vortex of drama like she always did. But after her frantic call and the gunshots in the background, adrenaline was still surging through his veins, seeking an outlet—and insisting that hot, sweaty sex was a fantastic idea.

Her hands tugged at his shirt, and then her soft palms splayed against his bare back, her nails digging into his skin just enough to be sexy as hell. She had always been bold in bed, and the reminder sent lust raging through him. He craved her pretty much every waking moment. And here she was, crawling all over him, hot and willing—

What the hell was he supposed to do with her? His brain said to run screaming from her. His body…well, that was a different matter. And what about his heart? It was torn between strangling her and throwing her down on the couch and making wild love to her.

They still didn't know who'd been shooting at her. Did the shooter know where Outlaw Ranch was? Know she was here? Surely not, or bullets would already be flying in through the window. God. He would never forget the sound of those gunshots coming through the phone, getting closer and closer to her.

In his residual terror, the desire raging through him won out over logic. He was too raw, too shaken to fight the feelings right now.

He carried her down to his sofa, shoving aside her clothing and his with clumsy hands. It was awkward and cushions went flying, but then he was pumping into her tight, welcoming heat, with each thrust reassuring himself that she was alive. That she was here. Safe. With him.

The lust that always flared in his gut with her was as bright and sharp as ever, as blinding as a blowtorch and every bit as dangerous. A torch could create things—build structures and form beautiful art. It could also destroy, incinerating everything in its path. Such was this thing between them.

But for the moment, he lost himself in it. He let the pleasure roar through him, wiping out thought or reason or caution. His entire existence narrowed down to her. How her eyes glazed over with desire. How her slim, athletic body writhed beneath him in the throes of pleasure. How the cries torn from her throat resonated through his own chest. How the slick glide of her body against his made for unbearably fantastic friction. She stroked his body to a place where he was overwhelmed, stripped bare and flung out of his mind into pure ecstasy.

He threw back his head and closed his eyes, completely lost in the sensations, glutted with lust yet greedy for more. He couldn't take much more of this. It was too much. Too good.

His entire body clenched and then exploded. He

surged into her as everything inside him broke loose. It felt like a raging river had burst through a dam in his mind, annihilating everything else within him with its fury.

He collapsed, exhausted, hanging between his elbows, which were propped on either side of her head. Her chest heaved beneath him, too. They'd had some intense sex in the past, but this… This was a new level altogether.

She totally wrecked him.

It was long minutes before he was able to gather himself enough to press up and away from her. He turned his back and put his clothes to rights. When he finally looked over his shoulder, her clothes were back in place and she was sitting upright, her hands folded primly in her lap. She looked like a teen who'd just gotten caught making out under the bleachers. The mental whiplash was severe. She threw herself into sex with him with wanton abandon and then retreated into this other persona that was polite, cautious and contrite.

Yeah. That probably had been a mistake.

But, hard as he tried, he couldn't muster any regret over it. Sex with Jessica was like no other sex he'd ever had.

She opened her mouth to speak, and he cut her off. "If you apologize again, I'm throwing you out on your ear. Besides, I'm not sorry for that."

"Good. Then I'm not either."

He moved over to the raised stone hearth and sat down on it, cautiously placing the coffee table between them. As if that would stop them from tearing off each other's clothes and crawling all over each other when they lost control the next time. Ha.

No doubt about it. This woman was bad news, although, to be fair, they brought out the absolute worst in each other.

"We need to talk, Jessica."

Caution danced across her mobile features. "About what?"

"About who was shooting at you. I called the sheriff, and he's going to try to find out where the shooter was and look for evidence to identify him or her. He's going to want to talk with you, too. The first thing he's going to ask is who has a grudge against you."

"Besides you?" she asked wryly.

He rolled his eyes.

She answered seriously, "The only person I can think of is the guy who drugged me and whom you pummeled."

That was what he'd figured. Jessica was spoiled and wild, and at her worst she could be a brat, but she wasn't a hateful person. She didn't tend to make enemies out of anybody. He asked, "Can you think of anyone, besides that guy, who was obsessed with you? Maybe showed stalker tendencies?"

She was thoughtful for a minute and then shook her head. "Nope. I've got nothing."

"So you really weren't kidding when you said someone had threatened you—and me," he commented.

"Uh, no," she retorted.

"This is nuts. Who would want to hurt you? Who did you tell that you were coming to Montana?"

"Nobody!"

"Surely you told your father."

"No. Not even him. I just got in my car as if I was going out to run an errand and kept on driving."

"Did you check your car for a tracking device?"

"Why on earth would I do that?" she responded. "Who would secretly track me? It's not as if I'm a spy."

"If someone really was following you, they could easily have planted a tracker on your car."

To that end, he pulled out his cell phone and gave his cousin, the county sheriff, Joe Westlake, another call on his cousin's private cell phone.

Joe picked up immediately. "Hey, Wes. Is Jessica okay?"

"She's rattled, but she's fine. She's here with me."

"Cool. I'll stop by to interview her when we're done on scene."

"Any luck ID'ing the shooter?"

"We found the spot he was shooting from, but he policed all his brass and didn't leave behind any evidence to speak of."

"Did any slugs lodge in the car itself?" Wes asked.

"Yup. We'll at least find out the caliber and type of weapon he was shooting. It appears the shot that took out her tire happened from almost directly behind Jessica."

"So he was driving behind her?"

"That's how it looks. Then, once she pulled over to change her tire, he exited his own vehicle and commenced sniping at her," Joe explained. "I can tell you it appears that one individual did all the shooting."

"Good to know. Hey, I called to let you know you need to check for a tracking device on Jessica's car. And not just the undercarriage. You'll need to fine-tooth comb the car and engine for one. The person who might be after Jess could be sophisticated and have money."

"Ohh…kay. That sounds ominous. Guess I'll be

doing that interview with your girl sooner rather than later." Joe hung up, and Wes stared unseeing at his phone.

Your girl? His gut tightened at Jessica being called his girl, but he couldn't tell if it was a good tightening or a bad one. Either way, it was weird. Even when they'd been dating, he had been worried about what General Blankenship would think of him sleeping with Jessica, and they'd been extremely secretive about their relationship. Indeed, as soon as the Old Man had found out about them, he'd put his foot down and told Wes to end it with his daughter.

By then, Wes had already figured out that Jessica—as amazing a chemistry as they had—was not going to make for a quiet, supportive, conservative military wife. Not that all military wives had to be that way. He would just need a politically correct wife if he planned to climb high in the Pentagon power structure like his boss had. And like his father had expected of him.

Word had it Blankenship's wife had been from a powerful East Coast fortune built in the defense contracting industry. She might have come from a politically advantageous background, but from what little the general had said of her, Wes gathered she'd been wild and artistic and creative—a lot like Jessica—and had been nothing but trouble for his career.

Of course, by his wife dying young and tragically and leaving him with a small daughter, George had garnered all kinds of sympathy and support. The tragedy had ultimately landed him the job that had catapulted his career from ordinary to the fast track.

All of that was moot, now. Wes had no career to

worry about. And he doubted his cattle would care if his wife was a free spirit or not—

"Where did you go just then?" Jessica startled him by asking.

"I was thinking about your mother."

"My mother! What for?"

"I was thinking about the parallels in your lives."

"She wasn't shot. She drowned."

"True. But, according to your father, you're a lot like her."

Jessica shrugged. "I wouldn't know. I barely remember her. And her family had nothing to do with my dad or me after her death."

"Why is that?"

"I suppose they blame him for taking her away from them and maybe indirectly for her death."

"That's pretty harsh. I can't imagine my parents shunning a grandchild, no matter how much they disliked the remaining parent."

Jessica shuddered. "I've met your parents. I would hate to test that theory."

He grinned crookedly. "Me, too." He added, "Joe's going to stop by here in a little while to talk with you."

She nodded and then asked him shyly, "Any chance I can go out to the barn and see the new calf again?"

He couldn't help smiling. "Sure."

He led her out to the barn and to the stall where Number 19 was resting with her calf. Both were lying down. Mama raised her head briefly and then went back to placidly chewing her cud. The scent of hay and corn and warm cattle surrounded him in familiar comfort. It was peaceful in the calving barn, with a deep quiet that sank into his bones.

Funny how much he'd hated ranching when he was a kid and thought it was the only future available to him. But now, after traveling the world, after seeing war and famine and suffering, the simple goodness of living off the land was starting to appeal to him. Even the idea of putting down roots didn't scare him as much as it once had.

"The calf is so adorable," Jessica murmured. "Have you named her yet?"

"Cows don't have names."

"Why not? You're not going to eat her, are you? Your dad explained to me the other night at supper that ranchers keep the heifers to have more calves and grow the herd, and sell off the steers to pay the bills."

"He's right about that." Wes shrugged. "I suppose you can name her if you want to."

Jessica tried out a half-dozen names and settled on Daisy, declaring it perfect.

He rolled his eyes indulgently. "Fine. Daisy it is."

Then Jessica surprised him by asking, "Do you have long-term plans for your ranch?"

He actually felt a little embarrassed as he admitted, "Yeah. Get bigger and richer than Runaway Ranch."

"Daddy issues, much?" she replied, twirling a piece of straw in her fingers.

"Pot calling the kettle black, much?" he retorted.

Jessica rolled her eyes. "Touché. I'll pit my father against yours anytime for who's the craziest, though."

Wes answered seriously, "Your father would win, hands down. Mine is tough as nails and can be a bastard, but he doesn't have the mean streak yours has."

Jessica glanced at him, looking surprised. "You saw that side of him, huh? He doesn't let many people see it."

"I worked with the man day and night for four years. It was inevitable that he would show his true colors around me. Your father was ruthless in pursuit of his ambitions."

"Huh. Yeah. That didn't work out so well for him," she commented. "He found out last month that he didn't get the job in the Secretary of Defense's office he wanted. And he just got passed over for his fourth star."

Wes hadn't heard that. Getting passed over for a promotion at that level was the kiss of death for any further advancement in rank for Blankenship. So, the Old Man was going to top out at three stars and not make it all the way to the pinnacle of the food chain? Wes wasn't sorry to hear that. "Your father must not be happy about getting passed over."

"He's livid."

"Is the military going to force him to retire soon?"

She grimaced. "Any day. God knows what he'll do with himself after that. He's a Marine and *nothing* else. He's talked for years about looking forward to retiring, but I think he's been lying all along."

Wes snorted. "He can always go into cattle ranching. My dad made the transition to it, okay."

"Your dad had your mom to help him make the transition."

"Well, your dad has you."

Jessica rolled her eyes. "Except he treats me like I'm fifteen and the boys are just starting to come sniffing around. I'm twenty-six, for crying out loud. The last thing I need is him hanging around, hovering over every aspect of my life more than he already tries to."

Wes grinned crookedly. "I'll probably be the same way with my daughters, so I can't really fault the guy for being protective." He added soberly, "And as it turned out, he was not wrong. You nearly got into some serious trouble."

Jessica snapped, "He's not protective. He's obsessive."

When they'd been dating, she had always refused to talk about her father. He was intrigued that she would use such strong language now to describe her only parent. Wes studied Jessica intently. "Really? Tell me about it."

"When he gets drunk, he calls me Rebecca. That was my mother's name."

Okay. That was creepy.

She continued, "Once, when he was talking to me like I was her, he told me he'd kill me before he would let me leave him. When I was a little girl, he used to say that she might have died and left him, but that he knew I never would. I used to think it was just his way of telling me he loved me. Now, looking back, it was a bit sinister."

Wow. That did go beyond overprotective a little too far. Aloud, he said carefully, "Your father does have a rather...extreme...personality."

Jessica snorted loudly enough that Number 19's head jerked up. She murmured to the cow, "It's all right, girl. I'm sorry I woke you. Go back to sleep."

He just shook his head. If Jess wanted to talk to his cows like they understood her, more power to her.

"My father is big about putting up a good front for the rest of the world. Behind it, he's an entirely different person, particularly when he's under a lot of stress or he's been drinking."

"I saw that at work with him. He was all jovial and

friendly when anyone else was around. But get alone in an office with him, and more often than not, he was a born-again sonofabitch. Impossible to please. Obsessive about the tiniest details." Wes added reflectively, "Do you think it's fear of failure that drives him or something else?"

Jessica frowned. "I always thought he secretly felt unworthy. Or felt like a fraud. I could never really put my finger on it, but it was as if he was pretending to be someone he wasn't and was terrified of getting caught."

"Rough way to live a life," Wes commented.

"Agreed. That's part of why it was so important for me to clear the air with you. I truly didn't expect you to forgive me. I have no right to ask for that after what I did. But I wanted you to know why I did it and not obsess over why I turned on you like that. I saw what obsessing has done to my father. It has eaten him up from the inside out."

Quiet fell between them as they watched the newborn calf wake and stumble to its feet, still sorting out the whole business of managing four legs. Mama got up immediately and moved into position for the calf to nurse, nudging the little heifer with her nose. Wes smiled. "She's a good mother. You never know with a first-time mama cow. Sometimes they get the hang of it right away, and every now and then, one doesn't."

"What do you do with the calves whose mothers don't take care of them?"

"Bottle feed them. Ideally, you can milk the mother and feed the baby the milk it's supposed to be getting. If a cow dies or doesn't make enough milk, I'll supplement the calf's diet with milk from another cow or with a commercial milk substitute. But I like to try to get calves real milk as much as possible. If I'm lucky, another cow might have just calved and may accept the orphan calf as her own. I can tell you, it's a rough, round-the-clock job, though, feeding a newborn calf every two hours."

"It sounds like fun."

He snorted. "It is until that alarm clock goes off at two in the morning for the fifth or sixth day in a row and you're so exhausted you can hardly see straight."

"Sounds like new motherhood for human women."

He shrugged. "Any farmer who has hand-raised a baby animal can sympathize with a new human mother."

Jessica murmured, "You'll make a good father someday."

"I hope so."

"You want kids?"

He nodded, a little surprised to be doing so. He'd always assumed that family was a "sometime in the future" thing for him—when his career settled down and wasn't quite so demanding of his time and mental energy. That, and he hated the idea of leaving a wife and kids at home while he went off to war for months on end.

"What about you?" he asked Jessica. "Do you want children someday?"

"I never thought about it much before now, but I guess I do. Assuming I can get it right and not mess it up like my father did."

Wow. She'd always been guarded and polite in the past when it came to talking about the general. Had that been because he worked for the guy? Maybe she'd feared that he would tattle to Daddy.

He turned around with his back to the stall, leaning

one hip against the oak boards. "What's the worst thing your father ever did to you?"

Jessica stared at him, her eyes wide, as if the question had taken her by surprise. He could practically count the memories scrolling through her mind as her expression changed from one moment to the next. Unfortunately, most of the memories were bad if the look in her eyes was any indication.

She finally answered, "He didn't love me when I messed up. Love has always been transactional for him."

"That's pretty esoteric," he commented.

She shrugged. "I couldn't pick a single thing as the worst. Overall, he mistook smothering me for loving me. Any number of my worst memories spring from that."

Wes frowned. "I can't imagine anyone smothering you successfully. It would be like trying to bottle the wind. You have too big and free a spirit to contain for long."

She smiled sadly at him. "I wish that were still true."

Hearing something like that from her was shocking. Stunned, he replied, "Look, Jess. Don't let what a low-life jerk tried to do to you snuff out your zest for life. Don't give him that power over you. He doesn't deserve it."

"My therapist said pretty much the same thing, but he took two months to say it and charged me a fortune."

Never, in a million years, would he have guessed he would ever see Jessica Blankenship beaten down emotionally or even depressed. Reluctant sympathy coursed through him.

He shrugged. "Happiness is a choice. Not always an

easy one, but a choice. Choose to be happy and don't look back. Do things that make you happy. Your whole life is in front of you."

"Easy for you to say. You've already made a new start and are moving forward. I feel stuck in a giant sinkhole and can't get out of it. Every time I try to climb out, the sides collapse and I slide right back in."

It really bothered him to hear brave, irrepressible Jessica talk like this. Her wildness might be infuriating sometimes, but it was one of her most appealing qualities. "Tell me this. If there was one thing you could do right now—anything at all—that would make you truly happy, what would it be?"

She answered quickly, without hesitation, "Redecorate your house."

A burst of reluctant laughter escaped him. "Man. I walked into that one, didn't I?"

She stood up straight. "I'm serious. I've actually had dreams about redoing your place. It goes against my interior designer's religion for anyone to live in a home with so much undeveloped potential." She warmed to the topic, speaking enthusiastically. "The bones are great. Classic ranch architecture. It just needs a face-lift. It would look *so* good—"

She broke off, scowling at his broad grin. "Don't laugh at me. I'm serious."

"I know you are. You always have had a passion for restoring old, broken things."

She glared at him. "If you don't watch out, I'll restore you, mister."

"Ha. I dare you."

As soon as the words were out of his mouth, he knew

better. Jessica had never been one to turn her back on any kind of dare.

"Now you've done it," she replied archly. "I'm redoing your house, and then I'm coming after you."

Oh, Lord.

Except, in the midst of his chagrin he noticed something else. A tiny sliver of—joy?—had taken root in his soul. What in the world had he just gotten himself into?

Chapter 10

Plans swirled in her head, stacking one on top of another so quickly Jessica could hardly catalog them all. She needed a notebook—and soon—to start making lists. She hurried back to the house and sat down at Wes's kitchen table, sketching and imagining in a massive rush of excitement.

She demanded a measuring tape and drafted Wes to hold the end of it while she measured his house from top to bottom. She'd never been in his bedroom before and stopped cold at the threshold. His bed was as beautifully carved as his front door, with stylized tree branches and leaves covering the whimsically shaped headboard and tall posts. The piece looked as if it belonged in an enchanted fairy glade.

"Oh, Wes. It's beautiful." She ran her fingertips over the delicately carved wood. "I'm going to give you a bedroom worthy of this. It will be amazing."

"Don't go too crazy, eh? I'm not made of money."

"Oh, really, Mr. Trust Fund?"

"I'm not touching that money."

"Fine. I'll behave." And there was no law saying she couldn't touch her trust fund, which contained many millions of dollars. Her mother had been one of only two heirs to a massive defense-contracting fortune, and money still poured into her accounts every year from the business. Jessica already gave away money hand over fist to historical preservation societies and to groups that prevented animal abuse, and she still had more money than she knew what to do with.

Tapping a pencil against her front teeth, she stood in the middle of the otherwise Spartan bedroom and envisioned what the generous space could be. Oh, yes. It would be magnificent.

"Stop. I can see your mental wheels turning. I just need the basics. A bed. A dresser. A closet. Maybe a chair to sit in by the fireplace."

"Let me write those down." She made a note in her book and nodded to herself. "I have enough to get started on the design. I'll work on it while I finish up your parents' hunting cabin and will be ready to start on your place by the time I'm done with that."

He shook his head and muttered, "What the hell was I thinking when I asked what would make you happy?"

She paused in front of him and laid her palm against his cheek. "You're a good man, Wes Morgan."

"And a glutton for punishment, it seems."

She just smiled at him. She was going to give him a home worthy of his goodness whether he liked it or not.

Deep into detailed sketching an hour later at the kitchen table, she was startled when a knock sounded at the front door. Wes leaped up and peered out the window cautiously before opening it to admit a man in a brown uniform and wearing a badge.

"Jessica, this is my cousin, Joe Westlake. And as you can see by the khaki clown suit and tin star, he's also the county sheriff."

"Always were a jackass, Wes," Joe retorted cheerfully.

Jessica rose to greet him and smiled at the way his eyes widened. Most men reacted that way the first time they saw her. But she only cared when Wes's eyes lit up like that. "How can I help you, Sheriff?"

"I need you to make an official statement describing what happened to you today. If you don't mind, I'll record you telling it to me and have it transcribed. You can read over it and sign it later. Most people find it easier to talk with me than try to write it all out."

She nodded and sank onto the sofa while he sat in the armchair. She recounted the events as she remembered them, shuddering in recollection of how terrified she'd been when she'd finally realized someone was trying to kill her.

The sheriff nodded at the end of her recitation. "That pretty much jibes with the evidence I saw at the scene." He paused, then asked gently, "Any idea who might want to kill you?"

Jessica sighed and told the story of her drugging and near miss with being sexually assaulted. This time, she honestly described Wes's part in rescuing her. She left out the bit where Wes nearly killed the guy. That was Wes's story to tell or not as he chose.

Joe looked grim at the end of her recitation. "You were lucky to get away unscathed."

"I have Wes to thank for that."

Joe glanced up at his cousin. "How come you didn't tell anybody about this when you got home? Your old man thinks you left the military under a cloud. But you're a hero, dude."

Wes's blue gaze went as hard and cold as North Sea ice. "I did leave the military under a cloud. What Jessica failed to tell you is that I beat the crap out of the guy who drugged her. I damn near killed him. That's why I got kicked out of the Corps."

She stared at Wes, wide-eyed. Why on earth did he admit that when she'd protected him and left it out?

Wes's jaw rippled as if he was clenching it. Hard. As if he'd heard her unspoken question, he muttered, "I hate lies and secrets."

His honesty and directness—to his own detriment—were a blatant slap in the face to her. Her gaze shifted to Joe and she asked glumly, "Is there anything else you need to ask me?"

"I think that's everything for now. Where will you be staying if I need to get in touch with you again?"

When she opened her mouth to say that she would be at Runaway Ranch, Wes cut her off. "She'll be here. Where I can keep an eye on her until you catch whoever shot at her."

Joe nodded. "Glad to hear it. No telling if this was a random thing or if the shooter will come after her again."

Wes snorted. "I'm not an ex-Marine for nothing. Anyone wants to meddle with Jess, they're gonna have to go through me."

The sheriff left quickly after that, leaving the cabin in silence. Jessica turned to confront Wes. "Why do you want me to stay here with you? You hate my guts. Or at least you do anytime we're not making love."

He pushed a distracted hand through his shaggy hair, standing it up every which way. "Hell if I know."

"I can go back to Runaway Ranch and stay there until I'm done remodeling the cabin—"

"No! The last thing I want is for whatever danger is chasing you to follow you there!"

She frowned. "But it's okay if the danger comes here?"

"It's just me here. And I can protect myself."

"Your dad is ex-military, and the way I hear it, your mom's as good a shot as he is. Not to mention there are a dozen ranch hands around at any given time, and I imagine most of them can handle a shotgun, too."

Wes shook his head stubbornly. "That's my family. You stay away from them."

She knew he only meant to keep the danger she'd attracted away from them, but the words still hurt. He would never admit to having had a relationship with her, and he certainly wouldn't share that they had smoking-hot sex practically every time they were alone for any period of time.

Not that it meant anything at the end of the day. She would never be more than an…outlet…to him. He blew off his frustration with her by having sex with her. It was probably a really bad idea to keep aiding and abetting that habit of his. But darned if she could keep her hands off him when he got near her. She craved him like she craved food or water.

It was probably a really awful idea to stay with him for any length of time. Given their track record, it could only end badly for them.

But darned if she could bring herself to say no to him.

* * *

Wes fed the cows in a bit of a daze. What the hell had he been thinking, insisting that Jessica stay with him? He really was worried about her dragging violence to his parents' ranch, but he knew as well as she did that it was not the main reason he wanted her here.

What kind of sick idiot asked the woman who was worst in the world for him to shack up with him? He was a masochist, plain and simple. A dumber-than-dirt one.

When he went inside in the gathering dusk, he drew up short at the sight of Jessica in the kitchen serving up plates of sauerkraut and sausage with some sort of green-bean-and-almond sauté on the side. "How did you manage to make something tasty out of the assorted crap in my refrigerator?" he demanded as he sat down to eat with her.

She shrugged. "It just takes a little creativity and out-of-the-box thinking. I've always loved to mess around in a kitchen."

"I didn't know that about you. We always went out to eat."

"That's because you worked long hours and wanted instant food when you got out of the office. I couldn't plan meals for you because I never knew when my father would unchain you from your desk."

Live and learn. She hadn't known about his art. He hadn't known about her cooking. He supposed they were even. "This is tasty. Thanks."

"My pleasure. Maybe tomorrow we could make a run to a grocery store so I can properly stock your kitchen. I'll meal plan before we go, if you'd like, so I don't cook anything you hate."

He snorted. "After the grub I've eaten in the field

during military deployments, there's basically nothing you could make for me that I wouldn't eat."

"Still. What's your favorite food?"

He frowned. "I've always liked a good steak. But I really like my mother's beef Stroganoff. It's an old family recipe."

She nodded and looked pleased.

"Are you going to ask me my favorite color and zodiac sign next?" he asked wryly.

"Blue and Taurus. I know when your birthday is, Wes."

"How did you know blue's my favorite color?" he asked, surprised.

"Most of your clothes have blue in them, and the few places where you've bothered to decorate in your house have blue in them. And your bathroom towels are blue."

He scowled. "I didn't know I was so transparent."

She grinned. "If it would make you feel better, you can think of it as me just being incredibly observant."

He smiled back reluctantly in spite of himself. When she wasn't being a total brat, she'd always been pretty good company. Although in her defense, she hadn't behaved rotten once since she'd come to Montana.

Huh. That was a surprise.

Where, then, had he gotten the impression she was so awful? He thought back and was startled to realize that it had been her father who usually described her in negative terms. Oh, George hadn't come right out and called her names, but he was forever and always taking little digs at her that added up to a pretty terrible overall image. It hadn't even occurred to Wes that George had colored his impression of Jessica so heavily until this very moment. Subtle, that guy was. But why would the man sabotage his own daughter like that?

It made no sense.

At the end of the day, Jessica was beautiful, smart, talented and charming—when she wasn't off being wild and impulsive. George Blankenship ought to be proud of her. If nothing else, his daughter should remind him of his deceased wife. Supposedly, Jessica was a great deal like her mother.

It had started raining during supper, and Wes went out to his carving workshop, which he had set up in an old smokehouse that somebody had closed in a few decades ago. As rain beat a soothing rhythm on the old roof, he absently picked up a chair leg he was working on. The darkness and the quiet and the simple pleasure of carving wood into the shapes he envisioned in his mind calmed and centered him.

His mind drifted back to his earlier train of thought. Where else had Jessica's reputation as a diva in all the worst ways come from, anyway? Had other people supported George's vision of his daughter?

He thought back to meeting her friends. They'd tended to be wild children and had often made him feel old and boring. Still, they'd universally adored Jessica. Nope. It had just been George who'd taken subtle potshots at her every chance he got. Why would the man gaslight his own daughter as he had? Was he trying to keep men away from her or something?

"Whatchya doin'?" Jessica asked abruptly from the doorway.

He jumped, startled, and his knife slipped. "Ow!" he yelped. Crap. He'd sliced the index finger of his left hand, about halfway down on the underside, pretty bad.

"Ohmigosh! I'm so sorry!" Jessica rushed forward. "What can I do to help?"

He grabbed a towel he normally used to wipe sawdust off wood and wrapped it around his finger, holding it tightly. "Let's go to the house and clean it up."

She hovered worriedly beside him the whole way, and he finally glanced up at her wryly. "I didn't cut it off, Jess. It'll be okay. Accidents happen around a ranch."

She frowned at him. "I startled you. It's my fault. I'm so sorry."

He rolled his eyes, annoyed that she was apologizing. *Again*. He bit out, "I should have been more aware of my surroundings and heard you coming."

He headed for the kitchen sink to rinse off the blood while he sent her to the bathroom for the first aid kit. A good look at the cut revealed that it was deep and needed stitches.

"I'll drive you over to Hillsdale—" she started.

"No need. Miranda knows how to set sutures. Take me to Runaway Ranch."

"Okay. I'll drive your truck."

Oh, this was going to be fun. Jessica driving a truck? He climbed cautiously into the passenger seat. "So, this is a lot bigger than your car. You'll have to take corners more widely, and the brakes won't be as nimble as the ones in your Corvette—"

"Wes," she interrupted gently. "I've got this. I'll take care of you. I swear."

He subsided. Well. This was certainly a change. He was usually the one rescuing her.

She did, indeed, drive carefully to his parents' ranch and parked close to the main house. She led the way to the kitchen door and rang the bell while he kept pressure on the cut, which was still adding blood to the stain soaking through the towel.

Miranda opened the door, took one look at his towel-wrapped hand and said briskly, "Sit down at the kitchen table. I'll go get my supplies."

Wes honestly expected Jessica to be squeamish about the stitches, but she surprised him by hovering over Miranda's shoulder, asking copious questions as his mother applied a topical numbing cream and commenced setting tiny, neat stitches in his skin. For his part, he looked away.

In a few minutes, Miranda had finished, wrapping his finger in gauze and taping it carefully with waterproof tape. Jessica listened intently to the instructions Miranda gave her about caring for the wound, and he sensed with amusement that Jessica was going to be a tough nurse and make him toe the line.

They were driving back to Outlaw Ranch, the windshield wipers thunking back and forth in the rain, before he remembered to murmur, "Thanks."

"For what?" she asked, sounding surprised.

"For taking care of me."

She shrugged. "You've taken care of me plenty of times. I'm glad I was there to help out."

He leaned back against the seat. It was weird having anyone look out for him like this. He'd been alone for so long, both as a bachelor officer and now as a rancher, that he'd almost forgotten what it was like to have family and friends around him. For a moment, he felt the burden of being responsible for every single aspect of his ranch lift slightly from his shoulders.

They got back to his house, which looked like a

drowned rat in the rain, its warped, mildewed siding black and slick. He just prayed the metal roof would hold up one more season until he could afford to replace it. Maybe after this fall's sale of feeder calves he could replace the rusted mess.

His finger was starting to throb painfully, and as soon as they got inside, he took a handful of painkillers and headed for bed.

From the doorway of his bedroom, Jessica asked, "Do you need help getting your clothes off?"

He looked up at her, his mouth twitching in amusement. "I'm not an invalid. I cut my finger. Thanks anyway, though." And Lord knew, he was in no condition for a round of athletic sex with her. Although as soon as the thought crossed his mind, his crotch stirred with interest.

Down, boy. He needed to sleep off the stress of cutting himself badly and being rescued by Jessica.

He crawled into bed, his alarm set for six o'clock and the morning feeding. It was weird knowing Jessica was in the house, and that, for once, he wasn't alone. It was…nice. And that was his last thought before he crashed.

When Wes woke up, the sun was streaming in his window at far too high an angle. The sun shouldn't even be up yet! He looked at his alarm clock, saw it was pushing ten o'clock and bolted out of bed, swearing and leaping into clothes. He hated being late for the morning feeding. The cows got restless, and with so many of them close to calving, he didn't want to stress them out.

He charged into the living room and pulled up short. Jessica was sitting at the kitchen table drinking a cup of coffee. And, more to the point, she was wearing a pair of his jeans, which hung baggily on her slender frame, and one of his flannel shirts, which was covered in bits of hay.

"What have you done?" he blurted.

"I turned off your alarm clock so you could get some rest, and I fed the cows this morning. You probably ought to go out and check that I gave them enough hay. I was getting pretty tired by the end, and I may not have thrown down enough for them."

"You fed the cows?" he repeated blankly. Jessica Blankenship, jet-setter, trust fund baby and city girl extraordinaire, had fed his cows? Had he woken up in an alternate universe or something?

"I saw you do it before, and it's not exactly rocket science to put corn and hay into a feeder." She added, "There's a pot of coffee made, and I'll fry you up some eggs if you'd like."

Yup. Definitely an alternate universe.

"How's your finger feeling this morning?"

"It hurts a little. Nothing much."

"Since you can't work around the ranch today, I'd like to go over my thoughts about your house with you. Maybe take you on a shopping trip."

He groaned. "If you take me to a craft store, I may have to kill myself."

"The alternative is to trust me and let me make all the decisions for your renovation."

"Renovation?" he echoed in alarm. "I thought we were talking about a little facelift. A rug here and there. Maybe some new paint."

"Wesley Morgan. If you *ever* paint those glorious

ceiling beams and wood-planked walls, I will personally have to hurt you!"

His eyebrows lifted. "No paint. Got it."

"So what's it going to be? Shopping hell or do you
trust me?"

He lifted his gaze to hers across the table. "I guess
I trust you."

She stared back, her sky blue eyes wide and beautiful and surprised. "Well, okay then," she breathed. She
shook herself out of her apparent shock. "I've got some
phone calls to make."

"I'm going to go check on the cows while you do
your designer thing," he announced. "And then I'm
going to do some work in the woodshed—and no, I
won't try to carve anything one-handed. I've got some
sanding and staining to do."

"No heavy lifting or hard work for you!" she called
after him.

"Yes, ma'am!" he called back over his shoulder, feeling more cheerful than he had in a very long time.

Chapter 11

Jessica made calls to the contractors she'd been using on the Runaway Ranch cabin and lined up a whole list of people to come in and start work. Since she couldn't safely leave Outlaw Ranch to go shopping by herself, she resorted to the internet, which wasn't her favorite way to work since colors couldn't be relied upon to be accurate from pictures. But she did her best.

She placed a large order for furniture and guessed at the colors. If they were awful, she could always have Charlotte Adams re-cover the upholstered pieces. In the meantime, she needed to start clearing the space. She chose the guest bedroom, which was sparsely furnished with only a single bed and a chest of drawers, as her base of operations. She emptied drawers and cabinets in the kitchen into plastic bins she found stacked in the mudroom.

And then she moved on to Wes's bedroom, stacking his clothing, which was as neatly folded as she would have expected of a career Marine, in the drawers in the guest room. It was strangely intimate handling his personal possessions. The scent of his aftershave rose faintly from the folded shirts, and she resisted an urge to bury her nose in them. After all, it wasn't like she was in love with the guy—

The thought stopped her cold. How *did* she feel about him, anyway? Goodness knows, she was attracted to him. And fascinated by him. She hadn't been able to get him out of her mind ever since she'd briefly dated him. And when she'd been in fear for her life, her thoughts had turned to him first. That had to say something about how she felt, didn't it?

If he had stayed in the military, she would have known what to expect of a long-term relationship with him. But this life of his in Montana, on a ranch no less, was completely foreign to her. Would she go stir-crazy in a place like this? Or would the lure of making a life with a man like Wes be enough to make her want to settle down and put down roots?

Her father's career had moved the two of them to a brand-new place every few years. If Wes had stayed in the Corps, his career would have been the same way. She'd never even considered the notion of staying in one place for long before. But then, she'd never considered the notion of having an actual family, either. Had Wes becoming a rancher changed the equation?

She finished putting all the things she planned to keep through the renovation in the guest bedroom just in time for the first workers who arrived. She wasted no time putting them to work demolishing the kitchen, bathrooms and ripping out fixtures. The more stuff that could be gone before Wes returned to the house, the less he could complain about her plans for renovating his home.

The construction crew was efficient and had mostly gutted the kitchen before Wes stopped in the doorway, staring around in shock. "Jessica!" he shouted over the din.

She poked her head out of his bedroom where she was directing the removal of the ceiling. "Oh, hey," she replied casually.

"What in the *hell* are you doing?" he demanded.

"You said I could redo you house. I'm redoing it."

"I thought you were going to redecorate it, not destroy it!"

"I'm not destroying it. I'm restoring it. That's different." She smiled winningly at him, but he didn't seem to be buying it if that scowl thundering on his brow was any indication.

"I can't afford all of this—" he started.

She cut him off breezily. "I'm extremely good at my job. I won't cost you any more than you can afford. Trust me."

His gaze narrowed into a full-on glare at that. "We need to talk about this—"

"Later. I need to keep an eye on the crew and make sure they do exactly what I want. Otherwise, you may end up having to pay for replacing more than you need to." It was a lie because she planned to foot the whole bill for this project, but she really didn't want to have an all-out fight with him in front of the crew she'd hired.

He whirled and retreated from the combat zone that

the house had become, which was just as well. She really did have a lot to do today.

By midafternoon, demolition was mostly done, and the crew had transferred most of the debris to a dumpster that had been delivered.

She rode over to the cabin at Runaway Ranch with the construction crew's foreman to check on the latest work there and was delighted to see that the floor was installed, the new kitchen cabinets hung and the light fixtures in place. The rough-honed granite counters needed to be installed, a little touch-up painting finished and the furniture delivered, and the cabin would be done.

The foreman dropped her off back at Wes's house in the late afternoon, and she called a thank-you to him and headed for Wes's front door. The porch floor had been stripped away, with only a three-foot-wide walkway of wood planks left intact. She picked her way carefully to the front door.

She looked up and realized Wes was looming in the doorway. And he looked furious. She stepped inside as the last workmen packed up for the day and left, promising to be back first thing in the morning.

The door closed and silence fell in the gutted house.

"Just out of curiosity," Wes asked with ominous calm, "how long is this renovation going to take?"

She shrugged. "Four to six weeks if we don't hit any snags and the wiring and plumbing turn out to be sound."

"How am I supposed to live in the middle of this? Do I even have a working toilet?"

"I left a toilet and sink in your bathroom, and the shower in the guest bath still works."

"How am I supposed to eat?" he asked.

She shrugged. "We can eat out."

"You do realize it's a solid half-hour drive to Sunny Creek, right? Each way."

"The microwave oven is in the guest bedroom, and I'll get us a hot plate." She added cheerfully, "Oh, and the coffeepot still works. It'll be fun. Like camping."

The look on his face announced that he saw no possibility of camping in his own house to be fun.

She rolled her eyes. "If you're not up for an adventure, you can always go stay in the hunting cabin at your parents' place. The furniture's being delivered there tomorrow and it will be finished."

"What part of 'I don't want anything to do with my parents' don't you get?"

"You called your dad when you needed help with Number 19 and Daisy."

"That's different. An animal was suffering and needed help."

"No, it isn't different," she disagreed. "You need help and your parents have the means to offer it to you. Why won't you let them assist you in any way?"

"Because I want to do this on my own."

"Then quit whining about not having a kitchen and help me with the renovation instead of fighting me on it."

"I never wanted all of this."

Oh, *now* he chose to complain? He gave her permission to do the job and then, when the reality of it was staring him in the face, he wanted to back out? Wow. That was a whole lot like their entire relationship, now that she stopped to think of it. She, for one, was sick of his whole on-again off-again games.

She wagged an accusing finger at him. "You know what, Wes? You're a hypocrite. You climb up on your high horse when it's convenient for you, but heaven forbid that you should take a little help from your parents or admit that you have feelings for me when it's not to your advantage to do so."

"What does my having feelings for you have to do with my not being able to stay in my own home because you've wrecked it?"

She ignored his attempt to turn the topic and warmed to her own point. "You're all happy to sleep with me when you feel like doing it, but then you push me away when I'm interested in being with you. You want me to admit I have feelings for you, but I don't see you admitting that you have feelings for me, even though we both know you do."

"I…what?" He sounded blank, as if he didn't know what she was talking about.

Men. They were all a bunch of unconscious, un-self-aware jerks at times. Wes was acting just like her father. She rolled her eyes.

"Oh, puh-lease, Wes. Nobody has the kind of chemistry in bed that we do without real feelings for each other being involved."

"That's not true—" he started.

She cut him off, well and truly irritated now. "You know what? You seriously need to get over yourself. You're so busy hanging on to your grudge against me that you can't see how you really feel about me, even though it's staring you straight in the face."

"I know how I feel about you. I—"

She cut him off again, finishing his sentence for him. "You hate me. Despise me. You'll never forgive me," she snapped. "But you're all kinds of willing to jump in the sack with me. How do you reconcile *that* with your big words about not being able to stand the sight of me, Mr. Mega-Morals?"

It was probably a low blow to attack his morals, but it was high time someone hit him over the head with a big, fat dose of reality.

Yes, he'd been wronged. But she wasn't entirely at fault in being drugged, either. A tiny bit of wrong had been done to her, too. She hadn't asked to be threatened and blackmailed nor to be put in the impossible situation of trying to protect a man she cared about deeply by having to hurt him. And she surely didn't deserve his hate for choosing to save his life.

She glared at him, hoping that at least a tiny bit of what she was thinking showed in her eyes. He deserved a swift kick in the shins, and she was apparently the person the universe had chosen to deliver it.

Lord knew, those bullets flying at her on an isolated mountain road—when she'd thought she was safe—had been a kick in the shins to her.

Wes interrupted her internal rant, which she privately thought was a pretty good one as rants went. "Look, Jessica. I get that you're enjoying playing house with me. But we both know this won't last for you. You'll get bored and restless, and then your wild streak will rear its ugly head and you'll do something unpredictable."

Her wild streak was ugly? "Gee, I thought you rather liked my wild streak," she retorted. "Particularly in bed. I dare you to tell me you don't."

He opened his mouth. Closed it again.

Uh-huh. That was what she thought. She pressed her point, continuing, "Without my wild streak, you'd be just another boring stick-in-the-mud. I keep you stirred up. Feeling alive. Admit it."

"Being around you is…interesting. I'll grant you that."

Ha. Just interesting? She was a three-ring circus of fun! And he loved it, whether he admitted it or not.

"You disappoint me, Wes. I thought you were more honest than this. But now I see you're lying to yourself in addition to lying to me."

She scored a hit with that salvo. He whirled away from her and stomped across the bare living room to stare out the big windows at the back of the room, opening onto a magnificent Rocky Mountain tableau.

He looked as solid and immovable as the mountains beyond him. And, face it, his strength was one of the reasons she loved him a little. She never had been the kind of person to hold a grudge. And as she stared at his broad shoulders, narrow waist and long legs, her irritation at him waned, replaced by aching longing.

She said more reasonably to his back, "I don't have to stay here. I'll be perfectly safe at Runaway, and if I'm there, you and I won't have to keep tearing each other apart."

She still had little more than the clothes on her back by way of possessions, and it was an easy matter to fetch the keys for her repaired car and her purse from the guest room and head for the front door.

Wes moved fast, meeting her at the door, his big hand closing around hers as she gripped the door latch. "Stay," he said roughly.

She looked up at him candidly. "I'm sorry. You can't have it both ways, Wes. You can't hate me and want me with you."

His frown deepened even more. She felt a frisson of sympathy for him, but this wasn't her problem. He had to work it out for himself.

She continued gently, "I know how I feel. But until you figure out how you feel, I can't be with you. I'll see the renovation through, of course. And then I'll honor your wishes and leave for good."

Wes stared at the closed front door that Jessica had just left through. A combination of high indignation and impotent fury tore through him. His head might acknowledge the validity of her arguments, but his heart howled in frustration that she'd walked away from him and left him here, alone. Again.

What was up with that? He shouldn't care if she left. Hell, he should be relieved that she was gone. He'd survived a near miss with getting tangled up in her insane life once more. He'd barely escaped the last time; no way would he have made it clear of her twice. The odds just didn't stack up that way.

He turned and stared at the war zone she'd made of his house. Somehow, it was an apt analogy for what she did to his head and heart.

Gah! He stomped out to the calving barn and was relieved to see the signs that another cow would give birth tonight. Something, anything, to keep his mind off the most exasperating female he'd ever had the misfortune of knowing.

When he finally made his way back to the house in the wee hours of the morning as mama and new calf, a nice-looking bull, rested comfortably, he prayed that Jessica had at least left him a bed to sleep in. He was startled to realize she'd torn the entire ceiling out of his bedroom. The wood beams that held up the roof were visible now, and the space felt huge and cavernous. Wow. What a change. The last thing he wanted to do was acknowledge that she was good at her job, but she really was a talented designer.

And there was no place in his life for her.

Jessica felt bad shacking up with Wes's parents again, but it wasn't like she had anyplace else to go. Miranda had thrown her an understanding look that communicated her sympathy at loving a Morgan man, and then insisted she stay in the newly renovated cabin. Sure, she could return to the B and B in Sunny Creek, but after having been shot at she would hate to draw trouble to Annabelle Cooper's doorstep, and the B and B wasn't exactly an armed fortress.

As it was, she couldn't avoid going into Sunny Creek and doing a little shopping for herself soon. She needed more clothes and toiletries and an actual computer. If she was going to do design work, she couldn't keep doing it on her phone.

Hank Mathers, who turned out to be a fascinating man of deep thoughts and few words, acted as her driver and bodyguard. He was a full-blooded Lakota Sioux Indian, and his people had lived on the land that was now Runaway Ranch for as long as there was oral history of it in his family, apparently.

She finished her impromptu shopping trip in Sunny Creek with a visit to Pittypat's for another piece of lemon meringue pie while Hank ducked into the hardware store across the street for something he needed. The pie tasted just as amazing as it had the first time.

Patricia came out of the office when Jessica was

about halfway through her dessert and sat down in the booth with her. "So, you're still in town, are you? Did you get your business with Wes Morgan taken care of?"

Jessica smiled politely. "For the most part. But then his mother hired me to redecorate a hunting cabin, and here I am. Still in Sunny Creek."

"Well, we're glad to have you. A pretty girl like you will have every young man in town sniffing after her before long."

That sounded purely awful. Besides, there was only one man whom she cared about doing any…sniffing.

In a blatant attempt to change the subject, Jessica asked, "I need to order some custom kitchen cabinets. Do you know anywhere around here I can get something like that?"

"Most folks drive into Butte to shop for major purchases."

"And how do I get to Butte from here?"

She listened carefully to the woman's directions and supplemented them by pulling up a portable GPS system on her phone. Hank was up for a road trip, and they reached Butte around two in the afternoon. It wasn't that big a city, and she found a kitchen design and supply store without too much trouble.

Hank took off, leaving her the truck's keys and his cell phone number, promising to be ready to go whenever she was done with her decorating stuff.

She spent a couple of hours finalizing the design for Wes's kitchen, ordering everything she would need and paying extra for rush delivery. Across the street from the kitchen design store, she spotted a gaming store and internet café and jogged over to it.

She had been avoiding her email account on the assumption that someone might be able to track her location if she opened her mail. But now that a shooter clearly knew where she was, she wasn't so worried about electronic security. And it had been weeks since she'd checked her email. Which, in her life, was tantamount to having been in solitary confinement for a year.

A bunch of her girlfriends had sent her worried and increasingly frantic messages. She replied to all of them, apologizing for worrying everyone and explaining that she had decided at the last minute to go on a personal retreat to get her head together. She scrolled through a bunch of junk and then a recent post caught her eye. It had been sent last night.

She opened it and started to read.

You may have slipped away from me on that mountain road. But I'll get you next time. I know where to find you.

Of course, it wasn't signed. And it was clearly a reference to the shooting outside of Sunny Creek. With the exception of Wes, his family, the sheriff and his men, no one else knew about the attack. Which meant this was almost certainly from the shooter himself.

She eyed the exit of the little store warily. Even the hundred feet of asphalt between her and the truck now loomed threateningly.

Who kept coming after her like this? It made no sense. She pulled out her cell phone and called the police officer who had taken her statement after the incident in the club.

"Officer Demoyne," a brisk voice said at the other end of the line.

"Hi, this is Jessica Blankenship from the roofie case you worked on a few months back in Washington, DC."

"Miss Blankenship, of course I remember you. What can I do for you?"

"I've received a couple of threats recently. I just got a threatening email, in fact. I was wondering if there's any way they're connected to my case."

"It's possible. If you'll forward me the email, I'll have our cybersecurity guys track down the IP address. Maybe we can ID who's harassing you."

"That would be great."

"In the meantime, do you need personal protection?"

She debated before answering. "I don't think so. I'm not anywhere near Washington, DC, and the local sheriff seems competent. Also, I'm staying with people who seem well able to defend themselves. Can I call you if that changes?"

"Of course. I'll be in touch."

She sat back, staring at her phone. Would this nightmare never end? It was just one mistake. One drink from a stranger. One bad decision to go out alone without being with friends. A handful of words in a military court of law. How could so little be screwing up her life so much?

And it wasn't all about her anymore, either. Wes was still paying for her mistakes.

Chapter 12

Jessica glanced at the time and realized with a start that she needed to get back to Runaway Ranch to tell the furniture delivery guys where to put the pieces she'd ordered for the hunting cabin. She texted Hank, who showed up in a matter of minutes, as promised. They hurried outside, climbed in the truck and headed back to Runaway Ranch.

Partway there, her cell phone rang. "Hey, Miss Blankenship. It's Sheriff Westlake."

"Call me Jessica, please."

"Only if you'll call me Joe."

"That's a deal, Joe. What can I do for you today?"

"It's what I can do for you. We got a preliminary report back on the slugs we dug out of your car. They came from a rifle called an M21."

"I'm familiar with it. The military used to use them

for short-range sniping. They were replaced a while back by the M24 and more exotic weapons."

Joe laughed. "Color me impressed. A girl who knows her guns!"

"My father is a Marine and didn't have a son. He taught me more than I ever cared to know about military-grade weapons. And for what it's worth, I hate guns in all forms."

"Too bad. At any rate, we sent the slug off to the FBI to run through their weapon identification database. It's a long shot that the bullets came from a registered weapon, but we'll check anyway."

"Thanks. I appreciate the update."

"You're sure you don't want my guys to keep an eye on you until we figure out who took those shots at you?"

"I'm fine. I'm sure it was just a random nutjob out messing around. After all, not a single shot hit me. And given the number of rounds fired, even pure luck would suggest that at least one bullet should have hit me."

"You're a lot calmer about this than I expected," Joe commented.

She smiled. "I'm nothing if not my father's daughter."

"Still. Don't hesitate to call me if you get scared or even get a funny feeling that something's not right."

"I will."

"Promise?" he demanded.

She laughed. "Cross my heart and hope to die. Or in this case, I hope not to die."

She rode back to the ranch in a reflective frame of mind. M21s had been common during Vietnam and then retired as military weapons. There had to be mass quantities of them available in military surplus stores pretty much everywhere. So, the fact that a military weapon had been used didn't necessarily mean some-one from the military had shot at her. The good news was her father had more or less kept her away from his career—he'd hated the idea of horny young Marines sniffing around her skirts. She doubted someone she'd met in conjunction with her father's work was behind the shooting in McMinn Pass.

Which left them no closer to knowing who had it in for her.

She spent the next few hours putting the finishing touches on the hunting cabin. As the sun set outside in glorious streaks of orange and purple behind the black silhouettes of the mountains, she stepped out onto the porch, well satisfied with her work. The porch swing was comfortably cushioned, and she sat down on it while she waited for Miranda to drive up and give the cabin her final approval.

Crickets were starting to sing, and some sort of frog was making a high-pitched chirping sound that she'd always associated with early spring. The air smelled of melting snow and wet dirt and the first hints of green, growing things. The colors of nature faded around her into the soft gray of twilight, and she found herself breathing more deeply and slowly, inhaling the night as it fell gently around her.

A ranch truck came up the road, its headlights cutting through the encroaching darkness. Miranda stepped out of the vehicle and immediately began to smile. "You didn't tell me you were redoing the porch, too."

"I just spruced it up a little. I refinished the floor, cleaned and stained the railing and posts, added some flowerpots and hung this swing."

Miranda surprised her by not being in a rush to go

inside. Instead, the older woman sat down on the swing beside her. "Sometimes I forget how pretty it is up here."

Jessica nodded. "And loud."

"Those are spring peepers drowning out the crickets. They signal that the snows are over for the year. Ranchers love to hear them, especially when calving season is getting going."

"It's really all about living with the land out here, isn't it?" Jessica asked.

"Indeed it is," Miranda replied. "It gets into your bones. People born and raised in these mountains, who make their livings off the land, can't ever really shake it. It stays with you, no matter how far you try to run from it. I tried to tell my children that, but they're all having to learn it for themselves."

"Wes seems to be settling in at his ranch. I think maybe he's figured out that he's part of all of this," Jessica commented.

Miranda smiled. "I'm glad to hear it. I just worry about him spending too much time alone on that wreck of a ranch. Getting started in the ranching business is damned hard work. My grandparents built this cabin and started Runaway Ranch in this very valley. They raised four children in this house."

Jessica looked over her shoulder at the tiny cabin in surprise. "That had to be a tight fit."

"Folks spent all their time outside. They only slept indoors or stayed in when the weather was terrible. But, even then, I suppose there's a reason they only had four kids. It had to have cramped their style to sleep in a two-room cabin with the children listening in on everything."

They traded knowing grins.

"I was born in this cabin," Miranda commented. "But my mother insisted on a bigger house before she had any more children. Hank and Willa Mathers live in the house I grew up in."

Jessica knew the structure. It wasn't unlike Wes's house—a long, single-story log cabin with a huge, inviting porch.

Miranda continued, "My boys were born in that house. We started building what's the main house now right before I had the twins. You haven't met them, but you'd like them. They're strong young women. Like you."

Jessica shrugged. "I don't feel all that strong. I had a bad scare a few months back, and I still jump at my own shadow."

"Joe told John and me about the attack on you up on the Westlake Road. Any idea who did it?"

Jessica's eyebrows lifted. "He told you?"

"Sweetie, this is a small town. Everyone tells everyone else everything. You won't have any secrets around Sunny Creek for long."

Huh. Was that one of the reasons Wes had left in the first place? He never had been fond of other people interfering in his business.

"You'll get used to it," Miranda said as she stood up.

"I'm not planning on staying for the long term—" Jessica started.

Miranda cut her off. "I've seen how you look at these mountains and how you look at my son. You'll be staying."

Jessica stared. The last thing she would ever consider doing would be settling down in some tiny town in the middle of nowhere. Sure, she had feelings for Wes, but did they run *that* deep?

"Show me what you've done to the cabin," Miranda declared.

Still in minor shock, Jessica opened the front door and let Miranda enter first. The older woman stopped just inside the door and took a long look around, long enough to register every detail. Jessica was confident in her own ability, but tonight she was nervous about how this opinionated and demanding client would respond.

Finally Miranda breathed, "Oh, my. It's perfect. Absolutely perfect."

Jessica let out a big sigh of relief. "I'm so glad you like it."

Miranda nodded slowly. "Wes is a lucky man. I can see the passion you bring to your work."

Too bad Wes didn't see it that way.

"Is there any chance you could redo my office to look like this? I love how it retains the rustic feel, but it's light and modern, too."

"Of course, I can do it."

"I think you have a great future in the field of interior design, my dear."

People back in Washington, DC, used to say that to her, too, but there she'd done mostly chic, elaborate, pretentious designs. It was fun stretching her wings here and trying something different. It had been a risk, but if she'd crashed and burned at rustic-lodge-chic design, she still had more money than she could ever use—even if she chose to live like a spoiled jet-set baby.

Privately, it chafed her a little that Wes never touched his trust fund and chose to earn a living completely on his own. She had considered giving that a try over the years but had never had the courage to go through with it. Or maybe she'd never believed in herself enough to give it a try.

She could probably open up a bank account in Sunny Creek. Start depositing the checks she earned from these design jobs. Maybe see if they eventually produced enough cash to live on. It could be an interesting experiment. And, if nothing else, it would give her a goal.

An hour later, as she walked through the main house with Miranda, the talk of redecorating Miranda's office was quickly expanding into a complete redo of the interior of the main house. Jessica thought the overall design was fantastic, but it could be updated and refreshed here and there—new fabrics for upholstered furniture, new window treatments that were less dark and heavy. A change of accent colors. Nothing too dramatic. Unlike Wes's house.

As the evening aged, she finally begged off, saying, "I have to be at Wes's house bright and early in the morning. My construction crew is starting to refinish his ceilings and beams, and I've got an electrician and a plumber stopping by to make a few repairs."

"You got him to agree to work on that shack he's been living in?" Miranda exclaimed. "How did you manage that?"

Jessica cracked a smile. "Long story."

"That's amazing. He seemed determined to punish himself for something. I was worried he would let that place fall down around his head before he would do any work on it. He seemed to relish how awful it was."

That sounded like Wes. Self-flagellation always had been a strong suit of his.

Miranda continued, "I'm so glad he's let you into his life."

"Well, I'm not sure I'd go that far," Jessica disagreed.

"I know my children. He's got feelings for you whether he wants to admit it or not."

"He's a wee bit miffed that I gutted his house. But a restoration to its original architecture required it. That wasn't what he expected when he told me I could re-decorate his place, though."

Miranda smiled broadly. "Good for you. Wes is the most like his father of all my boys. Stubborn and will-ful to a fault. John and Wes both need someone to take then down a peg from time to time. And you're woman enough to do it for Wes."

Warmth spread through Jessica's belly. Was this what it felt like to have a mother to talk with and who would back her up when life got messy? Everyone else seemed afraid of Miranda, but she rather loved the woman, as formidable as she was.

"Stay in the hunting cabin as long as you'd like to, Jessica. No one else is using it, and it's all gussied up, now. You can work on the main house, and you're a short drive over to Wes's place to manage that job." She added archly, "And you know what they say about ab-sence making the heart grow fonder. It'll be good for Wes to have to work to get you."

Jessica blinked, staring at Miranda. Apparently, the woman had decided that she and Wes were supposed to end up together. She wished she shared the woman's confidence.

"You know, dear, I think you'll be comfortable up at the hunting cabin. There's more privacy up there in case my hard-headed son wants to come around and make a proper apology to you." The twinkle in Miranda's eyes made it clear exactly what form she thought that apology should take.

Wes apologize? Not very likely. But still. The idea of a little time to herself, to think about her future and figure out a way forward in spite of having a stalker tailing her, was very appealing.

Plus, she would be ensconced deep inside Runaway Ranch, far from prying eyes and flying bullets. No way would anyone find her way out here. "If it wouldn't inconvenience you, I might just take you up on that offer," Jessica declared.

"Perfect." Miranda added, "I'm having the family over for dinner on Sunday. You have to join us."

"I don't want to intrude on family—"

"You're coming. I won't hear any arguments over it."

Ah. There was the iron-willed matriarch everyone talked about. Jessica smiled, rather fond of being bullied by this woman. "In that case, I guess I'll be there on Sunday."

Wes was notably absent the next two days as Jessica supervised and pitched in to help the construction crew work on his house. The job was going fast because it turned out the place had fairly new plumbing and wiring, and the crew wasn't moving any walls. The new roof looked out of place above the disastrous siding, but the new wood siding wouldn't arrive until next week.

The interior ceiling and its massive beams gleamed a warm golden color now, and the sanded and refinished plank floors had been stained to match. Slate flooring had been laid in the bathrooms and kitchen, and shower tile was curing before it could be grouted.

She spent Saturday turning a series of carved poles

she'd found in a closet into curtain rods. Wes had created them and they were probably walking sticks, but they were far too beautiful to take outside and ruin, thank you very much. She hung the new curtains using cast iron rings and stood back to admire the effect.

Her laptop dinged an incoming email, and she went over to check it. Officer Demoyne had sent her something. Stomach tight, she opened the email.

It turns out the threatening email to you was sent from a proxy server in Billings, Montana. It's my best guess that whoever sent you that threatening email has nothing to do with the guy who roofied you. I confirmed today that he's still here in the DC metro area.

Billings, Montana? Jessica's blood ran cold. Whoever was threatening her was close. So, as she'd suspected, those gunshots on the road *hadn't* been random. Someone had deliberately tried to kill her. All hope, however far-fetched, that it had been a prank or a mistake of some kind evaporated.

She sat down heavily on the lone kitchen chair she'd left for Wes.

The back door opened and she looked up bleakly. Wes stepped into the remains of his kitchen and stopped abruptly, looking chagrined. "I thought you left already," he mumbled.

"I'll leave now," she replied glumly.

"What's wrong?"

She lifted her gaze to him. "I beg your pardon?"

"You look like you've just seen a ghost. What's wrong?"

"I just got a message from the police. A threatening

email I got was sent from Billings, Montana. It couldn't have come from the guy who drugged me at the party in Washington."

"What threatening email?" he exclaimed.

"The one I got a few days ago."

"What did it say?"

"Nothing much. Just, I'm coming for you soon. I know where you are, and you'll die. The usual stuff you'd expect in a threatening note."

"Why didn't you tell me?" Wes demanded.

"Because it's not your problem." She shrugged. "The police officer I talked with doesn't believe the guy from the club is stalking me. Which means whoever's after me probably doesn't have anything to do with you. You're in the clear."

"If it wasn't that guy, then who shot at you?" Wes demanded.

She shrugged, feeling defeated. Helpless, even. "I have no idea. Apparently, I have enemies I'm not even aware of."

He took a quick step forward as if to hug her, but then checked himself, stopping in the middle of the space. Of course he stopped. He hated her guts.

She picked up her purse, tucked her new laptop under her arm and headed for the door. She paused long enough to say tiredly, "The crew has the day off tomorrow, so you won't have to hide from me. We'll be back Monday midmorning. The flooring guys will be refinishing these beautiful, hand-scraped pine floors. Your cabinets should be done being refinished next week. The cabinet guy still had to build a couple of new cabinets because of the reconfiguration of the kitchen, too. He's hoping to finish those this weekend. But after that, the granite counters can go in. There's been a delay on your kitchen appliances, but I'll try to have a more or less functional kitchen for you by the end of next week."

It was just so darned exhausting trying to keep up a good front all the time, especially for Wes, who could read her so easily and well.

She climbed into the Jeep she'd leased for the next several months while a Corvette specialist in Bozeman did more work on repairing and restoring her car. She barely made it out the front gate of the Outlaw Ranch before she had to pull over at the side of the road and rest her forehead on the steering wheel, blinded by tears that filled her eyes but refused to fall.

Her entire life she'd been petted and adored, first by her father and then by her friends, teachers and, well, pretty much everybody. And now, the one person whose opinion she cared about judged and despised her. How could her life go so far off track so fast? She wasn't a bad person, at least not intentionally.

Even walking into the calm comfort of the hunting cabin a little while later failed to make her feel better. She ate something from the freezer and microwave without registering any taste at all, and then she flopped on the couch, facing yet another lonely Saturday night with only her regrets for company.

She dealt with her misery by going to bed at barely eight o'clock and escaping into sleep. It was the coward's way out, but she'd had a really rotten week.

Wes stared up at the gorgeous new vaulted ceiling in his bedroom as sleep eluded him. Moonlight filtered in past the sheers Jessica had hung behind the new curtains, which were made of a pale tan burlap. The silvery moonlight played with shadows cast by the heavy wood beams crisscrossing overhead. The room felt twice as large now and had a stately quality to it that he reluctantly admitted was great. She knew his taste, and he couldn't complain about the new, raised stone hearth for his fireplace nor about the thick Navajo rugs on the hardwood floors or the overstuffed armchair and ottoman beside the window.

The new double-paned windows with handmade wooden frames didn't rattle in the wind at night anymore, which was a blessing, too. They'd driven him a little crazy over the long winter just past.

Yup, his bedroom had been transformed into a gracious but masculine space where he could unwind and relax after a hard day's work. And every inch of it reminded him of Jessica, no matter where his gaze landed in the space. She had touched or transformed every square inch of it.

What was he going to do about her, anyway? She had all but accused him of being in love with her in one breath, and then had called him a hypocrite in the next. Was it even possible to be both? More to the point, was she right?

His heart had about jumped out of his chest when he'd come into the house and spotted her this afternoon. He wanted to tell her how much he liked the things she was doing to the house, but the words of praise had refused to come out of his mouth. Was he really that petty?

He fell asleep thinking about what she felt like in his arms and woke up the next morning imagining making love to her. He groaned and tried to get back to sleep, but to no avail. Irritated as hell at himself and at her, he got up, fed the cows and stomped out to his workshop to do a little carving.

His finger was healing enough for him to start using his whittling tools again, and he needed to take out his anger on a good piece of wood, forcing it into the shape in his mind.

His cell phone rang at noon, startling him out of the concentration he often lost himself in when he was creating a piece of carving. It was the ranch phone number. If it was Jessica bugging him one more time about some detail having to do with his house, he was going to scream.

"What?" he snapped into the phone.

"Since when do you take that tone with me, young man?" his mother snapped back. "You're late. Have you forgotten about dinner at the main house today?"

"Crap. I didn't realize what time it was."

"Everyone's here. I'll hold the meal until you get here," his mother replied sternly.

Which was Mirandaspeak for he had better get his butt over to her house ASAP. He tossed down his tools and headed out. He loved his mother, but he would always be a little intimidated by her. She was a fierce woman as strong as the mountains she'd grown up in.

He barged into the kitchen of the big house about five minutes later and pulled up short at the sight of Jessica and his brother, Chase, laughing at something Chase's fiancée, Anna, was saying. "What's *she* doing here?" Wes demanded.

Chase looked up, his gaze narrowed in warning. "She's my future wife."

"Not Anna. Jessica."

Chase smirked. "The way I hear it, she's *your* future wife."

Wes rounded on Jessica to rip her a new one, but she'd gone pale and looked fully as horrified as he felt at Chase's gibe.

He turned back to his older brother and snarled, "Am I going to have to take you out back and kick your ass, or are you going to keep a civil tongue in your head and not embarrass Mother's guest?" For there was no question at all who had invited Jessica to a family dinner. Miranda was famous for interfering in every Morgan's personal business.

Chase's smirk widened into a grin. "A mite touchy, are we, little brother?"

Wes told Chase where he could go and how he could get there, in the most succinct and impolite of terms.

Mild-mannered Anna started to laugh and then announced, "Wow. You really do have it bad for her, don't you, Wes?"

He glared, but knew better than to say anything rude to her. Chase hadn't been a Special Forces soldier for nothing, and the guy was lethal in a fight. Wes didn't relish pissing off Chase enough to actually provoke a fistfight or even just a wrestling match.

He glanced over at Jessica and was gratified to see her face flushed scarlet with embarrassment. Good. At least he wasn't the only one bothered by the jokes about the two of them.

John Morgan strode toward him and Wes braced himself. The two of them might have declared a silent truce over Number 19 and her calf, but there was no animal in distress to buffer them now. "Glad you came," John said gruffly.

Whoa. Miranda must have hog-tied him and threatened him within an inch of his life to get the Old Man to be that civil to his errant son. Their last fight, when he'd gotten home, disgraced and ejected from the Marines, had been epic.

Wes nodded back stiffly.

John turned to Jessica, and Wes was shocked to see his father's gruff expression fade into a fond smile. "I haven't had a chance to tell you how much I like what you did to the cabin, young lady. Next time Miranda kicks me out to cool my heels in the barn, I'm heading up there to lick my wounds."

She replied, "Well then, I guess I'd better lay in a supply of good scotch up there."

Jessica smiled warmly at his father, and she was so dazzlingly beautiful that Wes actually staggered a little. She'd been so somber and unhappy around him recently that he'd forgotten just how magnificent she was when she expressed joy. She lit up a room, even a big one like his parents' great room.

Anna looped her arm in Jessica's and led her away. Wes strained to hear what they were talking about and was surprised to hear that Miranda had hired Jess to freshen up the entire main house. Jessica was describing what she was planning to Anna, who listened raptly.

Wes realized with a jolt that he was listening raptly, too. And he didn't give a flying flip about color palettes and accent pillows. He spun away, scowling.

"What's up, Wes?" Chase asked quietly, holding out a beer to him.

"Mom hates it when we drink on Sunday."

"It's after noon. She'll get over it."

Wes took the beer and tossed back a long slug.

"You got problems with your girl?" Chase asked.

"She's not my girl."

"But you want her to be," Chase commented. "Don't deny it. You can't take your eyes off her, and she practically glows when she looks at you."

Wes huffed. "It's complicated."

"Always is with the good ones."

He shot his brother a candid look and was surprised to see sympathy in Chase's eyes. His older brother clapped him on the back. "You might as well give in, now. It's no use fighting them when you love 'em. They always win. Haven't you figured that out after growing up with our mother?"

"Anna's nothing like Mom."

Chase laughed heartily. "And yet, she's got me wrapped round her little finger. I'll do anything for her. *Anything*."

Wes stared. "Really? Like what?"

"She's got me helping plan our wedding. Do you have any idea how many kinds of wedding invitations there are?" Chase rolled his eyes. "I thought it was a piece of cardboard with the date and time on it. Have you ever heard of a save-the-date invitation?" He shook his head in disgust.

"I had no idea you'd fallen so far, bro," Wes replied sympathetically. "Sounds like you've lost your man card for good."

Chase grinned. "Yeah. But I found Anna."

Wes just shook his head.

They strolled over to the long dining room table, and Wes wasn't the least bit surprised that Miranda had maneuvered the seating arrangement so he was beside Jessica. His mother hadn't put an extra leaf in the table, either, so Wes was sitting elbow to elbow, knee to knee with Jess. He was close enough to smell her gardenia perfume. The scent never failed to remind him of old money, beach estates and fast cars.

An image flashed through his head of Jessica in dark sunglasses with a silk scarf wrapped around her head, wearing white leather gloves, driving her vintage Corvette with the top down. She had looked like a movie star from the 1950s. It had been the day they'd taken a road trip to the coast. The sun had been shining, the salt smell of the sea mingling with her perfume. They'd had a picnic and too much wine and ended up making love on the beach. Yeah, that had been a damned near perfect day.

Jessica did know how to live each moment to the fullest, that was for sure.

"Earth to Wes, come in," she murmured beside him.

He looked up, startled out of the memory, which was secretly one of his all-time favorites.

"Your mother just asked you if you like what I'm doing to your place."

He glanced down to the foot of the table. "Jessica's doing a fantastic job on my place." He added wryly, "I'm just worried she won't stop with the house."

"What do you mean?" Jessica interjected.

"I'm afraid I'm going to walk out to the barn one morning and find the damn thing wallpapered and curtained and accessorized."

Everyone laughed, but he caught the brief look of hurt that passed through her eyes. Beneath the talk and clatter of dishes passing around, he murmured, "I didn't mean anything by that. I was just joking. We kid each other a lot in this family."

She nodded, but he frowned, not convinced she'd forgiven him. He forgot sometimes that she'd grown up with just her father for family. Poor kid.

Why did he give a damn if he'd hurt her feelings, anyway? If she couldn't take being teased a little, she surely wouldn't last long in his family—

Whoa. Time-out. He didn't *want* her to last long in his family!

Cripes, the woman tied him in knots.

Scowling, he ate in silence, letting the banter and discussion of Chase and Anna's upcoming wedding flow around him without touching him.

He should have known Miranda would try to throw him and Jess together. He should have turned down today's dinner invitation, except it was lonely in his nuked house after Jessica left.

He'd been okay before she'd come, but now the place echoed hollowly. He occasionally caught a whiff of gardenia or found a paper with a scribbled sketch on it in her handwriting. Even her sketches were talented, conveying artistically what she wanted workmen to do, be it installing a hearth or hanging the new wrought iron chandelier where the kitchen table was going to go.

Each reminder of her caused him actual physical pain. His gut tightened like someone had reached into his body, grabbed a fistful of his innards and given them a good, hard twist.

"Are you okay?" Jessica whispered, startling him.

"Yeah."

"You looked like you were in pain."

"I was."

"Are you sick?" she asked in quick concern. "Or is your finger hurting?"

He glanced down at the bandage on his finger. "It's fine. Doc says I can take the tape off tomorrow."

"That's wonderful! Can you go back to carving?"

He threw her a sheepish, sidelong look. "Already did."

"Wes—"

He cut her off, muttering urgently, "Don't tell Doc Cooper. And, for God's sake, don't tell my mother."

Jessica smiled fondly down the table. "Miranda's great, isn't she?"

He blinked, taken aback. "Are we talking about Miranda Morgan? You didn't have to grow up with her. She's a terror."

"I didn't have a mother at all. You should be grateful for her, even if she can be a bit of a mama bear. She loves all of you guys immensely."

"True. But she's an inveterate meddler. Take you being here today and conveniently seated beside me."

"She means well."

He harrumphed.

Miranda looked over at him, an eyebrow raised, and he smiled lamely at her. No need to cause a scene when he and his father were just starting to bury the hatchet after their last falling-out. The fastest way to piss off John Morgan besides dissing the United States Marine Corps was to upset his wife.

The meal ended, and Chase invited Anna out to the horse barn to see the new foal that had been born a few days ago. Miranda bred champion quarter horses and had some beautiful specimens in her barn.

Wes looked over at Jessica reluctantly. If she thought calves were cute, wait till she got a load of a foal. "You wanna go, too?"

"Will you come with us?" she asked hopefully.

He sighed. "Yeah, sure. The alternative is to get drafted to do the dishes with Mother and suffer through an interrogation from her."

Jessica chuckled. "I'm glad to know that I rate higher than slave labor and hostile interrogations."

"Just barely," he allowed drily.

They followed Chase and Anna, who walked ahead, their arms twined around each other. It was hard to look at. The pair were a vivid reminder of what he lacked in his life. Since when was he all hot and bothered about finding a woman and settling down, anyway?

The answer, which came to him unwillingly, made his jaw tighten. *Since Jessica Blankenship had shown up at his front door and started playing house with him.*

What in the *hell* was he going to do with her?

Chapter 13

Wes fled Monday morning as a dozen contractors and workers and Jessica descended upon his house. He couldn't believe how fast she was getting the job done. Then again, he supposed no man could refuse her when she batted her gorgeous eyes and smiled that winning smile of hers at him.

On the one hand, he was eager to get his damned house back to himself. On the other hand, Jessica's promise to leave for good when it was done loomed ominously in the back of his mind. He wanted her to leave, right?

Aw, hell. Who was he trying to kid? He didn't want her to go.

He was riding fence again today, making sure his herd hadn't broken through the fence to get to greener grass on the other side. He'd seeded his pastures last fall and should get better, thicker forage for his cattle this year, but the new seed wasn't coming up as fast as his father's older, more established pastures, which continued to tempt his cattle.

He was paying attention to his horse's footing and stewing over Jessica's imminent departure when he heard a faint bang and something zinged past him. A sharp crack of sound made his horse shy. He managed to keep his seat, but barely, as his horse jigged, agitated, beneath him.

"Easy, Mac," he soothed the horse. Usually Mac was as steady as a rock, and nothing fazed him. Except for snakes, of course. Mac was terrified of them and ran like a little girl from them. All thirteen hundred pounds of him.

Wes looked around cautiously. He was near the top of the valley his ranch shared with a portion of the Runaway Ranch property. The trees were thin, and the pastures were giving way to fields of boulders and patches of late snow.

Thunderclouds were roiling over the mountain peaks in the west, and he'd assumed that loud bang was thunder. What if it wasn't?

Jessica's shooting incident fresh on his mind, he turned Mac back down toward the barn and gave the horse his head. Mac was as good a trail horse as he'd ever had, and the animal could be trusted to choose his own footing and not twist an ankle on a loose rock or unseen gully.

They'd gone perhaps a hundred yards when another bang sounded and bark flew off a pine tree a few yards ahead of him.

Sonofabitch. Someone was shooting at him!

Leaning low over his horse's neck, he clucked to Mac and squeezed his legs against the horse's ribs. Picking up on Wes's stress, the horse jumped forward, stretching out in a gallop. Even then, Wes left the horse to pick his own path. Mac had been born and raised in this valley and would know the terrain better than any human ever could.

Fat drops of rain began to pelt his back, and Wes pulled his cowboy hat lower on his brow. They charged down the mountain, and the barns and house came into view. He didn't ease back on Mac's reins until they'd almost reached the barn, and even then he trotted directly into its sheltering cover.

He slid from the winded gelding, quickly stripped off the saddle and bridle and threw a wool cooling blanket over the animal's heaving sides. "Good job, Mac."

He patted the horse's neck and commenced walking the horse up and down the long aisle between the decrepit stalls. He'd fixed up a big double stall for Mac when he'd bought the horse. It was bedded with fresh sawdust and weatherproofed against wind and wet. When Mac was dry and breathing normally after his hard run back to the barn, Wes put him away.

He checked the horse's water, tossed him a heaping helping of grain and threw in a couple flakes of good alfalfa hay. God knew, the horse had earned it. Mac's speed and familiarity with the mountain had likely saved Wes's life.

He pulled out his cell phone and dialed his cousin, Joe.

"What's up, cuz?" the sheriff answered.

"You know how someone took potshots at Jessica last week? Someone just did the same to me on my own damned property. Two shots were fired at me before my horse got me the hell out of there. I was up in the high pasture. Unfortunately, it's gonna take horses or helicopters to get up there and have a look around."

"Is it raining up there? It's pouring down here in town."

"Yup. Cats and dogs up here."

"Damn. The rain will erase evidence that could have been helpful. But maybe we can still retrieve a slug to compare to the ones used to shoot at Miss Blankenship."

"I only have one horse. If you want to go up there tomorrow, you'll need to bring your own ride."

Joe laughed. "Cheapskate."

"Naw, man. Just a cash-poor rancher trying to get started in the business. All my money went to cattle."

"I'll bring one of the sheriff-patrol horses first thing in the morning, and we'll ride up there."

Wes ran back to the house, not only because it was raining harder now, but also because he hated the sensation of being outside and exposed to a potential sniper. Lord, it was like being back overseas at a forward operating base with enemy combatants on the lookout for any chance to take out an American soldier.

He ducked into the house, which wasn't much less of a combat zone than the high pasture had been. Men were working all over the place, doing last-minute trim work, installing stuff in the kitchen and who knew what all else.

He needed a little peace and quiet, and retreated to his bedroom, closing out all the noise with a sigh of relief. He turned and drew up short as something—someone—moved in the corner.

Jessica stepped out of the shadows beyond his bed.

"Oh! I wasn't expecting you back yet. I'm sorry. I was putting your clothes back into the new dresser for you. I think I got most of them back in the right place."

He shrugged impatiently. "I'm sure it'll be fine. Listen, Jessica. I need you to do me a favor."

"Anything. Name it."

"I need you not to go outside today for any reason. Promise me."

"Okay, but why?"

"Someone just shot at me up at the top end of my property. It could just be a poacher I stumbled across. Or," he added reluctantly, "it could be the same person who shot at you."

"Ohmigod! Are you all right?" she cried, rushing over to him. Her hands roamed frantically up his arms and across his shoulders, fluttering in panic down his ribs and around his sides.

He captured her hands and held them against his chest. "I'm fine. But with the rain, the sheriff and I won't be able to get back up there until tomorrow morning."

"Should we leave?" she asked urgently.

"I'm not about to get chased off my own land. Not to mention I'm a Marine. I can handle myself when someone threatens me."

"But I don't want anything bad to happen to you—"

He released one of her hands and pressed his fingertips against her lips. "Nothing bad will happen to me or to you. I promise."

He became aware of how soft and plump her lips were against his fingers, how warm and kissable. Her eyes were wide with fright and worry for him, and something warm surged through his gut at the sight.

His fingers drifted down to her chin, lifting her face slightly, to the perfect angle for kissing. His other arm went around her and he drew her close. She came to him without any hint of resistance, and when his lips replaced his fingertips, lightly touching her mouth, she sighed like this was a homecoming she'd been waiting for for a very long time.

In an instant, the kiss transformed from sweet and grateful to smoking hot and carnal. Before he hardly knew what was happening, her hands fumbled at his belt buckle, his zipper made a metallic slithering noise and her fingers wrapped around his rock-hard shaft. He was always rock hard around her, it seemed.

He grabbed at handfuls of her puffy retro skirt, dragging them up around her waist. He felt bare bottom and grinned against her mouth. She might be wearing a demure fifties-throwback dress with a little lace collar, but she was wearing a naughty, barely there thong beneath it. He shoved the scrap of fabric aside and plunged a finger into her wet desire. It was too much. He had to have her.

He hoisted her by the hips, and her legs wrapped around him eagerly. He backed her up against the new wood planks covering his wall and lowered her onto his straining erection.

He buried his face against her neck, groaning his pleasure into her satin-smooth skin. Jessica threw her head back, riding him with abandon. She was lithe and athletic and slender and curvy all at once.

Relieved as hell to be alive, he surged up into her with abandon to match hers. How was it that he could never get enough of her? Every time he was inside her like this, he only craved her more. Every time he felt her pulse racing frantically beneath her skin, his raced harder. Every time he tasted her mouth, he grew starved to taste her more deeply.

He found release in her body, joy in her muffled cries against his neck now, security in how tightly she clung to him and freedom in how she made his spirit soar. Sex with her was more than just physical pleasure. It was life.

He had never been a woo-woo kind of guy, but ever since she'd come to Montana, sex with Jessica had been…more. It wasn't just sex anymore. It had become something life affirming, spiritual, even. Which was ridiculous, of course. But undeniably true.

Blessedly, the wanderings of his mind were taken over by the physical sensations of Jessica's tight, hot body cupping his sex, by the glory of plunging so deep into her that he could feel her womb, the instinctive clenching of his glutes as he drove into her, the fantastic feel of trapping her between him and the wall at her back, losing himself in the pleasure clawing at the back of his eyeballs and closing his throat and constricting his heart.

His entire body braced as the coming explosion built and built. And built some more. Holding his breath, he plunged into her harder and faster, racing toward a finish that he sensed would be epic. Jessica's fingernails clawed at his back and she surged against him as mindlessly as he was pumping into her.

And when the dam was on the verge of bursting in a spectacular fashion, he whispered, "Look at me."

Jessica's sex-glazed eyes opened, and he dived into their azure depths, reveling in the helpless love he saw there. Her beautiful, kiss-reddened mouth curved into a smile of pure bliss, and her internal muscles gripped him so strongly he thought he might cry.

Staring through the naked windows of their joined souls, their joined bodies sought the explosion together, straining against one another frantically.

All at once, his entire universe froze. Clenched. Drew one last, apocalyptic breath and then exploded. This was a supernova—a flash of light blinding all the way across the universe, followed by a crash of pleasure so intense that no matter, no planet, no sun could survive its utter and perfect devastation.

Thank God his knees were locked, or he would have fallen to the ground under the weight of the ecstasy ripping through him, destroying him.

Vaguely he realized he was leaning heavily against Jessica, smashing her against the rough wall at her back. He tried to push away from her and let her breathe, but her arms tightened around his neck and one of her legs slid from around his hips to touch the floor.

"Don't move," she mumbled.

"Not sure I can," he mumbled back.

Eventually, her lips moved against his neck, kissing lazily. Her hot, wet tongue touched his skin and roused him slightly from his stupor.

"You've killed me." He managed to sigh.

"What a way to go."

He smiled against her temple, too spent for a response. More time passed, and he murmured, "I give up."

"Give up what?"

"Fighting against you."

"Were we fighting?" she asked, sounding more alert.

He lifted his head to look down at her. God, she was

beautiful. Her features were delicate, elfin even. Her bones were exquisite, her cheekbones sleek and elegant, her jaw just square enough to have character yet not so much as to be masculine. And her eyes—the life brimming in them was impossible to look away from.

He pushed a strand of hair off her damp forehead from where it had stuck to her porcelain skin. It delighted him to see her mussed up by sex, her skin flushed with color he'd put in her cheeks, her eyes sparkling with pleasure he'd put in them. Normally, she was so polished, so put together. But this side of Jessica, breathless and messy, was his absolute favorite version of her.

"I wasn't fighting with you," he explained. "I was fighting against myself. Against my desire for you. I'm done fighting this, whatever this is that we have between us."

Her eyes lit with excitement. "You mean we get to do that again…a lot?"

He laughed under his breath. "God help me, but yes. You and I may end up burning each other to the ground and completely wrecking each other's lives, but so be it. You're an addiction I can't shake."

"Just call me nicotine and heroin."

He eased her other leg off his hip and took a step back from her, righting his clothes. "That's what I'm afraid of. Both of those kill the foolish and unwary."

"Is that what we are?" she asked softly. "Foolish and unwary?"

"How would you describe us?"

She tilted her head, considering him more seriously than he'd expected. "Star-crossed, maybe. Inevitable, definitely." She paused and then added, "And who says being foolish and unwary is a bad thing, anyway?"

He dropped a kiss on the end of her elegant, perfect nose. "I do. But damned if I can stop being either."

Jessica snuggled deeper under the new down-filled duvet she'd put on Wes's bed. This was a lightweight one, appropriate for the warmer nights of spring and summer, and its gentle warmth was weightless and wonderful.

Or maybe that was Wes's body heat wrapping around her so perfectly—effortless and natural beside her.

Why on earth had it taken them so long to find this simpatico again? They never should have broken up the first time, her father's wishes be damned. She was just grateful that Wes had finally stopped fighting his feelings for her and given in to them. If only it hadn't taken someone shooting at each of them to bring them to this point.

She was worried about this shooter of his. She didn't believe for a minute that it was a simple poacher that Wes had stumbled across. Her instinct told her in no uncertain terms that it was the same person who'd tried to kill her on the Westlake Road.

Her contentment destroyed, she lay awake, staring at the new ceiling, idly counting the planks lining the roofline between the heavy, gorgeous ceiling beams.

How long she lay there, she didn't know. An hour maybe.

She heard a strange sound faintly—like a woman screaming a long ways away. Must be a coyote howling or something.

She heard the noise again, and it was louder this

time. That didn't sound like any canine howl she'd ever heard before.

"Wes," she whispered.

He was awake instantly, his consciousness tangible in the darkness.

"What's that sound?" she asked him. "You'll hear it in a minute. It's like a woman screaming."

He sat up, the duvet and flannel sheets pooling around his waist. She reached up to touch the shadowed planes and valleys of his muscular back. She never got tired of looking at him.

The sound came again, and Wes swore. He leaped out of bed, yanking on jeans and his cowboy boots and forgoing even a shirt before he raced out of the bedroom at a dead run.

Alarmed, she followed suit, pulling on her own jeans, a T-shirt and her new cowboy boots. She stepped out into the living room and stopped, staring at a strange flickering light coming in the new picture windows. What was that—

And then it dawned on her. The flickering light was yellow and orange and red.

Fire.

Stone-cold terror roared through her.

The animals.

Wes.

Oh, God. Not Wes. She tore outside and flew across the front yard toward the old horse barn. The north end of it was engulfed in flames, spiraling up into the night, throwing sparks easily a hundred feet in the air as the old, dry, seasoned wood went up like an enormous pile of tinder.

She saw Wes's shirtless form race inside the south

end of the barn, from which heavy smoke was pouring like a river of death, and her heart stopped beating. No kidding, stopped.

She sprinted toward him, flying over the wet grass with speed born of sheer terror at the idea of losing the man she loved.

No way was he going in there alone.

The cloud of smoke began to swirl around her, blinding her eyes with agonizing pain and making her cough so hard she couldn't draw a breath. She slowed. She'd lost her bearings when the smoke had blinded her. Panicked, she stumbled back to figure out where she was before charging forward again.

As she squinted into the smoke, she thought she saw tongues of flame licking at something overhead in front of her.

And then a black apparition raced toward her, fast, bearing down on her as if to run her over and consume her. The fire itself had come to life and was coming for her to kill her—

The giant shape took form, and she realized with a start that it was Wes, leading a squealing and lunging horse beside him. The beast was blindfolded with a white towel, but every time an ember fell on his hide, the horse kicked and screamed.

"Get the hose!" Wes shouted hoarsely at her, coughing violently on the last word. His face was black and sweat had drawn hellish streaks through the soot coating his face and chest.

She ran over toward the big loafing shed he kept the entire herd of cattle in when it was wet or windy and turned on the faucet to the garden hose he used to water the cattle. Surely one lousy hose wouldn't begin to fight the conflagration now engulfing the entire barn!

"Hose us down!" he shouted over the rising roar of the fire.

Who knew a fire could be that loud? She could barely hear him over it.

And then the wisdom of his order hit her. He was making sure neither he nor the horse had any live embers on them that would further burn them. She sprayed him and the horse with the water until both of them were drenched and shivering.

"Water the roof of the loafing barn!" he shouted as he led the trembling horse toward the calving barn.

She pointed the spray at the roof of the next closest barn to the fire, frantically wetting the wood to protect it from flying sparks and embers. She spotted a tiny fire licking at a spot on the roof and sprayed it immediately.

Her back was roasting with the heat, so painfully hot it felt as if her skin was starting to peel off her body. She spared a second to hit herself with the hose, and steam rose from her shirt. She went back to work trying to save the barn.

Wes came over to her and took over the hose.

She ran to the calving barn and turned the water faucet there on, and she sprayed the far side of the loafing barn, as well.

The fire itself rose up a good fifty feet in the air, and a tornado-like vortex of fire whirled up demonically. The heat was unbelievable. She heard cattle bellowing and stomping behind her in the calving barn, terrified. She prayed the calves weren't being trampled, but there was no help for it. They had to save the barn and prevent the spread of the fire. If the loafing barn went up, it could very well light up the calving barn, too, and then they would start losing cattle.

She couldn't even bring herself to consider the horrifying possibility of Wes's prized cows being burned alive.

Three sets of headlights tore across the pasture, and a dozen men spilled out of pickup trucks, John and Miranda Morgan leading the charge. "We saw the fire!" John shouted. "What can we do?"

For a gray-haired guy of at least sixty years, the man could *move*. He ran up to his son, embracing him fiercely for a second, and then took the hose from Wes's hands and passed it to one of his men.

Several of John's ranch hands opened the calving barn and let the terrified cattle streak out into a pasture, well away from the fire, while other ranch hands commenced spraying the wall of the loafing barn that faced the fire with foam from big metal canisters. She assumed it was some kind of fire retardant.

After that was done, a couple of intrepid guys in heavy canvas duster coats climbed a ladder onto the roof of the loafing barn and walked around on it with fire extinguishers.

The hands took turns going up on the roof, spelling each other from the intense heat every five minutes or so.

Miranda served cold water and hot coffee to the men, and Jessica helped her, running back and forth from the house with fresh jugs of water for the men to drink. Grateful to have a job, she ran off and returned over and over, staggering under the weight of a big orange cooler she filled with ice water. She and Miranda passed out cups and the men guzzled water continuously.

Somewhere in the nightmare, Joe Westlake and several of his deputies showed up, and they too pitched in to keep the fire from spreading to the other barns.

The horse barn was a total loss. But as the fire finally began to burn itself out, it became clear that they'd saved all the other barns. No animals or humans had been seriously hurt. There were minor burns here and there where embers had landed on exposed flesh, and the cattle were agitated and restless, refusing to settle down or even to come back into the calving barn to eat.

The men monitored the loafing barn carefully for hours after the main fire had died down to make sure there were no flare-ups. With daybreak came exhaustion, and Jessica sagged over the water jug, her eyes gritty, the taste of smoke thick and acrid on her tongue, her arms so weak she could barely lift them.

Miranda had left sometime before, and she returned now with Willa and the cook, Ella, in tow, with a veritable truckload of food prepared for the men. Everyone grabbed sandwiches and ate in exhausted silence for the most part.

The men finally started to congregate on the front porch of the house. They were filthy, blackened and streaked with sweat and water and grime. They loaded up in trucks and started to head out, back to Runaway Ranch.

John looped an arm around Wes's shoulders and the two men walked toward her, one the carbon copy of the other. They were much more alike than they were different, at the end of the day, and they shared a common love of their land, their homes and their animals.

Wes disengaged himself from his father's arms as they approached, and he walked into her arms wordlessly. She hugged him as hard as she could, doing her best to share whatever strength she had left with him.

John said from behind Wes, "The good news is the cattle are fine. Everything else can be rebuilt as long as the herd is safe."

"Thank goodness you're safe," she murmured to Wes. "I died when I saw you run into the fire."

"I had to save Mac. He saved my life today. He didn't deserve to die like that."

John rumbled, "What do you mean, he saved your life today? What happened?"

Wes turned wearily to head for the house with her tucked under his arm. "You'd better come inside, Dad. We need to talk."

The minute John heard about the attempt on Wes's life, which had been followed immediately by one of his barns going up in flames, John ordered a half dozen of his remaining men to go back to Runaway, get shotguns and ammunition and come back to Outlaw Ranch.

Grim faced, his men complied with alacrity.

Except when the trucks came back a half hour later, Miranda Morgan climbed out of the first one. And, God love her, she was carrying a deadly looking rifle.

Jessica hugged her tightly. "You're a lifesaver. What would we do without you?"

"I expect you'd all perish, eventually," Miranda replied tartly. But beneath the woman's crusty tone, Jessica sensed terror and profound relief that her son was alive and unharmed.

An SUV turned into the drive, and Jessica recognized Joe Westlake's official sheriff vehicle. He must have gone home, cleaned up and come right back out here, this time in an official capacity. He went straight to the burned-out hull of the barn and began poking around and taking pictures.

"At this rate, all of Sunny Creek will be here soon," Jessica commented.

Joe said without looking up, "Welcome to a small town. We rally around each other in times of trouble."

Wes remarked quietly, "I don't think this was trouble. I think it was arson."

Jessica stared at him in dismay. "The shooter?"

He shrugged. "Maybe. That whole damned end of the barn went up all at once. The whole thing was engulfed in a matter of minutes. If you hadn't heard Mac screaming when you did, he would have died."

"Speaking of your horse," Miranda said, "let me trailer him over to my barn. We'll have Doc Hamilton take a look at him. Make sure he doesn't get sick from inhaling all that smoke."

"He's got some bad burns where embers landed on him," Wes replied.

Miranda smiled. "I'll treat him like one of my own babies."

"Oh, Lord. He'll come back so spoiled he'll be unridable," Wes groaned.

Miranda just smiled serenely. She went outside to talk to one of the ranch hands and send him back for a horse trailer.

Jessica turned to Wes. "If Mac was burned, does that mean you were, too? Take off that sweatshirt and let me check you out."

She didn't know where he'd gotten the garment from, and she watched in alarm as Wes winced, pulling it over his head cautiously.

"Uh-huh. As I thought. You've got some burns yourself, mister. Any chance I can get you to go to a hospital and get these properly treated?" she asked.

"Nah. I'm fine."

"Knowing you, you'd throw a piece of duct tape over them and call it a bandage, and then you'd press on with your life," she accused.

"I would probably use electrical tape, but yeah," he replied sheepishly.

"Sit down," she ordered. "And don't move till I get back." Jessica fetched the first aid kit and opened it on the kitchen table. She cleaned his burns as gently as she could, but he hissed with pain as antiseptic hit the raw wounds. She smeared them liberally with antibiotic cream, covered them with squares of rayon and then covered them with gauze and medical adhesive tape.

When she was finished, she realized her legs were about to give out from under her and she sank into one of the brand-new kitchen chairs. "You took ten years off my life when you ran into that barn, Wes. Please never scare me like that again. I don't ever need you to be a hero again."

He shrugged. "I did what I had to do."

"What will you do next?"

"I'll rebuild the barn, I suppose. This time with a metal roof and siding. The good news is I can lay it out more efficiently than the last barn."

"What about the shooter? What's to stop him from coming back and torching another barn, this time with livestock in it?"

"My dad is lending me some of his hands to guard the place until we can figure out who's been shooting at the two of us."

She sagged with relief. Thank goodness his pride

wasn't so inflexible that he wouldn't take help from his family. It was one thing to be stubborn and independent. It was another thing entirely to be suicidally pigheaded.

"I want you to leave," Wes announced.

"No!"

"You're not safe here. I'm not willing to take chances with your life, Jessica."

"And I'm not willing to take chances with yours!" she exclaimed. "I'm not leaving your side."

"It's not open to debate. I already talked with my father about it, and he agrees with me. You should go stay at Runaway where there are a bunch of people who can protect you."

"Wes, you're all the protection I need. I trust you with my life."

"I'm not doing a hell of a good job keeping you safe so far," he muttered.

"I would be a nervous wreck without you," she declared.

"And I'll be a nervous wreck if you stay."

"We're in this together. Let me stand by you and fight with you. I can shoot a gun and handle myself under stress." His expression remained stubborn. "Please," she begged. "You and I let circumstances separate us once before, and look how much harm was done and how long it has taken for us to get back together."

He didn't budge.

"You need me, Wes. You draw strength and comfort from me, and I do the same from you."

"She's got a point," a new voice said from behind her. Miranda had come inside and stopped just behind Jessica.

"She's not safe out here—" Wes started.

"No one's *safe* living on a ranch in wild country like this. This is a hard life and requires strong women."

"She's a city girl. She knows nothing about this life!"

"Don't sell Jessica short, son. I've seen her backbone. She's got what it takes to stand beside you and make a go of this place. Goodness knows, she's plenty smart enough to learn how to live and work on a ranch. What would it hurt to let her try?"

"For starters, there's the whole business of her, oh, I don't know, *dying.*"

"She's not dead yet, and she's been shot at and survived a fire. Not to mention she managed to talk you into remodeling this ramshackle excuse of a house. Which looks lovely, by the way, dear."

"Thanks, Miranda," Jessica replied, pleased.

Wes scowled back and forth between the two women. Perhaps he sensed defeat at hand when both his mother and Jessica ganged up on him. "Fine," he huffed. "But she's not setting one foot outside this house without an armed bodyguard. Not until this bastard is caught."

The front door opened again. This time it was Joe Westlake. "Wes? Can I talk to you outside? There's something I need to show you."

Jessica watched the two men's tall figures move toward the blackened skeleton of the burned barn. Certainty that Joe had found proof of arson coursed through her. For all her brave talk to the contrary, she was not so naive that she wasn't terrified at the prospect of staying here with Wes.

However, someone was out to harm or kill them. And until that person was caught, neither she nor Wes would be safe anywhere.

Chapter 14

Calving season went into full swing, and perhaps the stress of the fire triggered more of his cows than usual to give birth, but for the next week, Wes was up around the clock babysitting his cows through their first deliveries. Most of them went fine, and a few required visits from Dr. Hamilton to expedite. But so far, Wes had yet to lose a single cow or calf.

It was about damned time a bit of luck went his way.

An official arson investigator came to the ranch and poked around in the remains of the burned barn for about three minutes before confirming Joe's finding and declaring the fire to have been arson. Not that it was news to him. He'd known the second he'd heard Mac screaming that night that someone had deliberately torched the barn.

He was just grateful that the bastard hadn't gone

after the calving barn, where over half his herd and a half-dozen newborn calves had been housed. Had the arsonist merely been sending a warning by torching the big, mostly deserted barn? Or was it possible the guy had gone after the biggest structure without realizing it wasn't the most important structure on the ranch? If that was the case, it would mean the arsonist was a city slicker and not a local.

Wes and Joe ended up driving a four-wheeler up into the high pasture and hunting around until they found a pair of trees with bullets buried in their trunks. It took them a couple of hours to find the first distinctive hole in a tree trunk. After that they found the second slug quickly. They dug out the slugs and took a close look at them.

Joe commented, "These look a lot like the rounds we dug out of Jessica's car."

"You'll run them through a forensic comparison, though, won't you?"

"Dude. They'll get mailed off to the FBI this very day."

As Joe bagged and tagged the bullets, noting the time and location where they were found, Wes said, "Those aren't very deformed, which means they were moving at a slow rate of speed when they impacted the trees."

"Which means what?" Joe asked.

"They were fired from very near the limit of the weapon's effective range. The slugs were slowing down. Losing velocity. They traveled a long way and bled off a lot of energy before they reached those trees. They were only buried a half inch or so deep in the wood. Had they been fired from close range, they'd have smashed into the trees and buried themselves four or five inches deep, at least."

Joe grinned. "You're good at this stuff. Ever consider a career in law enforcement?"

"Nope. I'm happy to leave the handcuffs and speeding tickets to you, big guy."

"Aw, the handcuffs can be fun to play with…with the right partner. And you ought to hear the crazy things people say and do to get out of a speeding ticket. I live for those excuses."

Wes just shook his head. He'd take a nice, quiet life as a rancher any day. Although, it hadn't been the least bit quiet since Jessica had shown up on his front porch.

Several times over the next week, his father's ranch hands, standing guard at Outlaw Ranch, heard movement in the middle of the night. But when they pursued the source of the intrusion, whatever or whoever it was took off.

Wes continued to argue daily with Jessica to leave Outlaw and, potentially, to leave Montana altogether, until the sheriff and the Morgans caught whoever was attacking them. She refused to budge. She was adamant that any risk he faced was a risk she would face, too. He had to give her credit. She was made of sterner stuff than he would ever have guessed.

Jessica had almost finished the interior of his house, and today the crew had torn the exterior siding off the house, wrapped it in some sort of insulation and was now installing beautiful golden siding—vertical wooden planks that had been stained and coated to maintain their freshly cut color indefinitely.

He barely recognized the house anymore. In a matter

of weeks, it had become a gracious and inviting place full of light and color. Everywhere he looked, he saw something pleasing. Who knew how big a difference it would make to his mental state to live in a space that reflected his tastes and made him happy and relaxed.

Or maybe it was Jessica who'd done all of that for his mental state. He never knew where another reminder of her free spirit would show up around the ranch. She named his calves and thought he should massage the cows that were still expecting, and she'd even installed a stereo in the calving barn that played relaxing music for the expectant mothers. There were always wildflowers in a vase on the kitchen table now, and his bathroom and bedsheets smelled of gardenias. She'd invaded his workshop, building new shelves and installing dozens of drawers and bins that neatly held all of his tools and bits of raw wood. She'd even moved in a ridiculously comfortable chair for him to sit in while he carved. He looked up the brand name online and was stunned to discover it was a thousand-dollar-plus ergonomic chair.

She cooked for him and all the guards from Runaway Ranch, laying out huge spreads of tasty food that rivaled his mother's cooking—which was saying something.

If he didn't know better, he would say she was settling in beautifully to ranch life. Thing was, he knew in the back of his mind that this wouldn't last. She was a flight risk. Someday she would tire of playing rancher's girlfriend, and she would take off. Without warning, she would up and leave, and never look back.

He would be left with reminders of her everywhere he looked. And it would kill him.

Jessica was shocked to discover how much she loved the steady rhythms of ranch life. Each day was tied to the weather and the land and the animals—no two days were the same. And yet, the progression of spring, of calving, of renewal and growth was slow and steady, as inevitable as sunrise and sunset.

The incursions into the ranch stopped, and John's ranch hands went back to Runaway Ranch. Even Wes finally relaxed and quit worrying constantly. Oh, he still kept a loaded shotgun by the bed, within arm's reach, but he slept through the night now. They both did. Running and growing a new ranch was hard work, and there was always more for both of them to do in a day than there was time. But she found deep satisfaction in working beside Wes and helping him make his dream come true.

At long last, she did a final walk-through of the renovated house with the general contractor, clearing the last few items from her checklist of fixes and tweaks before the project was done to her exacting satisfaction.

She had just watched the contractor's truck retreat down the newly paved asphalt driveway when her cell phone rang in the back pocket of her jeans. A moment's amusement that she now more or less lived in jeans struck her as she dug out her phone.

She stared in shock at the caller ID. "Dad? Hi. Is something wrong? Why are you calling me?"

More to the point, had he run a find-my-phone app and figured out where she was? God, why hadn't she thought of that before? If her dad could do it, her stalker could probably do it, too.

Her father was speaking angrily. "...you're the one who up and ran away from home without a single word to anyone." He devolved into a tirade about how she was selfish and ungrateful, and she tuned it out, walking back up the porch steps and sitting down in one of the pair of beautifully carved bench swings Wes had made for her as a surprise to say thank you for redoing the house.

Eventually she tired of her father's ranting and interrupted. "Do you have something specific to say to me, or are you just calling me to vent?"

Her father stopped speaking abruptly. Then he continued, "Since when do you think I'll stand for that kind of insubordination from you?"

"Insubordination comes from a soldier to his superior officer or an employee to his boss. I am neither a soldier nor your employee," she snapped.

"You're my daughter. I raised you and fed you and housed you and clothed you, and you'll by God show me the respect I deserve!" he bellowed.

"Every parent has those responsibilities to their children. You didn't do anything special by providing for my needs. You merely did what was required of you. And, let the record show, I paid for my own clothes and my own housing and needs out of my trust fund for a good chunk of my youth."

And he was off and running on another tirade, shouting this time. She put him on speakerphone, lowered the volume and laid the phone in her lap to wait for him to wind down. A few months ago, she would have hung up on him and given him the silent treatment for a few weeks until she got over her petty tantrum and he cooled off. She'd grown up a lot since then.

She could forgive the man for being lost after his wife died and for never finding himself again. Now that she'd experienced the partnership a man and woman could share, she understood how devastating Rebecca's death must have been to George. God knew, he hadn't signed up to be a single parent of a little girl. That had to have been a terrible shock to a military man like him. Not only had he had to be both mother and father, he'd had to learn how to parent a girly girl, totally unlike his rough-and-ready Marine troops.

Some of his words penetrated her thoughts, and she listened in dismay as he shouted, "You're just like your mother, and, mark my words, you'll come to the same bad end she did!"

The old pain, the empty place in her heart that should have been filled by her mother's love, reared its ugly head. She hated it when George played that card. How could she be anything like her mother? She'd never gotten a chance to even know Rebecca.

While George continued to rage through the phone beside her on the bench, demanding that she come home *immediately*, she reflected that, truth be told, he hadn't really been that much of a father to her over the years. He'd expected her, at age six, to learn how to make her own lunches, do her own laundry, get herself to and from school every day and do her own homework.

Honestly, she'd felt like a trained pet most of the time, marched out to perform for his guests, and then put away and forgotten until it was time for her to perform again. When she'd gotten a little older, he'd expected her to act as his social aide, planning and hosting business dinners and meetings by the dozens.

Of course, as a kid she hadn't known any other life or anything different. And she had learned to be independent. To take care of herself.

But as she reflected back on that little girl, she saw now how lonely she'd been. That she'd been starved for love. That she had become a flamboyant class clown so the other kids and teachers and her friends' moms would like her and fill the gaping void in her heart.

She liked the person she had become for the most part. And, thanks to Wes, she'd discovered that she wasn't as broken and unavailable emotionally as her father liked to accuse her of being. Which was ironic. The man had the emotional depth of a spoon.

She would like to think that all his love had died with Rebecca and that he had never recovered from that tragic loss. But when he was being an ass like right now, she wasn't so sure. Maybe he really was just a cold, hard shell of a human being after all.

"…sick of waiting for you to come crawling back home. I give up. Where the hell are you, anyway?"

She snorted. He must have an important dinner meeting coming up and had finally noticed her absence. She'd been gone over two months, and he was just now bothering to call and ask her where she was?

She just shook her head. How in the world had she ever mistaken his sporadic attention for real love?

She started, jolted out of her own wandering thoughts. "I'm with Wes, Dad. And I'm happy."

"Are you insane? That bastard tried to ruin you! He was prepared to drag you into court and force you to describe in public the humiliation you suffered, so his own precious career wouldn't be ruined. He was going to destroy you to save his own sorry, worthless hide."

"That's not how it happened, Dad."

"Don't you tell me how it happened! I was there. That sonofabitch was going to drag you down into the mud with him."

What kind of drugs was her father smoking? She'd

called Wes and dragged him into the middle of her mess. The only reason she hadn't suffered serious harm and humiliation—life-destroying, horrible emotional damage—was because Wes had come charging to her rescue the instant she'd called him. The fact that she'd escaped the bastard who'd drugged her pretty much unscathed was wholly due to Wes.

"You've got it all wrong, Dad—"

He yelled right over her, ranting about how Wes had ruined her life and, furthermore, ruined *his* life.

"Hell, for all I know, that disloyal, selfish bastard set you up just to get back at me!" George shouted. "My career tanked because of him! My personal aide forced to resign or face court-martial—it was a fatal stain on my flawless record!"

Really? Her father was going to make this all about him? She had escaped rape by the skin of her teeth, and somehow the whole nightmare was all a giant plot to ruin his precious career? Wow. Her father really had gone off the rails.

On a hunch, she asked, "So. Have you retired yet, Dad?"

"Bastards put me out to a pasture like some broken-down old mule. No matter that I have forty years' experience. That I was a general, for crying out loud. That I wanted to keep working. Oh, no. They had to make room for new goddamned blood."

Or maybe they were getting rid of the crazy old man who'd fallen *way* off his rocker. She'd known for a while that her father was becoming increasingly unstable, but she had no idea he'd gotten this bad.

"Have you thought about talking to somebody about

your feelings? Someone who can help you deal with them?" she tried.

"Like a shrink?" her father squawked. "You think I'm crazy? You? You're just like your mother, and she was completely unhinged!"

"You just seem really upset. Maybe if you talked to a counselor, they could help you let go of your anger. Show you some ways to help calm your emotions—"

Nope. The rant was back on.

Having been away from him for a few months, maybe that was why his deranged emotions were so striking to her now. Or maybe he'd just completely lost it since she'd left Washington. Either way, she was shocked. Her father had been a formidable man in his day. A hard taskmaster, yes. Tough as nails and leading by intimidation rather than inspiration. But he hadn't been crazy. This man, the one yelling and sputtering incoherently, was a stranger to her.

And then something her father said made her sit up straight and stare at her phone in dismay.

"Wesley Morgan ruined my life. And, mark my words, he's out to ruin yours. You need to leave him. Now."

"I'm not leaving Wes, Dad."

"Then he's going to break you. You're more fragile than you know. When he rips your heart out and stomps on it, you're going to fall apart. And then you'll pull some stupid stunt like your mother did and end up dying."

"That's ridiculous." But a chill rippled down her spine at his dire prediction. Was he right? Would she crumble if Wes left her? It wasn't entirely out of the realm of possibility. She'd laid her heart bare to Wes and had thrown herself into this relationship with everything she had. She'd held nothing back from him this time.

"Leave him, Jessica. I'm ordering you."

"I'm. Not. A. Soldier," she huffed. "You can't order me around. I'm an adult, and I'll make my own choices."

"Leave him. Or else," her father growled angrily.

"Or else what? What will you do to me?" she challenged. "You can't touch me or my trust fund. I don't need you anymore."

"Wanna bet?" he snarled. Lord, she'd never heard her father sound quite this enraged—and she'd seen him get pretty darned furious over the years.

She'd had it with him. He could just get over himself and get over trying to push her around. She declared sharply, "I'm not leaving Wes, no matter what you say." Her voice rising, she added, "Do you hear me? I love him!"

She disconnected the call, jabbing furiously at the off button.

A movement out of the corner of her eye caused her to look up.

Wes.

He was standing on the steps, leaning against one of the new porch posts.

"Who was that?" he asked evenly.

"My father."

"What the hell did he want?"

She was abjectly grateful to Wes for not dwelling on her last, shouted assertion to her father. She shrugged. "He called to demand that I leave here and go back to Washington. Apparently, he thinks my place is there, taking care of him."

Wes snorted. "Last time I checked, he's not in his dotage. He's what? Fifty-eight? Sixty?"

"He'll be sixty next month." Her hands were shaking, and the aftermath of the call was starting to hit her. She felt tears well up in her eyes, although she couldn't tell if they were from sadness or anger. Who did her father think he was, yelling at her like that and trying to order her around like she was a child?

"Aw, Jess. I'm sorry you had to deal with him." Wes opened his arms, and she ran into them, sobbing in earnest as all the pent-up emotions precipitated by her father's hatefulness came flooding out.

Wes didn't know what to say to make it better for Jessica. He knew full well how mean her father could be. The man had a gift for going for the jugular. How she'd turned out loving and kind and warm and generous with George Blankenship for a father, he had no idea.

He kissed Jessica's hair and felt the front of his shirt get wet, and his heart hurt for her. His kisses shifted to her temple, then to her satin cheek, where he tasted the salt of her tears, and on to her jaw. And when Jessica lifted her face to him, he kissed her lips, offering comfort and support in the only way he knew how.

He bent and swept her into his arms, carrying her inside, through the beautiful home she'd made, and into his bedroom. Their bedroom. He laid her down on the bed and stretched out beside her, kissing her tenderly. She turned in to him, pressing hungrily against him, suddenly frantic for him.

He understood the impulse. She wanted a distraction. Needed a distraction. She wanted to feel better, and he was the lucky man she had turned to, looking for love.

Love.

Her shouted declaration to her father rang in his ears as he undressed her gently, kissing a path in the wake of his hands as he pushed her clothing aside. Warmth flowed through him that had nothing to do with the heat of her body. Smiling against her stomach, he kissed a path of destruction up to the valley of her breasts and back down to the core of her womanhood, savoring every inch of her, relishing every cry of pleasure slipping from her throat.

He kissed away the last tears from her cheeks, abjectly grateful that he seemed to have successfully distracted her. He'd never been around women who cried, and he had no idea how to deal with it other than panic and chocolate. And sex. Apparently, this worked, too. Thank goodness.

Jessica's hands speared into his hair, and she laughed a little as she tugged him up her body to kiss him on the mouth. "Are you ever going to cut your hair, or are you planning to be a wild mountain man the rest of your life?"

He grinned and kissed her smile, savoring the sweet berry taste of her. He murmured against her soft lips, "I did it to punish myself. To erase any sign of the Marine I used to be."

Her smile grew. "I'd say you obliterated that guy when you went for the beard."

He moved his chin, rubbing his beard against her neck, and she giggled. "That tickles!"

"Oh, so now you like the wild mountain man?" he teased. He dragged his beard down her throat and across the sensitive peak of her breast.

She laughed and pushed on his shoulders, rolling

him over onto his back. "Am I going to have to pin you down and make love to you until you agree to shave that thing off?"

He grinned up at her. "That sounds like a challenge to me."

Her eyes danced with humor and affection and desire, and he pulled her down to him, kissing her with all the ardor he couldn't find words to express.

Their lovemaking was tender and funny, punctuated by laughter and teasing, and, finally, when words deserted him, he resorted to staring deep into her eyes. He loved how they glazed with pleasure and then went blind with ecstasy, and he was right there with her, losing himself completely in her and in them and in the magic they made between them.

In the aftermath, as she dozed on his chest, Wes reflected that life couldn't get a whole lot more perfect than this.

If only he could be sure of Jessica. She might yell at her father that she was in love, but he knew how fractious their relationship had always been. He'd witnessed plenty of fights between the two of them in George's office when Jessica would storm out in tears after ugly words were exchanged. He got that she would fling her relationship with him in her father's face by way of hurting her father back.

He just wished she really meant it. That she was willing to commit to him. To stay with him forever. Then he might finally be able to let down the last walls in his heart, too.

Of course, Jessica was nothing if not observant. She didn't say anything about it, but surely she felt his reservations about her. That was probably why she was trying so damned hard to prove herself to him. She was possibly the only woman he'd ever met who was as competitive as him. The one way to get her to do something was to tell her she couldn't do it.

The cloud of doubt that followed him around constantly settled upon his shoulders like a lead blanket. Funny, but it felt almost comfortable, so long had he been carrying it around with him. Making love with Jessica might drive it away temporarily, but until she promised him forever, the doubt would always be with him. Of that, he was sure.

He got that she had daddy issues. Hell, he had some of his own. But at some point she had to grow up. Break away from George and live her own life. And until she did that, Wes knew—*knew*—she would keep on running from her demons.

Jessica woke up in the early evening to the delicious smell of steak sizzling on a grill. She smiled lazily. Wes must be playing with the grill feature on the new stove. Memories of how they'd spent the late afternoon made a smile play on her lips as she stretched her arms over her head.

Then her father's disturbing phone call came back, and her smile faded. She was actually worried about his mental stability. He'd been mercurial in the best of times. Had forced retirement finally pushed him over the edge?

Of course, the question was, what edge? How much of a handle on reality had he lost? Or was he merely obsessing over her abrupt departure and blaming it all on Wes?

Frowning, she climbed out of bed, pulled on jeans

and a cute tank top and strolled barefoot into the kitchen. Wes was at the stove, tending to a pair of mouthwatering sirloins. But, more to the point, he was shirtless, his jeans riding low on his narrow hips. The V of his back and the play of muscles across it were enough to make her mouth water.

She stepped close behind him and wrapped her arms around his waist. "Hey, handsome. What can I do to help?"

"Pour yourself a glass of wine and go sit by the fire. I'm cooking supper tonight."

"To what do I owe this treat?"

"You've been cooking for me and my father's men nonstop for the past two weeks. You deserve a break. Go. Sit. Drink. Relax."

Well, then. She could get used to this! She sipped on a crisp Washington State wine she'd found in Butte the last time she'd been there and did her best not to let worry about her father creep into the quiet of the evening.

Wes carried two plates over to the couch, and they ate in front of the fire while a John Wayne movie played on the TV. She was amused to listen to Wes critique the details of ranching, horseback riding, roping and a myriad of other cowboy skills portrayed in the black-and-white film.

Of course, she was known to nitpick set details in historical movies, too, so she wasn't going to cast any stones at Wes over it.

The movie ended, and she helped Wes carry the empty plates back into the kitchen. They finished cleaning up and he turned off the lights, leaving only the dim light of the dying fire lighting the great room.

"About what you said to your father today," he commented.

She turned to look at him questioningly.

"I understand that you were just trying to make a point with him and to get him to back off."

"You mean the part where I told him I love you?" she asked ominously.

"Yeah. That. I just wanted to let you know that nothing has changed between us."

Nothing had changed, huh? She'd yelled at the top of her lungs that she loved him and Wes was totally blowing it off? Seriously?

A slow burn of anger began to simmer in her gut.

Wes continued, "Believe me. Of all people, I get what a gigantic ass he can be. I won't hold you to what you said."

God. What a fool she'd been. She'd thought this afternoon's tenderness in bed had been him reacting to hearing her declare her feelings for him. That he'd been pleased to know she loved him and had been trying to show her how he felt about her. Had she really been that wrong in reading him? Had she been so lost in her own euphoria at realizing how she felt about Wes that she'd totally mistaken his feelings in return?

Embarrassment joined in with the burgeoning anger.

Wes spoke over his shoulder as he piled ashes around the coals and damped the fire for the night. "My parents have been known to drive me crazy, too. I've said things to both of them in the heat of the moment that I regretted later."

He thought she should regret saying she loved him? But what if she didn't?

"It's late," he said, apparently oblivious to her dismay. "We should get some sleep. I have a big day to-morrow. I have to run the entire herd through the cattle chutes and vaccinate them. If you want to come out and kiss the calves, feel free to join me."

He looked up as she didn't move from her position next to the kitchen counter. "Are you coming?"

She planted her fists on her hips as her indignation broke loose. "Why is it you refuse to acknowledge that I'm capable of real, deep and lasting feelings?"

"I beg your pardon?"

"Men. Sometimes you're so clueless!"

She warmed to her topic, really irritated now. "Why do you just assume that I don't mean it if I say I love someone? Do you think I'm so shallow that I don't know how I feel? Or that I'm so vapid and unreliable that I would change how I feel in the blink of an eye?"

"Huh?" Wes managed to get in. She barged on without letting him get a word in edgewise.

"What have I ever done to you to convince you that I'm such a terrible human being? Is it me? Or is it my father? Do you believe the horrible things he says about me?"

A look of recognition flashed across Wes's features. Ha! She'd hit the nail on the head! He did believe her father!

"You do know that my father says awful things about me to chase off people who might take me away from him, right? He's a freaking psychopath. I don't even want to think about what he must have said to you to get you to break up with me when we dated the first time around."

"He pointed out that dating you was a conflict of interest to my career," Wes replied. "Which it was."

Her eyes narrowed. "And you were so willing to get rid of me that a mere bump in your career path was enough for you to dump me like a hot potato?"

"It was more than that. You were wild. Unpredictable."

She strode forward to stick a finger in his chest. "Name me one thing—*one thing*—I did that was wild or unpredictable while we were dating!"

He frowned as if trying to remember. Finally he said, "I don't remember. It was a long time ago."

"I'll tell you what I did that was wild and unpredictable. Nothing! I was nothing but decent and caring to you."

"Except for the whole ruining my career part."

"And I'll feel terrible about that until my dying day. I only lied because I believed wholeheartedly that you would be killed if I didn't do it! Even then, even when I hurt you, I did it one hundred percent with the intent to protect you."

"That's sure as hell not what it felt like."

She threw up her hands. "And, of course, the only thing that matters is how you felt. Heaven forbid that you should think for a second about how I felt, terrified and isolated, and scared to death that at any minute you would be murdered. Paco might have only been a dog and old, but he was mine. And I loved him. And someone *killed* him! I was *convinced* the same would happen to you if I didn't lie."

He frowned and took a step backward, away from her. Which was probably a pretty good call. She was ripsnorting mad now.

"I suppose you actually believed all the garbage my father spouted about me. You let my rotten, crazy, self-serving father poison your mind against me, didn't you? Are you really so gullible and weak-minded that you can't make a decision for yourself? Don't you trust the evidence of your own eyes? What the heck have I been doing around here if not working beside you and helping you build a home?"

"I appreciate your help…"

"But?" she demanded. "I want to know how you were going to finish that sentence."

His jaw tightened. "Fine. But I'm waiting for you to leave. You've run away before, and you'll do it again. You wouldn't know how to put down roots and stay in one place if the dirt reached out and bit you."

"You broke up with me! I never stopped caring about you. When I was in trouble, you're the first person I called! When I thought you were in trouble, you're the person I warned. I knew you hated me. I *knew* you would be terrible to me if I showed up on your doorstep, and I still came. Why? Because I've never stopped caring for you, Wes Morgan!"

He looked flabbergasted, but he also looked stubborn. Like he still refused to believe her.

She continued, "I never abandoned you. But you abandoned me. You're so eager and willing to believe the worst of me that you would ruin what we have between us rather than admit you were wrong."

Wes stared at her, saying nothing to refute her accusations, doing nothing to show her she was wrong.

She threw up her hands. "I give up. If you don't believe, we have no future together. If you can't trust my feelings to be real and lasting, I've got no chance with you. We're wasting our time here. I'm done."

Chapter 15

Wes had known she would ultimately leave him. He just hadn't expected it to end so spectacularly, with her making accusations against him that almost, but not quite, hit home. Their fight hadn't been about him. It had been about her, dammit. About her issues with her father. About her blaming her old man for all of her problems. Right?

It took him about forty-eight hours to cool down enough to start going back over her words, flung at him in anger. He could finally hear what she'd been trying to say. Did she have a point, after all?

Had George Blankenship engaged in a subtle and persistent campaign to tear down his daughter's reputation? Why would any father do that to his own flesh and blood? What did the guy have to gain from sabotaging Jessica? It made no sense at all.

Frustrated that she'd walked out on him, just like he'd predicted she would, and that she'd proved his point by doing so, he had no idea how to make things better between them. Until she realized she'd been childish and impulsive to just walk out, they had nothing to discuss.

The wildflowers in their vase on the kitchen table died. He tried to replace them with a new handful of flowers, but they just looked like weeds. And they died, too.

More calves were born, but Jessica wasn't around to coo over them and give them whimsical names. They got ear tags with numbers in them, and he tried to name them, but his heart wasn't in it.

He fed the cattle and cleaned barns; he did chores and made repairs, but he got no joy from it. He sat alone in his beautiful home, and with nobody to share it with, he hated it.

In short, with Jessica's departure, the light went out of his life. Again.

Wes went back to eating random frozen food out of his freezer and lost weight again. The hollows came back to his cheeks, the haunted look returned to his eyes. His beard and hair got longer and stragglier, and he didn't care.

He couldn't even find the energy to carve anymore and spent long hours in his wood shop holding a piece of wood in his hand, staring at nothing and not carving a single shaving off it.

Now and then, he worked up enough energy to ask himself where and when it had all gone so terribly wrong. But he didn't have the energy to find the answers or come to any conclusions.

He'd been in bad shape when he'd come home from

the military, but that was nothing compared to now. The only thing that got him out of bed in the morning was the insistent mooing of the cattle demanding their breakfasts. They were innocents in all of this, and he wouldn't let them suffer. Even if he could barely bear to look at them anymore. Their curly faces and big brown eyes only reminded him of Jessica's delight over how sweet and friendly they were. Their silly names stuck in his head, and he couldn't think of them by their number tags anymore.

He'd lost track of what day of the week it was or what the date was when he spied his mother's car racing across his front pasture one afternoon.

He groaned. Great. Just what he needed. A visit from Hurricane Miranda to further mess up his already wrecked life.

She got out of the car and came up the porch steps, stopping in front of him where he lounged in a porch swing. "You look like crap," she announced.

"Hello to you, too, Mother."

"Have you been drinking?"

He shrugged. "I had a beer a while ago." And he'd had several more beers before that. But she didn't need to know that. God knew, he didn't need a tirade from her on the evils of excessive alcohol consumption.

And yet, she drew a deep breath and launched into the mother of all tirades.

"Wesley James Morgan. I've been trying to give you the space you so loudly demanded from your father when you came home. I've been trying to respect that you're an adult and can live your own life, but enough is enough, young man. What did you do?" she demanded.

He squinted up at her. He really did have a headache,

and her strident tone of voice wasn't helping the throbbing in his skull. "What did I do about what?"

"What did you do to make Jessica leave?"

He threw up his hands. "Not you, too."

Her eyes narrowed to a menacing glare.

"I didn't do a damned thing. Why don't you ask her?"

"I did. She wouldn't say anything other than you knew what you'd done and it wasn't her place to tattle on you."

"Well, praise the Lord and pass the potatoes. She didn't throw me under the bus again."

"I'm going to throw you under a bus if you don't tell me what happened," Miranda threatened.

"It's none of your business."

"Apparently, it is, if my son's going to sit around wallowing in depression and refusing to do a damned thing to help himself."

Ugh. He hated it when his mother got into one of her zealous, fix-the-world moods. She was a human bulldozer when she got like this.

He leaned back with a long-suffering sigh. "All right. Say what you've got to say and get it off your chest. Then you can go home and leave me alone."

"I'm not here to give you a lecture. I want to know what you said to her that could drive her away from you. She loves you."

He snorted. "How the hell would you know what she feels for me?"

"It was written all over her face every time she looked at you."

"Infatuation is a far cry from love."

"You think I don't know the difference?" Miranda

snapped. "This isn't my first time around the block, son of mine."

He rolled his eyes.

"Did she tell you she loved you?" his mother demanded.

"Not that it's any of your business—yes, in fact, she did."

"Did you tell her you loved her back?"

"It's not that simple. She was having a fight with her father on the phone and shouted at him that she loved me by way of getting him to back off."

"So?"

He stared at his mother. "So. She didn't really mean it."

"How do you know what she meant? Did you ask her?"

He shrugged. "She said she meant it. Hell, for all I know she did mean it at the time. But I know Jessica. She's like trying to hold the wind in your hand. She'll slip right through your fingers."

"So, you didn't tell her you love her."

He glared at his mother. "No. I didn't."

Miranda nodded sagely, a knowing look on her face. "No wonder she left you high and dry. You're an idiot. Can't say as I blame her."

"Hey, now! She's the one who left me!"

Miranda glared down at him. "I thought I raised a smarter man than this. There's a huge difference between running away and being driven away. You drove her off."

"Did not." But his denial wasn't as heated as it had been in his own head for the past few weeks.

"Why are you always so fast to see the worst in that

girl? She's had a hard life and precious few people have shown her any love. It's not like she had any example of a loving relationship between her parents to show her what a real relationship looks like."

"Everybody has baggage from their pasts. She's not special in that regard."

Miranda shrugged. "I don't know about that. The fact that she's as warm and loving and caring a soul as she is without ever having had a mama—I think that makes her pretty darned special indeed. Downright extraordinary."

"She. Left. Me."

Miranda pointed an accusing finger at him. "You. Pushed. Her. Away."

He stuck his jaw out belligerently. "Yeah, well, I don't see her running back to me, do I? If she loved me so damned much, she wouldn't have left. The facts speak for themselves."

"Yes, indeed, they do. You're an ass."

And with that grand pronouncement, Miranda turned on her designer heel and stomped down the steps.

"Love you, too, Mom. Glad we had this little talk!" he called after her sarcastically.

Miranda didn't deign to answer but about tore up the asphalt of his driveway, she peeled out so fast.

He glared down into his beer bottle. *Jessica walked out on him.*

Jessica walked around in a fog for the most part. Thankfully, she was very good at her job and experienced enough at it to operate on autopilot. The beautiful Victorian mansion she was restoring next door to Annabelle's B and B was a walk in the park to renovate. She'd bought it on a whim to have something to do to keep her mind off how bad it hurt to have lost Wes. Again.

Not that it worked for a second, of course.

She was numb whenever she wasn't devastated by grief. She'd lost him for good this time. There would be no going back. She'd given him everything she had, even told him outright that she loved him, and it still hadn't been enough for him. She had nothing else left in her arsenal to fire at him.

The old home she'd bought had never been converted to apartments like so many of these large Victorians, which meant the floor plan had not been chopped up and altered from its original layout. With its bones intact, it was only a matter of figuring out how to route air-conditioning ducts, how to modernize the plumbing and wiring and how to fix a big crack in the foundation. Then the fun work of dressing up the grand old gal in authentic Victorian finery could begin.

She ought to be more enthusiastic about researching the home's original color scheme and figuring out how to pay homage to its past as the dwelling of a turn-of-the-twentieth-century copper baron. But her heart just wasn't in it.

The research librarian at the county library eventually found a description of the house in a lady's diary from the period. It detailed the exterior paint colors, and where they'd been applied. That and a few black-and-white photos were enough for Jessica to make an educated guess at how the house had been painted.

She put Charlotte Adams to work trying to find out exactly what paint pigments would have been used locally to achieve moss green, which had been the house's primary color and the white, hunter green and lavender that had been used as accent colors. Poor copper baron. His wife must have insisted on the lavender.

She only hoped it turned out to be a soft shade that would complement the moss green body of the house and not some garish purple tone. If it turned out to have been a loud violet trim paint, she would have to choose between historical authenticity and good taste—a decision she always hated to have to make as a designer.

She would cross that bridge when she came to it. For now, she was lucky to get through an entire day without falling apart. Sometimes she had to live hour to hour, or even minute to minute, to get through the pain of losing Wes.

Now and then she considered leaving Sunny Creek. But it was the first place that had ever felt like a home to her, and everyone in town had been so kind and welcoming to her. Wes notwithstanding.

More importantly, she was done moving around. She'd lived in fifteen different cities in the twenty years since her mother had died. Her father's two-year stint at the Pentagon had been the longest time the two of them had lived in a single city that she could remember. She'd had enough of it. She wanted to put down roots, and Sunny Creek was as good as anywhere else. She did love the mountains. And the clean air. And all the great folks she'd met.

Even if living here did mean she was going to run into Wes from time to time. The good news was he was such a hermit she would never see him. Honestly, she didn't think her pain could get any worse. Seeing him now and then wouldn't make her suffer any more than she already was.

The good news was there were dozens of historic

homes in need of repair and renovation in this town, and there was talk of a new ski resort opening up on the other side of the McMinn Mountain Range. If that happened, the market for newly updated, authentically historic homes, would soar. She could stay gainfully employed in the area for years to come.

Plus, it turned out she could live off her income as a designer. Particularly when she was so depressed she couldn't bring herself to even go out to dinner to eat, let alone go shopping for clothes or makeup or any other little luxuries.

Occasionally she dragged herself over to Pittypat's for a piece of pie, but that was only because the sisters would come and get her if she didn't visit them at least once a week.

Their worry was sweet. They were like a pair of dotty old aunts who fussed and fretted over her a little too much. But they meant well. Everyone did. Annabelle Cooper brought her supper a couple of nights a week. Anna Larkin, Chase Morgan's fiancée, had become a good friend as had Willa Mathers. Jessica found Willa's calm demeanor and Zen approach to life particularly soothing.

In fact, she was supposed to meet both Anna and Willa at Pittypat's in a few minutes for supper.

Forcing herself into motion, she laid aside paint chips and upholstery samples. She stopped in front of a mirror and winced at the sight of herself. Her hair was a mess and she wasn't wearing a lick of makeup. Which meant her skin was pale, her eyes more pale and the violent smudges under eyes so pronounced that she looked ill.

No help for it. A broken heart did that to a girl.

She raced into the diner a few minutes late and was alarmed to see Miranda Morgan sitting at the big booth in the back with Anna, Willa, Charlotte and Annabelle. Uh-oh. This wasn't some sort of intervention, was it?

"Hey, Miranda," she said cautiously.

"Hello there, Jessica. How have you been?"

She shrugged, unwilling to admit that she was miserable and life had sucked since the breakup with Wes. "Does something special bring you to town tonight?"

"I came to commiserate with you over what an ass my son is."

Jessica couldn't help but smile at that. "Which one? You have several sons."

Miranda scowled. "Sometimes I think they're all asses."

Anna and Willa hooted with laughter at that. Anna scooted over in the booth and Jessica slid in beside her. Patricia plopped a piece of lemon meringue pie down in front of her and declared it medicinal and to be consumed before dinner. Jessica dug in with enthusiasm, tasting food for the first time in days.

The women chatted companionably around her, trading stories about the dumbest things men had ever said and done around them. Jessica let the conversation flow over her and around her, a verbal blanket of love. So this was what it was like to have family. It was pretty nice, actually. She loved the perspective of women of multiple generations coming together to share their life experiences.

She felt the loss of her own mother most keenly in moments like this, but for once she also felt that hole being partially filled by the friendship of these women. Maybe, just maybe, she had finally found a home.

* * *

After the disastrous visit from Miranda, Wes settled into a pretty much permanent state of irritation at the entire human race. The whole world seemed against him. A cough went through his herd and kept him up for several long nights babysitting afflicted calves. Also, the vet bill for treating the whole herd had been steep. If it could break around the ranch, it did. Fences went down, doors broke—even his tractor broke down.

Fortunately, he diagnosed the tractor's problem quickly, and the hardware store in Sunny Creek stocked common tractor parts. He jumped in his truck and headed for town. As he pulled into the hardware store, he spied Jessica's Corvette parked across the street at Pittypat's. Great. What else could go wrong today?

Yup, there it was. His mother's German sedan was parked next to Jessica's car. Perfect. He loved it when every woman he knew decided to gang up on him. Miranda really should keep her big fat nose out of his personal business. He marched across Main Street with the intention of telling her that very thing.

He crossed the threshold into the vintage diner and stopped cold, immediately spying the large group of women laughing and talking together in the back of the room.

"Don't do it, man," a male voice said from the coffee counter.

Joe Westlake was the source of the warning, sitting hunched over a cup of coffee. Wes glared at his cousin. "My mother can stop hanging around with my ex any day now."

"It's a losing battle, Wes. I'm telling you. I grew up with four sisters, and I know what I'm talking about.

You don't want to mess with them when they close ranks and band together to hate on a guy. It's not a pretty sight."

"Willa and Anna are back there. They'll side with me."

Joe snorted. "Don't be so sure of that. They look pretty chummy with Jessica."

"She ditched me. I'm the injured party here," Wes declared.

Joe shrugged. "It's your funeral."

Scowling, Wes stomped past the grinning sheriff and headed for the big booth in the back corner. He caught sight of Jessica and his steps faltered. The impact of her beauty upon him was as great as ever. Maybe greater. Her features were so cleanly drawn, so purely lovely, they defied reason. No mere mortal was that perfect. Yet, there she sat. His gut twisted in desire and longing.

Truth be told, he suspected he would always react to her like that. God knew, she was the kind of woman who would be gorgeous at any age. Her bones, her eyes and her sunny spirit would all surely stand the test of time.

Jessica looked up and her gaze lit on him. Shock passed through her eyes, followed by wariness. Hurt. And then sadness. His gut twisted again, but for an entirely different reason. He'd put that unhappiness in her expression if everyone around him was right.

"Ladies," he said tersely.

"Wes!" Miranda exclaimed. "Whatever brings you here?"

"Can I talk with you for a minute, Mother?"

"Of course. What's going on?"

"In private?" he ground out.

She looked around the table at the other women

seated with her. "These women are all family. Anything you have to say to me, you can say in front of them. They'll find out what you said anyway. After all, the gossip network in this town is first-rate."

He felt his back molars grinding together like grist wheels. "Have you been drinking?" he snapped.

"Coffee? Yes. I'm drunk on caffeine."

Since when was his mother such a playful and annoying person? It was almost as if Jessica had rubbed off on her. Which was alarming in the extreme to contemplate. "Mother…"

Miranda's eyebrows sailed up. "Don't you go taking that tone with me, young man. I brought you into this world, and I can surely take you out. I'm here to have dinner with dear Jessica and her friends, so say your piece and go. You're disturbing us."

"It's not appropriate for you to be hanging out with my ex."

"Why not? She's a delight and I enjoy her company immensely. You, on the other hand, have become a gigantic sourpuss." Miranda shrugged. "I chose to keep her after your breakup."

"Oh really?" he spluttered.

"Really. The poor girl had to grow up without a mother, and she could surely use one now to help her navigate the vagaries of men who insist on acting like jackasses."

"Jackasses?"

"Giant ones," Miranda answered firmly.

Wes nodded slowly, anger building to a conflagration in his gut. He looked across the table at Jessica. "I hope you're proud of yourself, breaking up my family now."

She spoke lightly. "From where I'm sitting, it looks like you're doing that all by yourself."

"Wow. Anna, Willa, would you like to dive in here and pile on any more abuse?"

Anna looked a little cowed by the whole spat and retreated into the corner of the booth to do her best approximation of disappearing. Willa, however, planted her elbows on the table and leaned forward to study him intently.

"You don't have any idea why Jessica walked out on you, do you? You think it's her fault. That she up and decided to leave you. Am I right?"

He sensed the minefield he was walking into and cautiously made a noncommittal sound.

"You have no idea that you pushed her away from you, do you? You're so wrapped up in your own little world that you can't see beyond the end of your own nose. I never knew you had such narcissistic tendencies, Wes. I have to say, you don't wear them well."

"I'm not a narcissist!" he exclaimed. Why did he feel as if he was playing right into her hands by flaring up at her name-calling?

"What would you call it then? Selfishness? Immaturity? Plain old head-up-your-ass?"

The other women hooted with laughter, and he felt his face growing red. "What are you doing to me, Willa?" he bit out.

"I'm trying to give you a swift kick in the pants. You need to take a good hard look at yourself, my friend. I could help you if you'd like. I just got my official counseling license."

"Thanks, but no thanks," he retorted. Ugh. The last

thing he wanted was to have his basically little sister poking around inside his noggin.

"The offer stands. Whenever you're ready to figure out where you went wrong with Jessica, you know where to find me."

Ha. He could take care of his own damned relationships, thank you very much. Rather than stick around and take any more abuse from the tableful of women, he spun and stalked toward the exit.

"Told ya so," Joe muttered as Wes got close to him.

"Don't you start with me," Wes snapped.

"Actually, do you have a minute? There's something I'd like to show you at the sheriff's office."

"Unless it's the bottom of a bottle of beer, I'll pass."

"It's official business, actually."

Wes frowned. "Oh. Well, in that case, lead on."

He followed his cousin outside and down Main Street past a half-dozen buildings to the sheriff's office, which was housed in a quaint, old-fashioned building that looked more like a saloon than a police station. But once they passed inside, it was all modern law enforcement with computers, big monitors on the walls and several young, smart-looking deputies sitting at high-tech workstations, wearing headsets.

"What's up?" Wes asked.

Joe said hello to each deputy who looked up at him and led Wes across the open space to a desk inside a glass-walled office. "Have a seat." He indicated a chair in front of his desk, and Wes sank into it as Joe moved around behind the desk to sit.

"I've got some information for you. We got the ballistics report back on the bullets that were fired at you in your upper pasture. They're a match for the rounds we dug out of Jessica's car. The same weapon was used to shoot at both of you."

Wes leaned back hard, shocked. "Who in the hell has it in for both her and me?"

"That's what I was hoping you could tell me," Joe replied.

He shook his head. "I've been over and over the time I spent with her in Washington, all the mutual acquaintances we had. People I knew through her father. I've racked my brain, and I've got nothing, man."

Joe made a sympathetic sound. "Keep trying. If something or someone clicks, give me a shout. I've got Jessica working on it, too."

An urge to ask how she was doing danced on the tip of Wes's tongue, but he bit it back. Besides, he knew the answer for himself. She was partying it up with her girlfriends and restoring a fancy house. Life was going just great for her.

"There's something else," Joe said grimly.

Wes yanked his attention back to his cousin sharply. "What is it?"

Joe opened a drawer, pulled out a folder and pushed it across the desk toward Wes. "I've been in touch with the Washington, DC, police recently. The name Demoyne ring a bell?"

Wes looked up sharply. "He's the guy who arrested me after I beat up the guy who drugged and assaulted Jess."

"Officer Demoyne has been working with Jessica for a while, now. She has been getting threatening emails from an anonymous sender."

"Yeah, and she took long enough to tell me about it," Wes blurted.

"Probably because she hates your guts, man."

Wes scowled at his cousin. "I wasn't that big a jerk to her. She might have walked out on me, but I highly doubt she hates me outright."

Joe shrugged. "I try to stay out of relationship drama as much as possible."

"Good call," Wes replied drily.

"At any rate, Demoyne has been forwarding the emails to me. They're coming from a computer server in Billings, but the user could be signed in from anywhere in Southwestern Montana and be using the server wirelessly."

"Can't you track this person down?"

"Apparently not. I don't fully understand the technology, but the stalker is intentionally disguising his or her location and identity."

"What do you need from me?" Wes asked in concern. Joe didn't use words like *threatening* and *stalker* lightly. He was a cop, for crying out loud, and those words had specific and weighty meanings.

"Here's the thing. We've got no idea who might be sending these. Officer Demoyne has had an FBI profiler take a look at them, but the profiler says they're too generic to give him a handle on the psyche of the author. I was wondering if you'd take a look at the emails. See if they trigger anything for you."

Wes picked up the file and opened it. He thumbed through message after message, reading in growing horror. Why in the hell hadn't Jessica told him about the rest of these? The first messages were dated well before she'd moved out of his house. He could see what the profiler meant. The messages were similar, with several common themes running throughout them. The author wanted Jessica to leave Montana and go back to Washington, DC. And the author told her over and over that if she didn't leave Montana, and soon, both she and Wes would be in mortal danger.

"This bastard's threatening me?" Wes blurted. "Why?"

"If you'll notice, the threats against you subsided soon after she moved back to Sunny Creek and bought the Cleever house."

"She bought a house in Sunny Creek?" Wes exclaimed.

"Well, yeah. You didn't know?" Joe shrugged. "It's one of those big old Victorians on the north end of town. She's restoring it. I hear she's really turning it into a showplace. Folks are raving about it."

"She's not actually planning to stay in Sunny Creek, is she?" he asked in dismay. He didn't know whether to be thrilled that she hadn't bolted to some distant shore or royally pissed that she'd stuck around his hometown just to taunt him.

"How the hell should I know? I'm not her social secretary. Not that I'd mind applying for the job. She's one fine-looking woman. Nice lady, too. What the hell were you thinking, dumping her?"

"I didn't dump her," Wes ground out.

"Ah. She dumped you, huh? Tough luck."

Wes really didn't want to talk about his failed love life with his cousin, or anybody else for that matter. "Why didn't you tell me I was being threatened in these emails of Jessica's?"

"Because the threats against you had stopped by the time I was brought into the loop, but have recently started up again. Officer Demoyne is also worried about

Jessica's safety, and asked me and my guys to keep an eye on her as long as she's in town."

"Are you?" Wes challenged.

"Absolutely. We've got someone within a block of her place pretty much around the clock. When she goes over to Hillsdale to pick up stuff for her house, one of my guys almost always follows her."

"How long are you planning to keep up this security detail?"

Joe leaned forward. "As long as those threats continue to come to her inbox."

"How many are there, anyway?"

"Fifty-three and counting. She gets one or two a day, usually. Now and then she gets a cluster of several all at once."

"And there's no distinguishing words or phrases to help you identify this asshole?" Wes asked.

Joe shook his head.

Wes picked up the stack of emails again and went through them, more slowly this time. They were stiff. Formal. Almost like business letters. Something in the emails resonated with him but he couldn't put his finger on it.

Joe pulled out another folder. "You ready for the kicker, Wes?"

"There's more?"

"Yeah," Joe answered heavily. "A few days ago, the tenor of the emails changed. They stopped being threats and started being promises."

"That sounds ominous?"

"The FBI profiler thinks it's ominous. He's forecasting that our stalker has decided to take action to, uhh, punish both Jessica and you. Consider this an official warning from your local law enforcement official that you may be in danger. I'm formally offering you police protection if you desire it. Both the FBI and I deem your life to be in significant danger."

Wes just stared at his cousin. This was Sunny Creek. Where everyone knew each other and nothing really bad ever happened. Hell, they hadn't had a murder in close to twenty years, and the one that had happened in town had been from a drunken knife fight between two drifters passing through.

"Why the hell is Jessica showing herself in public?" he blurted. "She knows to take these threats seriously!"

Joe answered soberly, "I tried to convince her to lay low, but I get the impression she doesn't much care about her safety. I don't think she cares if the stalker kills her."

Wes stared at his cousin in dismay.

Reluctantly he picked up the second folder and read the last half-dozen posts. They were, indeed, different from the others. The blustering and threats were gone, replaced by cold calm and a declaration that his and Jessica's time was up to do what the writer wanted. Now they were going to pay for their crimes.

What crimes? Giving a damn about each other?

A shiver rattled down his spine. Whoever was writing these emails was certifiably crazy. And not just a little. This stuff was serial killer worthy. And the bastard's sights were firmly locked on him and Jessica.

Wes leaned back in his chair, staring at the files of threats. "How come I'm not getting any threats?"

"Do you have an email account?"

"Not at the moment. No need all by myself on my ranch."

"That's your reason, then," Joe said.

Wes blurted, "And she has no idea who's sending these to her?"

"None. She claims not to have any enemies, and not to know anyone who hates her enough to kill her. Would you say that's an accurate assessment? You knew her back in Washington, DC, didn't you?"

"Yes, I did know her. And yes, I'd say she's correct. Everyone who met Jess loved her."

"Someone apparently didn't. And he or she has developed a sick fixation on our girl."

"You have to protect her, Joe. She won't let me anywhere near her, or I'd do it myself. But stick to her like glue. Promise me."

"Dude, I've got this. Nobody's getting hurt around here on my watch."

Wes nodded grimly at his cousin. "If you need more manpower, deputize me. I've still got my concealed carry permit and weapons certifications from the Marines."

"You're not exactly an objective third party, my friend. And besides, I need you to keep a sharp eye on your own six o'clock."

"No one's sneaking up on me."

"Don't underestimate whoever's writing those emails. This guy's sitting around all day long plotting out whatever he's planning to do. He'll be meticulous and thorough, and potentially very dangerous."

Wes swore and didn't bother to hide his frustration from Joe. "You can't let anything happen to her. I'm the reason she came out here in the first place. If something bad happens to her, it will be all my fault."

"Unless you're the whack job writing those emails,

it won't be your fault. Get your head in the game, Wes. You have to set aside your guilt and whatever else you're feeling about her. I need your head clear and you thinking on all cylinders if you're going to help her. My gut feeling is that both of you know whoever's writing those emails. Go home tonight, stay sober and think as hard as you can about who might be stalking Jessica. Will you do that for me?"

"I'm not a damned drunk—"

"I'm not accusing you of anything. I just know that if I had lost a woman like Jessica I'd be hurting powerfully. And I might try to self-medicate away some of that pain so I could sleep and eat and breathe. Just sayin'."

Wes sighed. Joe was right. There was no need to rip off his cousin's head because Jessica had left. "I'll think on it."

"Call me if you come up with anything, Wes."

"Will do."

He stood up to leave, and a lump settled heavily in the pit of his stomach. Something bad was about to happen. He could feel it coming. He just didn't know what it was or what direction it would come from. He'd gotten this same instinctive intuition of impending danger when he'd been a combat officer in foreign war zones. The intuition had never let him down and had never been wrong. It was part of why he'd brought almost all of his men home alive—his gut was uncanny at warning him.

And it was screaming at him now. Something—someone—was coming for him, and more importantly, for Jessica.

Wes went straight out to the barn when he got home

to finish repairing his tractor. Although he got the machine up and running, it was too close to dark to start dragging the lower pasture today. The job would have to wait until tomorrow. He fed the cattle, checked on the cows still getting close to calving and then went into the house.

It was undoubtedly Joe's fault that the back of his neck tightened as he entered the house. He felt silly doing it, but he searched the place, peeking under beds and in closets and behind doors, wherever a human being could hide. Nobody was there, of course.

Shaking his head at his paranoia, he sat down in his armchair with a frozen pizza to watch a baseball game on TV. He was jumpy through the evening and finally had to laugh aloud at himself. He was a former Marine who had lived and fought in some of the most dangerous corners of the planet. And here he was acting like a nervous civilian without any idea how to handle himself.

He checked the shotgun he kept loaded by his bed, and he slept fitfully. All was quiet inside the house and out. But he couldn't shake the foreboding feeling that had settled in the pit of his stomach. Something bad was about to happen.

Chapter 16

The next morning, just as Jessica was knocking off for lunch after spending the morning stripping paint, her cell phone beeped an incoming text. She picked it up to glance at it and then gawked in shock.

Jessica, I need your help with a big problem. I wouldn't ask if it weren't important. And frankly, you owe me one. Please come up to West Lake, to the White Pine Forest State Park. Go to the cabins by the lake. I'll be in the last one. Number Eight. Hurry.

Holy cow. Wes really must be in trouble if he'd asked for her help the day after being so rude to her in the diner. Or maybe he'd only been that way yesterday because he was in front of his friends and family.

Why didn't he just call her? Why the text? Was

phone reception bad up by the lake? God knew, her cell phone hated these mountains and her coverage could be spotty in the high mountains.

Then there was the fact that he had never played the "you owe me one" card before. It was certainly true that she did owe him—many times over. But he'd always insisted that helping people in trouble was not the sort of thing he kept a tally of. He did it because it was the right thing to do. His problem must be dire, indeed, if he felt a need to twist her arm like that to get her to come to him.

She texted back, Leaving now. There as soon as possible.

Wes didn't reply. Which was also unlike him. In the past, his texts were generally chatty. Conversational. And always polite. He didn't just cut them off like that. What the heck was going on with him? He didn't sound like himself at all.

Worried, she pointed her sporty little car up into the mountains west of Sunny Creek. This wasn't an area she'd visited before, and she was amazed by the alpine beauty of the mountains rising up around her.

As advertised, the White Pine Forest State Park was full of tall, lush-needled white pine trees along with aspens, birches, spruces and a bunch of other trees she couldn't identify. A paved road wound into the state park, following the shore of a large lake, which she glimpsed through the trees from time to time. It was sapphire blue and the sun glittered across its rippled surface like a diamond. No matter that it was pretty. She still didn't like lakes. It looked deep and cold, and she shuddered a little at the reminder of how her mother had died.

Rebecca, an experienced swimmer and strong athlete, had gone out for a swim in the lake behind their house. The assumption was that she'd had a cramp or some kind of physical distress and never made it back to shore. Her body was found eventually, submerged in the middle of the lake, by rescue divers.

Jessica spotted the wooden sign pointing toward the cabins and took the turn. The road wound through a copse of pine trees that carpeted the ground in brown needles. The pines gave way to a thick stand of brush and deciduous trees, however, before she got to the last cabin, which was set a ways beyond the others.

She didn't see Wes's truck, which was weird. In fact, no vehicle at all was in sight. Was he even here? Or maybe she'd beat him. Frowning, she got out of her car and climbed the steps to the small, covered porch. She knocked on the door.

"Wes! It's me. Are you there?"

The door opened, and Wes was not standing there. In fact, the last person on earth she would have expected to see was standing there.

"Daddy? What on earth are you doing here? I got a text from Wes—"

He cut her off, ordering, "Come in, Jessica. We need to talk."

She stepped through the doorway, blinded by going from the bright light outside to the relative darkness of the tiny cabin's interior. She had started to turn toward her father to give him a hug when something—two sharp somethings—suddenly poked into her back.

A massive jolt of electricity slammed into her and her entire back clenched and spasmed, jerking uncontrollably. Her legs collapsed out from under her and she fell to the floor as she started to lose consciousness. *What the—*

Everything went black.

She regained consciousness sometime later. She was flat on her back on what felt like a bed. What the heck had happened to her? Had she fallen? Hit her head? No...

Good grief, her brain was sluggish. She'd gotten an electrical shock of some kind.

"Awake, are you? We can't have that, now, can we?" a gruff voice said from outside her line of sight. She tried to turn her head to see the source of the vaguely familiar voice, but her body wouldn't cooperate. At all. As in she was completely paralyzed. Fear surged through her, abruptly clearing the cobwebs from her mind.

What was wrong with her?

She tried to wiggle her fingers and was stunned when even that much movement took more energy than she could summon.

A wasp or a bee stung her in the upper arm, and the wooden walls and ceiling began to spin around her very slowly. She was sinking...sinking...

And the blackness absorbed her into its soothing embrace once more.

The next time she woke up, the first sensation she became aware of was thirst. Her lips were dry and cracked, and her throat felt bruised and tender, like she'd been swallowing rocks.

"Water," she whispered.

"Oh, now you want to drink," someone said sarcastically. "I try for hours to get you to swallow and nothing. But as soon as you wake up, you're begging for it. Ungrateful child."

She knew that raspy voice. Why couldn't she place its owner, though?

A plastic straw scratched her cracked and tender lips roughly, and she sucked greedily at it. A hand came under her head to lift it up, and she sucked even more thirstily. The water was tepid and tasted like sulphur. And she totally didn't care. It was wet.

That damned bee stung her arm once more, and she drifted away yet again, this time into a cloud of spun cotton that tangled around her arms and limbs so tightly she couldn't move a single inch.

The next time she woke, she desperately had to use the restroom. "I have to go to the bathroom. Now."

The raspy voice responded to her announcement with, "Oh, for Pete's sake. You'll have to stand up and walk to the john because I'll be damned if I'm gonna wipe your ass for you."

The crudity shocked her into a higher state of consciousness, but she was far from fully awake. Strong hands hoisted her upright and dragged her to her feet. Her legs felt oddly disconnected from her body, and her entire body felt puppetlike. Her limbs were weak, her joints uncooperative. If she had become a marionette, she really wished the puppet master would tighten up the strings a little. She felt all floppy and on the verge of collapsing.

"Stand up or you're going to pee in your pants."

Blinking, she squinted at the room. It was daylight again. Maybe late afternoon based on the rosy tint coming in the window. She had the sense of a full night having passed and most of another day. How could that be?

She was shoved roughly into a tiny bathroom and told to go and go fast. Or else.

Or else what? Too groggy to understand what was happening to her, she fumbled at her jeans button and zipper. How she managed to get her clothes out of the way before she sank onto the toilet seat, she had no idea. Instinct, maybe. And long years of muscle memory.

How long she sat there after relieving herself, she had no idea. She became aware of fists pounding on the door. A voice shouting that he would come in there and drag her off the toilet if she didn't hurry up.

It was an act of supreme effort to haul herself upright. She pulled up her pants, zipped them and belatedly remembered to flush the toilet. Man, she was out of it. The room began to spin and she clung to the towel rack convulsively, struggling to stay upright. Something was terribly wrong with her. But what? She couldn't focus her mind long enough or hard enough to puzzle out what was wrong with her.

She staggered out into the main room, which was now flooded with orange-red light. Yup. Sunset.

And then the bee sting, and night descended upon her again. The last thing she heard was that raspy voice, swearing as she thudded to the floor.

Wes finished dragging and seeding the lower pasture in the morning. Next up on the never-ending list of chores was to go to the grain elevator and buy a couple of tons of corn to restock his dwindling supply. He'd already planted a field of his own corn, but it would be late this fall before it was harvested, dried and ready to feed to the cows. Until then, he was stuck buying it. The sun was dropping behind the mountains, and the feed store would close in a half hour. But if he hurried, he could get there in time to buy the corn he needed.

He was heading for his truck when he spied a familiar SUV coming up his driveway. It parked beside him and the driver got out. Wes said, surprised, "Hey, Joe. What brings you up here?"

"I've been trying to get in touch with you all day, Wes. Why haven't you been answering your phone? You scared the hell out of me."

Wes frowned. "No one's called me."

"Are you kidding? I've called at least a dozen times. Left messages. Told you over and over to call me the second you got the messages."

"I lost my phone...yesterday, I think. What's up?"

"Jessica's gone missing."

"What?" Wes jolted as a surge of adrenaline ripped through him. "What do you know? When was she last seen? Have you got any leads?"

Joe threw up his hands as if to ward off the barrage of questions. "We've got nothing at the moment. I was hoping she was with you and that the two of you had decided to go off-grid, to ground, until the threat blows over."

"She's not here. You can look if you want."

"I believe you," Joe said briskly. "You may be a jerk, but you're an honest jerk. You wouldn't kidnap your ex."

"Gee, thanks for the vote of confidence," Wes replied sourly.

"Anytime."

Wes stared at Joe while his brain churned like mad. Something was trying to bubble up to his consciousness. A connection between recent events. Something important. It broke through and he blurted, "What are the odds my disappearing cell phone has something to do with Jessica's disappearance?"

Joe frowned. "I dunno. Do you lose your phone often?"

"Never. I always know where it is. There are specific places I lay it down, and nowhere else."

"Then I suppose it's possible the two are linked. You were included in the threats for a while. Do you have reason to believe someone broke into your house or truck to take your phone?"

"Two nights ago, when I got back from Sunny Creek, I was convinced someone had been in my house. But then I put it down to paranoia. What if someone *was* in the house and stole my phone?"

"Why? And how would that be connected to Jessica?" Joe asked.

"If someone called or texted Jess from my phone and said that I was in terrible trouble and needed her to come rescue me, she would go. At least, I think she would. My phone would be the perfect way to lure her into going somewhere she wouldn't normally go."

Joe grimaced. "Unfortunately, that makes a certain sick sense. The good news is I'm more optimistic about tracking down your phone than I am Jessica."

Wes frowned. "I have a tracer program installed on my phone. We can run it from my laptop computer in the house."

"Trace away. It may be the best lead we have on her."

Wes raced into the house and pulled up the phone-finder app on his computer. In a few seconds a message popped up on his screen. "That's weird. The tracer program says my phone is turned off. I never turn it off."

"Maybe the battery ran dead," Joe suggested.

"This tracer program would tell me that. But, instead, it says the phone is powered down."

"Does that tracer app have the ability to tell you where the phone was last used?"

Wes nodded and typed in the proper command. After a few seconds, a map popped up on the screen with a red dot in the middle of it. "Okay, that's wrong. It shows my phone being used at the Sapphire Club yesterday morning, late." The Sapphire Club was one step down from a strip club…one very shallow step, and not a place he routinely hung out.

"I gather you weren't there?" Joe asked drily.

Wes rolled his eyes at his cousin. "I was here on my tractor, seeding the lower pasture."

"So then, your theory that your phone was stolen is looking better. When's the last time you remember using it?"

Wes cast his mind back. "I guess that would have been day before yesterday."

"Before or after you decided to take on a pack of angry women and got handed your butt in a sling?"

"Before."

"Have you got any idea where Jessica might have gone off to without telling anyone?" Joe asked soberly.

"You would have to ask her girlfriends."

"Already did. The only thing they all agreed on was that she wasn't considering leaving town and had expressed being happy in Sunny Creek. Apparently, it feels like home to her."

Really? Jess liked life in a tiny town? Frankly, he was shocked at the notion.

"Look," Joe said, "it's possible she just left town for a few days without telling anyone. There may be nothing wrong."

"No, there's something wrong," Wes disagreed. "I feel it in my gut."

Joe grimaced. "Yeah, my gut's yelling at me, too."

"Can I help with the search?" Wes asked tersely.

"I wish you could. I've got my guys driving all over the county looking for her car, and I've notified all the neighboring counties. Tonight, I can officially put out a BOLO on her. Thankfully, that Corvette of hers is super distinctive. If someone sees her, I'll hear about it."

Wes nodded. "Yell if you can think of something for me to do. Anything."

"Okay. Call me if you hear from her. And stick by your landline so I can get in touch with you until you get a replacement cell phone."

Wes nodded and ushered his cousin outside. As he climbed into his SUV, Joe looked tired with dark smudges under his eyes. He'd obviously pulled an all-nighter last night looking for Jess. Poor guy. "Take care of yourself, Joe. You're no good to Jessica if you're dead on your feet."

"Easy for you to say. You haven't lost a citizen on your watch. One you promised to keep safe."

The thing was, Wes had also promised to keep Jessica safe. And he'd failed her. Again.

He went inside his house and paced restlessly for a while, his heart slamming against his ribs in stress. Something was wrong with Jessica. She was in huge trouble. He felt it.

There *had* to be a way to help her. But what? He felt physically ill with worry before an idea finally occurred to him. Maybe someone at the Sapphire Club would have an idea who might have stolen his phone. It was a long shot, but worth checking out. The local regulars there would be pretty well-known. Folks in these parts all knew each other, so the impulse to steal from one another was pretty small. If a stranger had come to the area, he or she should stand out to the staff of the Sapphire Club.

He drove to the bar and stepped into the dark, smoky interior. Loud music blared and a bored-looking go-go dancer gyrated to the beat on a stage at the back of the joint. Wes headed for the bar and the bartender, a guy he'd gone to high school with.

"Hey, Wes!" the guy shouted over the din. "Long time no see! What brings you in here?"

"I lost my cell phone and a tracker app showed it being last used in here late yesterday morning. You didn't happen to be working then, did you? Maybe see any strangers?"

"Nope, but Candy was here. She's the waitress in the red T-shirt." The bartender flagged her down as she approached with a tray of empty glasses, and she leaned forward to listen to the bartender shout Wes's question at her.

She nodded at Wes. "An older guy was in here yesterday. Almost bald. He was the only nonregular here during the whole lunch shift. Didn't look like the criminal type, though. But he was a terrible tipper, now that I think about it."

And clearly that was tantamount to a crime in her book. Wes smiled and thanked the woman, palming a twenty-dollar bill to her for her troubles. Her eyes lit up and she started to sidle closer to him.

"Sorry, I'm in a hurry tonight, Candy. Thanks for your help."

"No problem. Come back sometime when you're not in a hurry. I'll make sure you have a good time."

He smiled kindly at her. She was just trying to make a buck, after all. He left the club, his mind racing. An older, almost bald guy? Surely not. Surely George Blankenship wasn't lurking around Sunny Creek. He would have let Jessica know he was here, and he wouldn't stalk his own daughter. Would he?

The guy had always walked the razor's edge between reasonable and unhinged. Most people interpreted his brand of crazy as being a super-gung ho Marine, but Wes knew better. The guy had actually been a bit unbalanced. Had something pushed the Old Man all the way over the edge?

Wes drove back toward downtown Sunny Creek, and the more he thought about it, the more certain he was that the stranger at the Sapphire Club had been George Blankenship. It felt absolutely right in his gut.

He parked at the sheriff's office and went inside. "Is Joe here?"

"Nope, he's out cruising, looking for your girlfriend. Can I help you?" one of the other deputies said.

"I was just at the Sapphire Club, and I think Jessica's father is in the area."

"He's probably looking for his daughter, too."

Wes shook his head in the negative. "I don't think so…"

When he was done laying out his suspicions, the deputy started to type on his computer while he said,

"I'm going to run an occupancy and credit card search for this Blankenship guy and see if anything pops in this area."

Thank goodness the deputy believed him. Maybe, with the help of the sheriff's department, George could be located. The general's presence in the local area all tied in with his missing phone and Jessica somehow. He was *sure* of it.

Wes sank into a seat beside the deputy's desk. "Mind if I wait to see what you find on George?"

The guy shrugged. "It's an ongoing investigation, and we're not supposed to share information with the public."

"I know her well, and I know the area. I can help you guys," Wes pleaded. "I'm the closest thing to family Jessica has in Sunny Creek."

Huh. That was actually the truth. Even though they'd been on the outs for a while, they still shared a connection to each other. At least he hoped they did. No, they did. He was still totally hooked on Jessica, and there was no way her feelings for him had completely crumbled in the past several weeks.

Whatever they'd been fighting about before fell away to complete unimportance in the face of her disappearance. She had to be safe. She *had* to be.

The deputy responded slowly, "Joe thinks you're a stand-up guy. And if you're close to her, you might as well know what's going on."

Wes nodded tersely.

The computer beeped only a few seconds later. The deputy read aloud from the screen. "G. Blankenship's first purchase was in Billings, a full month ago, and then there's a list of gas and grocery bills here. He stayed at a motel there for two weeks."

"Any idea where he is now?"

"Last transaction I have is for a rental cabin at White Pine Forest State Park for one night about two weeks back. Is your guy a fan of camping?"

Wes shrugged. "He is a retired Marine. He would certainly know how to camp. Although he didn't strike me as the back-to-nature type."

"That's all I've got on him. He hasn't made any credit card purchases in the state of Montana since then. Maybe he left the state."

"Why would he do that without at least saying hello to his daughter?" Wes speculated. "And maybe he hasn't left. Maybe he has simply gone off-the-grid. He would know how to do that, too. If he's paying for stuff in cash, he wouldn't be leaving an electronic trail for you to find."

"True. But that sounds pretty paranoid."

Wes snorted at the deputy. "You haven't met George. *Paranoid* is his middle name."

The deputy was typing again. "Any idea what kind of vehicle he drives?"

"Assuming he hasn't rented a car to throw us off the trail, he owns a black Land Rover. It has Virginia license plates."

The deputy looked surprised at the detailed knowledge he had of George, but Wes didn't feel like explaining that he'd worked for the guy. Not now, when Jessica was in danger and every minute counted. The more he thought about it, the more certain he was that George had something to do with her disappearance. The general had always been a control freak where she was concerned. According to her, the man was known to obsess over her and even confused her for her mother sometimes. Talk about creepy.

Wes announced, "I'm going to run up to White Pine and ask the ranger if he knows anything about where George might have gone. If you'd let Joe know about all of this, I'd be mighty grateful."

"Yeah, sure. I'll get on the radio with him and relay it all."

"Perfect. Thanks, man."

The deputy grinned. "It would, in fact, be my job to help."

Wes nodded tersely over his shoulder but was already moving rapidly toward the door. *Hang on, Jessica. I'm coming for you.*

The next time Jessica made the slow swim toward consciousness, she actually made it all the way to full wakefulness. She had a raging headache and was thirsty again, and her stomach growled demandingly. As if she'd missed *several* meals. What in the world?

The room that took shape around her in the dark was Spartan. Linoleum floor. Raw wood planks on the walls and ceiling. Screens over the windows with mosquitoes and june bugs banging at them. A lantern sat on a small table beyond the foot of the bed, its light and steady hissing noise the only disturbances in the night and silence.

Outside, crickets and frogs made a deafeningly loud chorus. A whip-poor-will's distinctive call split the night outside, startling her.

She tried to sit up and was startled to realize her wrists were bound over her head and her ankles were tied to the footboard. The bed she lay in was made of logs and looked ridiculously sturdy. Panic surged through her. Had she been raped?

She took inventory and didn't feel any different. Plus, she was fully clothed. Whew. Had she been kidnapped, then? By whom? Why? Her memory was full of black, frustrating holes at the moment.

Recollection of multiple sharp pains in her arms came back to her. Injections. She'd been drugged! For how long? It was night now, and she recalled waking up to go to the bathroom twice. Maybe a day and a half? Or had it been even longer?

She appeared to be alone in the cabin, but there were two closed doors across the room. One was probably a bathroom. The other, she guessed, was a second bedroom. Was her captor in the cabin with her?

How in the world did this stuff keep happening to her? She was just trying to live a quiet life in a quiet town, for crying out loud. Was that too much to ask? An urge to cry tightened her throat and made her eyes fill with tears.

No! She had to hold it together. Survival was the priority right now, not feeling sorry for herself. She wasn't the daughter of a Marine officer for nothing. She knew she had to discipline herself and focus on the crisis at hand.

She tugged at her bindings and grimaced. They were painfully tight and left no room for her to even contemplate wiggling out of them. Worse, they were made of thick leather and didn't have the slightest bit of give in them.

Her muscles felt stiff and her entire body was sore. Memory of blinding pain, of spasming from head to foot while jolting agony ripped through her came back in a rush. She'd been electrocuted. A Taser, maybe? It had been the most excruciating agony she had ever experienced.

Anger swirled in her belly. Who in the hell had lured her up here, Tasered her then tied her up and drugged her? Surely Wes wasn't this desperate. Heck, all he had to do to get her back was apologize and promise not to be such a jerk anymore.

She blinked, startled, as the realization hit her. She'd never stopped loving him. No matter how mad she might be at him, her base feelings for him hadn't changed one bit. Too bad she was just figuring that out now. It would suck rocks if she never got a chance to tell him how she really felt. What if she died and he spent the rest of his life thinking she hated him? The idea of that caused a giant knot to form in her stomach. She *had* to get out of here and get back to him.

It was hard, but she pushed aside her panic at the idea of never seeing Wes again to concentrate on escaping her current predicament.

Who had kidnapped her? She had a very vague memory of seeing someone when she'd first entered the cabin. *C'mon, brain. Who was it?*

Maybe, as the drugs continued to clear from her system, full memory would return. In the meantime, she tried to remember the things she'd heard in speeches and discussions around her father's dinner table with former POWs over the years.

They talked about being stoic. Prepare for a long incarceration but know with certainty that you'll survive and someday get free. Set a goal in the distant future to focus on. Don't get too optimistic about a rescue or release soon or else you'll be disappointed and eventually break emotionally. But keep an eye out for opportunities to escape if they present themselves. Be willing to take the pain to get free.

Okay. She could do this. She might not get free tonight or tomorrow or even next week. But she would a) survive, and b) get loose, somehow. Stoic attitude in place. Check.

Next on the list: a distant goal. She needed a long-term goal.

As soon as she set her mind to it, that one was a no-brainer. She had to make it back to Wes. Tell him she was sorry for walking out on him. Beg him to do the counseling or other emotional work to get past his mental baggage so they could be together forever. Heck, maybe she should propose to him. Now *that* was a goal worth living for. Check.

What was the last bit? Oh, yes. Be on the lookout for chances to escape and be willing to take the pain to break loose. Heck, this kidnapping business had already hurt a lot. If Wes was the end goal, she could take the pain. All the pain. As much as the kidnapper wanted to dish out.

She didn't know how long she lay there. Long enough to decide that she was probably here alone. The night settled around her, and she listened idly to nature's concert outside. Gradually the cobwebs cleared from her brain. She remembered driving to the cabin because she'd gotten an urgent text from Wes. Which obviously hadn't actually been from Wes.

Who knew her well enough to use him as bait to lure her out here? That narrowed the circle of possible kidnappers by a lot—to someone she knew fairly well, in fact.

All of a sudden, the rest of her memory popped back into her head. One second it was gone, and the next it was there. Disbelief coursed through her as she remembered the face of the man who had met her at the door of the cabin. The man who had Tasered her and knocked her out.

Her. Own. Father.

Terror roared through her. Of all people, she knew how irrational he could be. She had always been afraid of him when he'd been drinking. Not because he got violent but because he got delusional. Had he had some sort of psychotic break when he got kicked out of the Marines? It was the only explanation she could think of for all of this insanity.

There had to be a way to talk him down off that bridge. After all, she was his daughter. He loved her, right?

Maybe *love* was too strong a word. But he surely considered her to be his responsibility. He expected loyalty from her and gave loyalty to her in return, if not actual love. She couldn't count how many times he'd said "Blankenships stick together" over the years. She would appeal to that side of him.

Assuming he returned here anytime soon. He hadn't abandoned her way out in the middle of nowhere, had he? She would give it till morning. If he didn't show himself by then, she would start screaming her head off. For now, though, she didn't want to risk waking him up if he was, in fact, asleep in the other room. He always had woken up more sane after sleeping off a good drunken bender.

She would reason with him in the morning, and he would untie her then and let her go. And the two of them would forget that this unfortunate little episode had ever occurred.

Except a frisson of warning somewhere in the back of her mind warned her that it might not be that simple.

The frisson turned into a shiver.

The shiver turned into fear.

And the fear turned into stone-cold terror.

Wes broke every speed limit between Sunny Creek and White Pine Forest State Park. Thankfully, at this time of the evening, the roads were deserted way out here. He drove up to the ranger's house with an angry spit of gravel from his tires, leaped out of his truck and knocked on the door urgently.

A gray-haired man of maybe fifty years answered him. "Can I help you? The park's closed for the night."

"My name's Wes Morgan, and a close friend of mine has gone missing. Sheriff Westlake, his men and I are looking for her."

"I haven't seen any lone women in the park recently."

Wes nodded impatiently. "I'm looking for a man who came through here a few weeks ago. It's important that I find him. It's actually his daughter who has gone missing. He's a retired Marine, in his late fifties. He would be balding, but otherwise have a very short military haircut. He's a wide, muscular guy with a barrel chest. His name is George Blankenship. He used a credit card to pay for an overnight stay here."

"We've got a guest in the park who matches that description, but that's not his name. Last name is Smith. And he's paying in cash."

Wes's gut tightened in anxiety. That sounded like George. Why would he be using an alias and cash if he was here for purely innocent reasons? Aloud, Wes said, "I need to know where he's staying. It's urgent."

"He's in the cabins. They're at the far end of the park, around the west end of the lake. Just this side of the boat ramp."

"How do I get there?"

"Follow the main road until you see the signs for the cabins, turn right, then left. He's in Number Eight. Last one on the end."

"Thanks. I need you to call the county sheriff's office and tell them everything you just told me. Tell them Wes Morgan thinks this Smith guy is George Blankenship and that he's up to no good. Have you got all that?"

"Uh, yes," the ranger replied in alarm.

Wes bolted from the house and ran for his truck.

The cabin's front door opened without warning and Jessica jolted in alarm. She forced herself to relax, however, when she saw who'd joined her. "Hey, Dad. I'm so glad to see you. How are you doing?"

"Don't try to sweet-talk me," he growled.

"I was just asking how you're doing," she replied carefully. She knew that tone of voice. He'd been drinking and was in an ugly mood.

He grumbled incoherently.

"Any chance I can go to the restroom? I'd hate to make a mess and stink up the place," she said as casually and calmly as she could. Which was a stretch. Her heart was pounding and warnings were screaming in her head that something was seriously wrong with her father. His eyes were wild. And his clothes were disheveled and dirty. Never in her life had she seen the man actually be *messy*. Not once.

Another grunt in response to her toilet request. However, he moved over to the bed and unbuckled her left hand. He stepped back, apparently expecting her to do the rest of the work of unbuckling her right hand and feet. She twisted to reach her right hand and then sat up slowly, her body creaky from inactivity. As she reached down for her feet, she heard the distinctive metallic click of a revolver being cocked.

Her blood ran cold. He was pointing a gun at her? Oh, yeah. Something was definitely extremely wrong with him. If he'd said it once, he'd said it a thousand times. *Never point a gun at a man unless you're willing to kill him.* Moving very slowly and deliberately, she unbuckled her feet and swung them over the edge of the bed. "Is it okay if I stand up?" she asked evenly.

"Slowly."

"No problem." She eased to her feet and walked slowly to the bathroom, her hands held well away from her sides. No need to make him any more jumpy than he already was.

She used the bathroom and splashed water on her face to help clear the last cobwebs from her mind. What the hell was she going to do now? She had to find a way to get away from him and that gun. But she dared not panic and do something stupid. She took a deep breath and stepped back out into the main room.

"How about I get the two of us something to eat? I'm hungry, and I bet you haven't been eating enough. You never do when you're working hard." She tried to sound fond of him but had no idea if she succeeded past the terror clogging her throat.

"No need to eat. You and I are going for a little ride."

"Oh. Okay. Cool. Where to?"

"Shut up, Rebecca. You always did talk too damned much."

Uh-oh. Not good. He always turned vicious when he lost himself in memories of his dead wife. She nodded silently.

He waved the barrel of the big Colt .45 revolver toward the front door, indicating that she should go ahead of him. Should she make a break for the trees or not? Thing was, George was a decent shot, and at a range of only a few feet he wouldn't miss her with that gun. He was also strong, fit and fast, thanks to a many-decades career as a Marine. She wouldn't likely be able to outrun him. Nope. It wasn't time to escape yet.

They stepped outside, and she didn't see her car anywhere. George must have moved it. He handcuffed her wrists together beside his black Land Rover using metal police-style handcuffs and shoved her into the vehicle's front passenger seat.

She wasn't surprised when he zip-tied her handcuffs to the door, thwarting any ideas she might have about leaping at the steering wheel. He always had been thorough and meticulous in planning things.

She sat quietly beside him as he pulled out onto the main road. Maybe she could make a fuss when they passed the ranger's house. Scream or maybe use her foot to hit the car horn. She was surprised, though, when George turned away from the park exit and drove deeper into the white pine forest.

Where in the world was he taking her?

Wes pulled up at the cabin and approached cautiously, pistol in hand. He snuck up under a side window and took a surreptitious peek over the sill. The main room was empty. He moved to the bedroom and had another look. Damn. Empty, too. He was startled to try the front door and find it unlocked. He went in fast, looking for signs of Jessica having been here.

His blood ran cold at the sight of the four shackles still attached to the headboard and footboard of the bed. He moved over to examine them, and the scent of gardenias rose from the sheets.

Jessica had been here. And recently.

Swearing, he bolted back out to his truck. The ranger had agreed to close the park exit gate, so if they were lucky, George and Jessica were still somewhere in the park. But where?

On the assumption that the ranger would stop them from exiting, Wes turned deeper into the park. *C'mon, George. Show yourself, you crazy bastard.*

Jessica stared in dismay as a boat dock with a dozen motorboats tied up at a long wooden pier came into view. She hated boats almost as much as she hated lakes. They both reminded her of her mother's tragic death.

Her father parked his Land Rover and came around to the passenger side of the car. Using a big, scary knife to sever the plastic zip tie, he cut her loose from the car door. But he didn't take the handcuffs off her wrists. He stepped back and waved the antique revolver that was his favorite at her, gesturing for her to head out to the dock.

She balked, stopping short of the wooden pier. "You know I don't like lakes or boats, Dad."

"Don't make me do you the way I did your mother," he snarled.

Ice froze in her belly. She asked carefully, "What do you mean, the way you did my mother? What did you do to her?"

"We never talk about that!" he shouted.

"I think maybe we need to talk about it now," she replied carefully.

"Get in the damned boat, Rebecca."

"I'm not Rebecca! I'm Jessica. Your daughter."

"Jessica's a baby. Asleep. Get in the goddamned boat or I'll kill you right here in the house with her."

"My mother went for a swim. She didn't get in a boat the night she died," Jessica tried. A tiny voice in the back of her head was screaming, *No...no...no*.

He didn't kill her. He couldn't have. He loved her, right? Her mother went for a swim and drowned.

George grabbed her upper arm and shoved her toward the dock. She stumbled, caught her balance and turned to face him. "Tell me what you did to her, Father. Did you kill my mother?"

"Of course I did."

The words were so shocking they knocked the breath right out of her lungs. She stood there in the sand in front of him, gasping for air. He might as well have punched her in the gut.

"Why?" she managed to gasp.

"Bitch thought she was going to leave me. Would have wrecked my career. I got my first job in the Pentagon because everyone thought I had pull with her family. That I could get the military a break on some huge contracts. But if she dumped me, I would lose it all. Selfish bitch didn't care. Said she wasn't happy. That I was mean. She didn't like moving all the time. Being alone. What the hell did she think being a military wife was all about?" he bellowed.

"How did you kill her?"

"Same way I'm gonna kill you. Hold your head under water until you drown, then push you in the lake."

Jessica stared at him in horror. "You'll never get away with this."

"Got away with it before."

"Yes, but I'm your daughter. My mother was weak, fragile, but I'm not. I'm a fighter. If you shoot me, everyone will know you killed me. They'll run the bullet through the FBI database and match it to your gun."

He raised the revolver as if to strike her and she said quickly, "Mark me with your gun, and they'll know you killed me, too."

Scowling ferociously at her, he grabbed her arm and tried to pull her onto the dock. But now that she knew what was at stake, she fought with all she was worth. If he was going to kill her, he was going to have to do it right here, on shore, where maybe someone would hear the gunshot and come to investigate.

Very few gunshots killed people outright. Maybe she wouldn't bleed to death before help came.

Her father was a powerful man and yanked her violently forward. She fell to her knees, her only option to become deadweight to him.

He swore violently, alternately calling her by her own name and her mother's.

She ended up sitting on her rear end, digging her feet into the sand for all she was worth, backpedaling every time he tried to shift his grip. Cold water lapped around her ankles and then around her knees.

She screamed then. At the top of her lungs, as piercingly loud a shriek as her throat would produce.

Her father's hands slipped around her throat from behind. She yelled, "You'll mark me. They'll know!" before his fingers tightened and cut off all her air.

She flung herself onto her back, kicking her feet up and back, connecting hard with her father's face. He howled and let her go. She rolled as fast as she could away from the water and came up onto her knees, her handcuffed hands in front of her.

She panted hard, catching her breath.

Her father charged her like a bull, and she waited till the last possible second and then dropped flat on the sand. He sailed past her and splashed several steps into the water before he could stop himself. She climbed awkwardly to her feet and ran a half-dozen steps up the beach before he tackled her from behind, knocking her flat once more.

Wes was out there. Waiting for her. She had to fight. For him.

She rolled onto her back and swung her hands as hard as she could, aiming her metal handcuffs at her father's face. He roared in pain as she slammed into his nose. She screamed again with all her might, a sound of rage and determination to prevail against this madman.

George's fist rose up and swung down toward her temple. She saws the blow coming, but too late. She threw up her hands, but he smashed past them with his fist. Blinding pain and white lights exploded inside her skull, and then nothing.

Wes spotted the boat ramp in his headlights, and seconds later the beams of light illuminated George's

Land Rover. He hit the gas pedal and shot right past the parking lot and onto the grass leading down to the dock. As he flung open his door, he heard a shriek that cut off sharply.

He sprinted forward toward two figures on the beach. One lay prone, unmoving in the sand. The second figure—male, muscular and familiar—stood up over the first person's body.

Rage exploded in Wes's skull. If that bastard had hurt Jessica—his mind wouldn't even allow him to contemplate the idea of her dying—George was a dead man.

Wes hit the sand at a dead run as he saw George brandish a big revolver, pointing it at Jessica. "No!" he shouted at the top of his lungs.

George lurched, jerking the gun up.

A deafening report shattered the night and a bright muzzle flash exploded. As he closed the gap between them, Wes spied the gun pointing directly at him. He staggered as something hot slammed into his left shoulder, but he righted himself and kept on running.

Wes ducked as the gun was leveled at him again. Another gunshot.

A miss.

He closed the last few yards between him and George and put on an extra burst of speed. He lowered his good shoulder and slammed into George, knocking the older man back a full body length from Jessica and laying him out flat in the sand. Wes dived for George, but the man rolled clear and jumped to his feet more quickly than Wes anticipated.

The bastard took off running down the dock and leaped into a speedboat.

Wes let him go and, instead, scrambled over to Jessica. *Please, God, let her be alive.*

He fell to his knees beside her and reached for her neck, searching frantically for a pulse. She was so damned still. *Be alive, be alive, be alive.*

His fingertips felt a heartbeat. Another one. It was slow. Thready. But it was there.

Behind him a motor roared and Wes glanced over his shoulder in time to see George accelerate away from the dock in a sleek motorboat.

Frantically, Wes ran his hands over Jessica's body, searching for wounds. For bleeding. For any life-threatening injury. "It's me, baby. It's Wes. I've got you. You're safe. Open your eyes for me, Jess. I love you, dammit."

Her eyelids fluttered.

"That's it. Look at me. You can do it," he begged.

She whispered something, but he couldn't hear it. He leaned down close and put his ear right next to her mouth. She whispered hoarsely, "Say it again."

He pushed up enough to look down at her. "Say what again?"

Her voice was a little stronger. "That you love me, you moron."

"Oh—that. I love you, Jess. Always have. Always will."

She smiled a little then and closed her eyes again.

Alarmed, he ordered her, "Stay with me! Don't close your eyes."

One eye peeled open. "Shh. Not so loud. Head hurts."

He rolled his eyes, torn between laughter and exasperation. "You may have a concussion, baby. I need you to stay awake. Can you do that for me?"

She looked up at him, starlight kissing her features with otherworldly beauty. "I love you, too."

He smiled down at her. "I would kiss you right now, but I don't want to move you until we know you don't have any serious injuries."

"Kiss me anyway."

He bent down and very carefully, very gently, kissed her. In spite of everything she'd been through, her mouth opened hungrily against his, seeking more from him. And Lord, he was tempted to give it. Her hands still cuffed together, she slipped them over his head and around his neck. He winced as fiery pain shot through his left shoulder. And his shirt felt wet against his skin.

Quickly, she yanked her hands over his head and used her fingertips to carefully pluck away the torn and bloody fabric of his shirt.

He looked down and was relieved to see that it looked as if he'd been winged. A furrow in his skin bled freely, but the joint moved normally, and he didn't see a bullet hole.

A single gunshot rang out loudly across the lake behind them and they both jumped hard.

"Oh, no," she said softly, as if she'd just absorbed a terrible blow.

And then it hit him what that shot signified.

"Oh, baby. I'm so sorry." He did gather her up in his arms then, as carefully as he could.

Tears ran down her cheeks unchecked. He completely understood. Her father had clearly been mentally ill and might have just tried to kill her, but he was still her father and, furthermore, her only living parent.

They clung to each other for a long time, grieving the death of her father. George might have been a bad man, an emotionally unbalanced man, but he'd been her father and a human being. His death was still a tragedy. Wes hated George for the suffering he'd put Jessica through—including this last, terrible blow. But Wes vowed to himself that he would protect Jessica from experiencing any more pain like this. Ever.

He was surprised to taste salt in his own mouth and realized tears were running down his face, as well. George Blankenship had been a force of nature, and this was a tragic way for his story to end. Anything that caused Jessica pain caused him pain, too.

He held Jessica in his arms, sharing warmth and silent comfort with her until he heard a siren in the distance.

Jessica roused herself and surprised him by saying, "There's something I have to do before anyone else gets here."

"What's that?"

"I set a goal for myself when I was tied up and didn't know if I was going to live. If I got free, I promised myself I would do it."

"Anything, Jessica. If it's in my power to make it happen for you, I will."

If he didn't know better, he would say it was a twinkle that entered her eyes. "Oh, you can make it happen."

"Name it."

"Wes Morgan, will you marry me?"

He stared down at her. His mind went totally hardcore, blue-screen-of-doom blank. "Marry? You?" he sputtered.

The twinkle in her eyes started to fade. "Never mind—"

"Yes, I'll marry you!" he exclaimed. "Hell, yes!"

Her entire face lit up this time. "You're not just saying that because I almost died, and my dad just died, and you're trying to make me feel better?"

"Now who's the moron? No, baby. I said yes because I want to wake up beside you every morning for the rest of my life and fall asleep beside you every night. I want every last cow on my farm to have a ridiculous name, and I want children—our children—lots of them. I want flowers on the kitchen table and girly underwear hanging in my shower. You can even hang decorated wreaths on my carved front door. I want to spend my youth with you and be with you in my old age. I want it all, Jess."

"Funny, but that's exactly what I had in mind. Except not the wreaths. Your carving is too pretty to cover up."

And so it was, when Joe Westlake and the park ranger pulled up behind them, that Wes and Jessica were laughing and crying together.

And so it was, that out of trauma and tragedy, they found light. And hope. And happily-ever-after.

* * * * *

Don't miss other thrilling stories by Cindy Dees:

Navy SEAL's Deadly Secret
Special Forces: The Recruit
Special Forces: The Spy
Special Forces: The Operator
Her Mission with a SEAL
Navy SEAL Cop

Available from Harlequin Romantic Suspense!

Get 4 FREE REWARDS!

We'll send you 2 FREE Books plus 2 FREE Mystery Gifts.

Harlequin Romantic Suspense books are heart-racing page-turners with unexpected plot twists and irresistible chemistry that will keep you guessing to the very end.

FREE
Value Over
$20